THE WAITER'S GAME

The Waiter's Game

M E GOLESWORTHY

Sospiro Publishing

ISBN: 978-1-8381343-3-4

This book is a work of fiction. Names, characters, places and incidents are either a product of the author's imagination or are used fictitiously.

A CIP catalogue record for this book is available from the British Library

Also by M E Golesworthy:

Intervention
The Parade
Tea and Moles in Brackenden Green

PROLOGUE

Z House - Scottish Highlands 1933

The cell door creaked open, and through half closed eyes he watched the yellow light from the corridor creep towards him. Curled up on the damp stone floor, his body involuntary tensed as he prepared for more interrogations, more pain, more tricks.

In a strange way he preferred the beatings and the threats to being left alone for what seemed like months when he thought they had forgotten about him. That he would be held in there forever, abandoned and left to rot.

He closed his eyes and tried to cling onto the thought that it was only a game. He knew it wasn't real, but solitude, pain and loneliness made it easy to doubt one's mind. He heard someone enter and briefly considered grabbing him, but he knew that there would be others outside, just waiting for him to try.

'Come on Erik. It's over now.' The man who had come in spoke gently, but still Erik didn't move. It might be a ploy, another game they played to try to catch him out, but slowly he recognised the voice. The boss had come, it really was over.

The head of Z Section bent down next to him, his expensive suit getting contaminated by the filthy floor. 'Let's get you upstairs. We haven't got much time to get you back into shape.'

Erik struggled to a sitting position and leaned his head against the wall.

'Thank God for that. How long have I been here?'

'Just over six weeks. It's the 15th of February.' Charles Johnson replied.

'Six weeks? Are you sure?'

He received a nod in return.

'Feels like a lot longer than that I can tell you.'

'You've done well. Can you stand up?'

His legs shook but he managed to get onto his feet, a defiant look in his light blue eyes.

'You didn't break me; and you never will.'

'Glad to hear it.' Charles stepped out of the way and Erik spat on the floor in front of the guard who'd escorted him further down the corridor so many times these last six weeks. He knew that he'd only been doing his job, but still, he should consider himself lucky not to get punched.

Charles helped him up the stairs to the main part of the old country house and into a large, warm lounge. Three tall, leaded windows on the far side were framed by thick stone walls where the lights from the room reflected and mingled with the beginnings of a new day outside.

'Mrs Line, can we have one of your special cups of tea please. This man is in need of it.' He sat Erik down on the sofa.

'Of course, Sir. Can I get you one too?'

'No thank you. We'll have some breakfast afterwards.'

The housekeeper looked with pity on the tall, fair haired man slouched on the sofa before she disappeared towards the kitchen.

The fire roared in its old stone surround and Erik moved himself closer to it.

To think that through his darkest and most painful hours, this warm cosy lounge had been a couple of floors above him. Had Charles sat there with a drink, perhaps entertained friends, whilst in the basement, he'd been in hell?

They had blindfolded him when they grabbed him from the London hotel he'd been staying in and he still did not know where he was. That had been his twenty-fifth birthday.

He wished he could have a proper drink, but he knew that it would do him more harm than good before he'd had some food. A faint smell of bacon came wafting from the door where Mrs Line had disappeared and his stomach growled as he sank further into the sofa.

The boss had gone somewhere to collect his file; it would be filled with reports written by the nameless bastards who had tried to break him.

How had he done? There were times he couldn't remember and was not sure what he'd said or admitted to.

Mrs Line brought the tea and poured him a large cup.

'You poor man. It will be alright now.' Her motherly face looked with pity on him and he felt, for the first time since he got there, like crying. A great lump in his throat for the kindness shown by this woman he didn't know. He swallowed hard and smiled reassuringly at her.

'I'm fine, really I am.' He drank a little of the tea and fought hard not to let it show on his face just how awful it tasted. Instead he smiled. 'Thank you.'

'It's my own blend; you make sure you drink it all. It will do the trick, you'll see.' Mrs Line went back to the kitchen as Charles came back with a thick brown file marked "Secret" in bold red letters under his arm.

'I know you probably just want to eat and have a good sleep, but I have to go through a couple of things with you,' he smiled. 'You came through the early training very well, and this last part you came through as well as can be expected, if not better. We do still have to monitor you for a few days to see...'

'Will I be staying here?'

'Initially yes.' Charles got back up and walked over to the window. The house stood alone in the Scottish wilderness, surrounded by winter bare trees and darkness. If one wanted to feel on the outskirts of the world, this is where one should go. He turned back towards the room and continued.

'You've received a telegram from your sister.'

Erik's eyes darted briefly to the file left on the sofa, but his face didn't register surprise. Charles sat down again and opened the folder on his lap.

'She's expecting you by the end of March; you have a job as assistant to her husband.'

Erik nodded slowly. 'So it's happening?'

'If all goes well, you'll be leaving for Germany within a month. That should be enough time for you to get fit again, and for us to go through the final preparations. It might be best if you have a bit of breakfast and some sleep, and then we'll discuss it over dinner. You have to be sure you still want to go. There will be no back up if you need it and the Government will deny all knowledge of you,' he paused. 'In other words, you will be all on your own.'

Erik managed to get up from the sofa and slowly went over to the drinks cabinet where he poured himself a large whiskey. He held his glass up in a toast and grinned at Charles. 'It's the only way my friend. - Sieg Heil.'

~ 1 ~

Marseille, France, March 1941

'Go on say it. It won't hurt you. Just this once.'

Emilie's face was close, smelling of the lavender soap she liked to use when she was down south. When he didn't respond, she got up from the bed and walked, undressed, over to the gramophone. Sunshine breaking in through the worn wooden shutters danced over her back as she moved.

The sweet tunes of Lady Ella had ended some while earlier and the needle left crackling on the last round of the record. She picked the needle up and carefully moved it back to the beginning. Music soothed her. It lifted her spirits and always, always made her believe she could achieve anything she set her mind to.

Her country may be under the thumb of fascists spreading their nets over Europe, but jazz kept her going, made anything possible. It even cheered her up from Tom's constant refusal to say that he loved her, which she knew that deep down he did. Not in the same way he'd loved Maria, but how could she compete with a dead woman.

'You know I do,' Tom finally said and sat himself up leaning against the bed's cold metal bars. His deep brown eyes followed her as she moved around the room.

'One day you'll say it of your own accord.' She smiled and started getting dressed in time with the music. 'Come on, get up. We can't be late for the club.'

'They'll wait. You're their star attraction. I think it's important for you to be fashionably late.' Tom tried to pull her back onto the bed but was rewarded with his shirt and trousers thrown at him. 'Fine, but I've only got you for another couple of days and I think we should make the most of it.'

'We have been making the most of it.' Fully dressed she opened the shutters and let the late afternoon sunshine fill the room. 'They all know what we've been up to. The good thing is that they'll think it's you and Anaise getting up to no good.'

She applied powder over her smooth face. 'You aren't, are you?' Some blusher to the cheeks. 'When I'm not here.'

Tom laughed and pulled his trousers on. 'I can guarantee you that there is nothing, nor has there ever been anything, between me and your sister.' He went over to the dressing table and kissed her neck whilst still chuckling away to himself. She didn't know her sister very well at all, and he was sworn to secrecy.

'Don't laugh at me. It's difficult for me living in Paris knowing you're down here. You mustn't forget that I know what you're like.'

'What am I like, darling?'

'You know.'

'Oh Em, you know it's only you. Besides, you're the one with the husband waiting for you back home. I'm the one who should be jealous.' He put a comb through his dark hair and glanced in the mirror to ensure there were no lipstick marks anywhere.

'That was only because you went to Spain and abandoned me.'

A shadow briefly passed over Tom's face and Emilie turned around.

'I'm sorry. I didn't mean to mention it. I'm all done now.' She stood up and twirled around, making her long blonde locks bounce around her shoulders and her heart shaped face. It was no surprise that she had been topping the music halls in Paris for years. 'Let's have fun tonight and leave the past where it is. God knows there's enough trouble in the present.'

'I have to deliver the ink to Rémy before the show, so you're going to have to make your own way there with Anaise. I should have done it earlier. Sorry.'

'That's fine. All the more attention for me.' She joked and Tom relaxed again. He knew that she'd been looking forward to this evening and he hadn't wanted to upset her.

The ink should have been delivered earlier in the day but the town had been full of gendarmes for some reason or other and he'd felt uneasy, almost like someone had been watching him and he'd decided to go home instead.

There was no reason for it, he'd not seen anyone, but when your life, and the life of others, depended on secrecy you didn't need proof to be extra careful. Now he couldn't wait any longer. The newspaper couldn't be printed without the ink and everything else was ready.

'Come on, let's see if Anaise managed to find some food.' His stomach growled as he uttered the words. Unless you had family in the country side who could supply food outside rationing restrictions, you were always hungry.

'I won't miss the food down here.' Emilie puffed some Vol de Nuit in the air and walked through the spicy bergamot mist with her eyes closed.

'Well, you enjoy the extra rations brought to you courtesy of your pro German husband.'

'Now that's unfair. He's just misguided, but yes, I do enjoy it and whatever I eat, the Germans won't get.' She put down the amber perfume bottle before opening the door, and Tom shook his head.

Misguided was one word for it. Collaborateur was another.

***

The strong Mistral wind arrived in Marseille the very moment Tom left the house to deliver his parcel. This time of year, when spring had not quite yet settled in, the Mistral brought winter back and reminded him that only a couple of months earlier, the whole of the south had been cut off from the world. Snow storms cancelled trains and closed the ports but it had been good from a work point of view due to the reluctance of the police and other Vichy government staff to leave their cosy offices. He pulled his coat tighter, his hat lower and hurried along the bustling streets of the city centre. Once through the throng of the market square, he turned towards the port and disappeared in the crowds of refugees hanging around, waiting for their tickets out of France.

Rémy's house was not very far away from theirs but it was a whole different world, and even if Tom was being followed he'd lose them easily enough where he was going. Anaise's house, where Tom was lodging, was in a clean and relatively respectable area, Rémy's was in the absolute opposite.

In a small part of the old town, just north of the harbour lay the unmapped area of Le Panier, where, if you knew where you were going, the tiny cobbled alleyways could lead to safety, and if you didn't, it would probably lead you to a place you'd rather not be. It was a safe place to keep the illegal roneo copier.

The narrow cobbled streets had got him lost in the beginning and the smell of waste and rubbish reminded him of how lucky he was to not live there.

Turning left down a one way street he came to a two story house with a window broken on the top floor and the handle missing from the front door. He knocked quietly and heard steps coming towards it.

Rémy opened the door and rather brusquely pulled Tom in from the street.

'This should have been here by lunchtime.' He held up the parcel containing the ink which he had helped himself to from Tom's pocket. 'We have to work all night now.' He glared at Tom and threw the parcel to his son who ran towards the back of the house with it.

'I'm sorry Rémy, but there was something going on in town and there were more gendarmes around than normal. I thought it would be safer to wait.'

Rémy sighed and shook his large bald head. 'I knew there would be a reason, but my nerves are on edge. My son reported someone following him yesterday and Alain said he saw someone keeping his house under surveillance.'

'Is it serious enough to close down the network for a while? Until things settle down?' Tom asked, still standing against the damp wall in the small hallway.

There were plates being loudly washed up in the kitchen behind the fireplace and Rémy looked over there briefly.

'No. Let's get this month's paper out. Most of the work has been done and we are ready to copy. Well, we are now.' He glared ever so slightly at Tom again.

'We'll come over tomorrow for the distribution.' Tom promised.

'Take extra care. If there is any chance of you being followed or compromised, don't come here. Get word to us somehow, but don't come here.' He opened the door for Tom.

'I know what to do. And the same goes for you.'

Rémy nodded and shut out both Tom and the Mistral with a bang.

When he arrived at the club, Emilie was already up on stage singing Baby Won't You Please Come Home. Dressed in a backless blue and white evening dress, high heels and bright red lipstick, she flirted with the piano player as she sang. He'd seen her on stage many times when she first started out, then the attention had mostly been from old men sipping cheap wine in some dark bar in the side streets of Paris. That had been before the wars came, both the Spanish one and the European one, when everything had been easy and they had both been very young. If he hadn't gone to Spain, they would probably be married now. Instead she'd done what she said she'd do; she had got on with her life and married her most admiring fan, her authoritarian manager Gérard.

Tom couldn't blame her, and refused to blame himself, but fate had in 1937 been cruel indeed.

'She's quite sensuous on stage. I hadn't expected that.' Anaise said proudly as Tom sat down at the round table she shared with some friends. 'Did you see Rémy?'

'I did. He was jittery, but we'll talk at home.' Tom took a gulp of his drink. They watched Emilie in silence until she'd finished her number and then a roar of applause lifted from the crowded tables.

'She is bloody marvellous your sister. She's wasted up in Paris. You should get her to stay down here,' a drunken Dominic shouted above the noise.

Anaise nodded and replied, 'I've given up trying.'

'Shame on you. That's Pétain's job.' Dominic responded and the table burst out laughing. Tom noticed Jérôme's eyes casually scanning the tables around them to see if anybody had paid attention to the comment. When his eyes met Tom's on the opposite side of the table, he smiled. They had been friends since he'd arrived in Marseille, and he was an important part of their group.

The club was full, and if Emilie hadn't asked the doorman to let him in, he would be standing outside queueing still. As it was, the doorman had frowned upon his attire and ushered him in to the darkness of the club quickly before anybody noticed his very casual appearance. Half the country may have been handed over on a plate to the Germans and the unoccupied part drowning in refugees from the north, but somehow there was still money and champagne slushing around. Who were they all? They were certainly not the tens of thousands who had clogged up the roads all through France the previous year, leaving behind their homes and losing their families in the crush to escape the Germans. He'd seen it all before in Spain, when the terrified population tried to escape Franco's army and he hoped he'd never have to see it again.

He turned his attention back to Emilie who was now slowly singing her heart out.

'Would anyone like a drink?' he asked.

'Yes, please. How rich are you feeling?' Anaise enquired with a wide smile.

'Have anything you like.' Tom sighed and hoped she wouldn't go overboard. His funds were dwindling faster than he would like, and even though he had plenty of money back in England, he didn't know if he'd ever be able to transfer it here.

'Oh, well I'll have a Ruby Champagne cocktail please.' She blew him a kiss. 'You are a darling man.' The rest of the table agreed in tandem and Tom went in search of a waiter. The area all around them had turned into a dance floor and he decided it would be easier to go to the bar and order.

He asked the barman to deliver the drinks to their table whilst lingering for a little while at the bar. Through the smoke from his cigarette he glanced at a man standing a couple of meters away by the kitchen doors. He didn't drink or dance, his attention wasn't on Emilie, and he didn't look like an employee of the club. He must be some government employee, one of the secret service bureaux or perhaps the Gendarmes. You never knew, he might even be German. There were enough anti fascists and other undesirables here in Marseille to warrant a lot of interest. A hive of spies and escapees of all nationalities trying to get on a boat, at any price, out of France.

Tom took a deep drag of his cigarette and tried to see where the man's attention lay when the waiter, who was picking up his table's drinks, spilled the contents of his tray over Tom. He apologised and Tom swore in return. The bartender's face had gone red with anger and the man Tom had been watching now stood next to him and discreetly, through his coat pocket, pointed a gun at him.

'Monsieur Prideux?' The man asked in a southern accent.

'Oui,' Tom answered reluctantly. He had nothing incriminating on him and even though he had a false identity as Alphonse Prideux, his papers were immaculate. They had been stolen by a former government employee who'd fled Normandy the previous summer. Still, Tom's heart rate increased.

'I have someone who'd like to meet you Monsieur.'

'Well, I'm just going back to my table. He's more than welcome to join me and my friends.'

'He's waiting for you upstairs. Don't let him wait any longer than he already has.'

Something in his voice, not to mention the hand he kept in his coat pocket, convinced Tom that maybe it was better to meet this man than not. He looked towards Emilie on the stage, still singing, her eyes searched the venue for him. He hoped this wouldn't turn out badly.

They squeezed past some dancing couples towards a partly hidden door at the far end of the club. It was opened for them by a large bald man who didn't utter a word as they went past.

The main part of the club was all mirrors and lights, but the back was gothically painted black, and for some reason or other, lit with candles rather than electric lights. Tom knew where the stairs that led up from the dark hall went, and he knew that the clientele that went there did not queue outside the main club, and that it was not advertised to the general public. He'd not visited himself, but had heard rumours from friends, who had heard them from other friends.

Upstairs there were more of the same and a couple of scantily clad girls smiled quietly at him from a round red velvet sofa. An owl turned its head from his post on a coat stand as they went past and up another set of stairs where, behind closed ornate oak doors, Tom was asked to wait.

The large mirrored room was dominated by a round bed with purple satin sheets and expensive perfume hung in the air. A cafe table and two chairs were set up in the corner and a whiskey bottle rested on top of it. Tom looked away, who knew what would be in the bottle. Maybe it was all a joke and someone had set him up for a surprise visit here. A present. He would have to say no though because he was a changed man.

The man with the gun spoilt that scenario.

Downstairs, his friends would be drinking their cocktails and Jérôme would wonder where he'd disappeared to. He'd not been gone long enough for them to worry, and he hoped that he'd be back at the table before they had to.

He nervously walked around the room before sitting down on the edge of the bed. His reflection was replicated in the mirrors lining the walls and the ceiling. How he'd changed these last few years. He would turn thirty in a couple of months, but he felt a lot older. There was no point worrying about being killed, a lot of good people had died fighting for what they believed in, and some for what others believed in, and some because they couldn't get away. He had worried once and he had loved once, it had got him nowhere, and life was so much easier when you didn't let things get too close. A clear head, a rational mind and a healthy dose of luck would see him through this war alive.

He decided that the whiskey was probably alright and was just about to try it out when the door opened and a tall slim man in a charcoal suit came in. Tom abruptly stood up.

'I hope I'm not disappointing you.' The man smiled and closed the door. 'I'm Martin Perrault, agent of the Bureau Cinquieme.' He indicated for Tom to join him at the table and poured some drinks. His face and manner were friendly enough, but these were not friendly times and he knew that Martin Perrault wanted something from him. He didn't know what, but there was no other reason for getting him up here at gunpoint.

'Monsieur Perrault, why have you brought me here? My friends will be wondering where I am.'

'Yes, I'm sure they will, but I won't keep you more than a few moments.' The rough Paris accent contradicted his sophisticated exterior.

Tom accepted a cigarette and blew a cloud of smoke towards the ceiling whilst waiting for Monsieur Perrault to start. He was quite a handsome chap, mid-thirties, dark hair slicked back from his high forehead and brown eyes that were a little too close together.

'Your girlfriend is quite a singer.' He indicated towards the main club. 'I had terrible trouble dragging myself away from her.'

'She's my cousin, not my girlfriend, but yes, she's rather fabulous.' Tom waited a moment for Monsieur Perrault to respond. When he only nodded and refilled his glass Tom continued. 'Your Bureau Cinquieme was disbanded last year.' He decided to take a chance and emptied his glass. 'Didn't anybody tell you?'

'You're very well informed. However, it never stopped existing, only now it's staffed by ghosts.'

'Ah, very sensible. Agents whose records have been wiped out as if they'd never existed. I guess, if the Germans don't know about it, they can't mind can they.'

The Bureau Cinquieme had been the information gathering part of the French intelligence network, but it had been closed down the previous year due to Germany not approving of the French Vichy government officially spying on them. It would seem that actually, they'd just gone underground.

'We're not anti German, we're pro French which brings me to the reason I asked to meet you.' He leaned back in his chair and locked his eyes onto Tom's. 'We know all about your little network here Monsieur Prideux. We have done for a little while now.'

Tom's muscles tensed but nothing showed on his face and he held Perrault's gaze without flinching.

'You, your "cousins", the dregs in Le Panier. We know what you do, and when you do it.' He stopped for a moment to let Tom respond.

'There has clearly been some mistake. If you had any proof we'd be having this chat in some prison cell.' His heart was beating hard and fast as he took a deep seemingly relaxed drag of his cigarette before crushing it into the ashtray.

Tom had felt that something was wrong for some time, but if they had evidence of his group's activities then they would have swooped down and arrested them already. Wouldn't they?

'I can assure you that there is no mistake, and we have plenty of proof. At this very moment in time, we could go to Le Panier and pick up some illegal papers and a printer together with your friends working on the latest issue even as we speak.'

Tom's eyes broke away from his gaze. How did they know all of this? He could see what was coming. They'd want him to spy on them.

'What do you want?' Tom asked neutrally, looking back up.

Perrault twirled the now empty glass in his hands and smiled.

'I knew we'd get on you and I. We both have France's best interest at heart,' he paused and put his glass down. 'I want you to kill a very special man.'

***

'So, it's finally happened. We're screwed.' Anaise closed her green eyes and held onto the edge of the large kitchen table, where the three of them had gathered after the club. Her shoulder length brown hair, smooth and shiny, fell over her face as she leaned forward. 'I think I'm going to be sick.' She took a few gulps of air and sipped the water Tom brought her before sitting down.

'There must be an informer in the group for them to know so much about us.' Tom said thoughtfully.

'Who? Most of us have known each other all our lives. Anaise and I grew up with them or their children. I would trust them with my life.' Emilie looked up from her glass of wine. 'They could have got some of the information from Vincent or Elise.'

Anaise nodded in agreement, but Tom wasn't convinced.

'They were based outside the city and only had Rémy as their contact here. Besides, it has been ten months since their arrest and all ties with them were severed at the time.'

'Has there been any news on what happened to them?'

'No. We know that Elise was sent to Ravensbrück camp and the British pilot they were hiding at the time was shot. There is still no news about Vincent.' Tom shook his head. 'This wasn't down to them.'

Silence settled over the room and the only noise heard were Anaise's fingers nervously tapping on the wooden table.

'We have some time to wrap up here and get you two out of France.' Tom said, hoping they'd listen to him.

'Don't be daft. They won't touch me. They have no evidence, and Gerard has friends in high places if they tried.' Emilie said matter-of-factly. 'I'll be fine and Anaise can come up and stay with me and we'll lie low for a while. Also, I have to let our people in Paris know what's happened as soon as possible. What about you Tom, what will you do?'

'I don't know. Stay here for a while. We're all safe until Perrault gets back in touch with details of what he wants me to do.'

Perrault had asked Tom not to leave Marseille and not to get involved in any further resistance work until he'd completed his task. He would be contacted with the details within the next couple of days and Tom didn't want to risk alienating him by leaving.

Rémy and his gang needed as much time as possible to relocate the equipment and maybe themselves too. They'd agreed no further contact unless there was an emergency.

Within an hour everything had been turned on its head. Everybody knew this could happen and it could have been a lot worse. They could all have been arrested. He was curious about the whole business of killing someone. Why couldn't they do it themselves? He wouldn't do it for them, they were after all a fascist government falling over themselves to gain favour with Hitler, and he would never help them in any way.

The fact that Emilie was convinced that her husband could, or more importantly, would, pull strings if he had to, was like a slap in the face. Tom could get her out of France, but she'd rather go back to Paris, to him.

'Make sure you don't take any unnecessary risks Tom.' Emile took his hand which he childishly moved away and instantly regretted it.

'I'll stay here for a couple of days too,' Anaise added. 'We'll be safe here for now and I'll come up to Paris at the end of the week as we originally planned.'

Emilie nodded, her eyes on the table where her hand still rested alone.

'I'll take the first train tomorrow morning.' She looked at the clock. 'Only five hours to go. I guess I should go and pack.' She got up to leave when Tom grabbed her hand.

'Sorry Em.'

'Help me pack?'

He nodded and got up from his chair, leaving Anaise alone at the table, staring into space.

~ 2 ~

Tom's steps echoed between the tall buildings along the tree-lined Rue Cours Gouffé. His low mood that morning was only matched by the miserable grey clouds speeding past across the rooftops towards the sea and into the distance. He walked purposefully towards the Eglise St Isabel where his official employment as homme d'entretien, maintenance man, lay. The work itself was for show only, he needed a place of employment to avoid being flagged up by the authorities. It was very convenient for meetings, but poor Father Michel despaired at Tom's upkeep of the church.

There had not been much sleep the previous night after Perrault's threat. Unfinished thoughts had kept both of them awake, staring at the once white ceiling, wondering what would happen next.

When the first morning light seeped in through the shutters, they had said their goodbyes.

'It's better like this,' she'd said quietly before they got up. 'I'd rather remember this than a stilted goodbye at the station.'

An hour later he'd watched her and Anaise walk arm in arm down the street towards Gare Saint Charles.

The Eglise St Isabel was in a quiet residential neighbourhood in the 6th arrondissement. Due to its proximity to the port, every street had been affected by the previous year's bombing one way or another. There were terrible gaps where buildings had once stood and others that had only partly collapsed and still had families living in them.

Some residents had tried to patch their homes up as best they could, but limited manpower and even more limited building supplies, meant that most of them had come to a halt. Under dried leaves and rubble along the cobbled streets, you could still find once treasured photographs and other personal possessions. One could only hope that their owners were still alive somewhere and well enough to miss them. These items were picked up when found and brought to the church where Father Michel kept them safe until they were claimed by their owners. Or put in one of the large boxes marked 'la mémoire' together with a prayer.

Tom found Father Michel in the rectory kitchen making tea. It was a sizable room dominated by a large square wooden table covered with a crisp white table cloth and a brown ceramic jug containing yellow wild flowers. A small loaf of black bread lay crudely cut on the side and two breakfast plates rested in the sink. Father Michel had company.

His old face lit up when he saw Tom. 'Ah, bien, très bien. I need help carrying these up to the loft.' He shakily handed two cups of grey liquid to Tom and led the way upstairs. 'Luckily Madam Ecout is off for a few days.' He looked over his shoulder towards Tom. 'You'll see what I mean.'

His soutane dragged against the wooden steps as he made his way slowly up the steep stairs. Tom followed and tried to not spill the contents of the cups. He hoped that the priest had not yet again taken in a stray. Father Michel had been the local Priest for over thirty years and there was not a secret in the neighbourhood he didn't know, or a sailor or sinner he'd ever turned away. Since the troubles started there had also been a regular supply of refugees from occupied countries. They could be found from time to time hiding in the shadows of the church to avoid spot checks on the streets.

They reached the loft, and as Tom had suspected, on the makeshift bed in the corner sat a girl. She jumped up and moved quickly into the shadows as Tom entered the gloomy room. Apart from the bed there was a small table with crumbs left behind from their breakfast and two chairs still pulled out. The floorboards were bare and a small cross hung above the wooden bed. Father Michel tutted.

'Don't worry child. He's one of us.'

Tom raised his eyebrows briefly behind the Priest's back. He'd given up his beliefs a long time ago. Father Michel was aware of this, but had made him one of his projects, convinced that he would, under his guidance, find his way back to the Catholic church. War makes for strange friendships, and theirs was now cemented solid by resistance to the invaders and the Vichy government.

The young woman came slowly back out into the dull light from the window and Father Michel took the cups from Tom and put them on the table. She was taller than she'd looked at first, about twenty years old with sand coloured hair combed back into a loose bun at the back and deep green eyes, filled to the brim with sadness.

'Sit down Sophia and drink your tea.' She did as Father Michel asked and looked curiously at Tom who still stood in the low doorway. He knew what this was all about and he wanted to tell Father Michel that it was getting too difficult, that refugees with no papers were less and less likely to get out of France. She would be better off going to one of the aid agencies and registering. He didn't want the girl to hear the hopelessness of her situation from him, Father Michel would be better at giving her the bad news than a stranger.

'Sophia needs help getting out. She's Austrian Jewish and has lost most of her family. She's got to get out.' Father Michel knew the difficulties, and he knew what Tom would tell him when they got back downstairs. He wanted Tom to feel Sophia's troubles before he gave a definite no. What he didn't know was the previous night's events and Tom wanted to tell him before they gave any information to the girl. Sure she looked the part, but how did he know that she wasn't just an informant. They already had all the information they needed, so Tom doubted that she was a plant, but there were other issues now.

'Can I talk to you downstairs?' Tom said to Father Michel.

'Of course. Can you please just talk to Sophia first and see what you can do.'

Reluctantly, Tom nodded and sat down on the other chair.

'Have you got any papers Sophia?' He looked at her and she shook her head.

'No. My mother has them. She carried all our papers,' she paused. 'I don't know where they are now. I don't know where my mother is.' Her eyes watered and her hands shook as she covered her face, and then her head, as if to hide from the world.

Father Michel put a hand on her shoulder. 'There, there Sophia. Your mother would want you to be strong.'

'I'm sorry.' She wiped her eyes and straightened up. 'No, Monsieur. I have no papers and no money.'

'It is very difficult getting out of France. We used to be able to send people into Spain, but now they send back anybody without papers. The escape lines are busy getting soldiers back to England. Have you got any relations in America? Their embassy is still open here and maybe they could get you an exit visa.'

'I have a brother in London. I'm not sure where he lives, but I can find him.' She saw Tom shake his head and continued. 'He lives in London and he will look after me. I have to go there. I have to go there.' She spoke faster and faster as she saw her hope of leaving disappear. 'I will do anything. Please, please don't say you can't help.' She looked to Father Michel and then back to Tom.

'It's not that I don't want to help you.' Tom sighed. Feeling sorry for her was useless, but he did all the same. He always did. It was just what Father Michel had aimed for. 'It will be alright. Something will come up but it might take some time. You stay here for now, and keep quiet so nobody else sees or hears you. Do you understand?'

She nodded with relief showing all over her face; a glimmer of hope in the distance to hold onto. Tom got up and told Father Michel he needed to talk to him downstairs. Once outside the door he could hear the Priest re-assuring the girl that all would be well.

'This must all have been sent to test our humanity and our faith. Tom, let's not find ourselves wanting in either. This is a precious life in need of saving.' Father Michel stood next to Tom in the kitchen, both leaning back against the wooden dresser that held what was left of the parish china.

Tom had explained the previous night's events, but Father Michel didn't seem to grasp the seriousness of their situation. Well, maybe he did grasp it, maybe he understood it better than anyone of them; that it was truly heroic men and women who continued when everything seemed lost. One saved life could so easily drown in the millions already dead.

'Father, I promise I will try but I don't know what my future holds. This time next week I could be in a cell or worse, but we'll see what happens...'

He was interrupted by loud knocking on the front door.

'That'll be Madam Maille. Her daughter is getting married tomorrow.' Father Michel shook his head. 'Sometimes I wonder if she has not been sent to test my faith also.' He smiled weakly before making his way towards the front of the house whilst Tom left quietly from the kitchen door.

***

Anaise stood at the end of the platform looking towards the tunnel where the train had disappeared. She stood there long after it had gone. Lack of sleep and a tearful goodbye had left her eyes puffy and tired. They'd spent most of their adult lives apart but this blasted war had made everything so fragile, and now, every time she said goodbye to anyone, she wondered if she'd ever see them again. Finally, she turned around and sauntered back along the platform and out of the station. The monumental steps leading down to street level were lined with statues reminding visitors of Marseille's past and the glorious destinations that could be reached via her port before the war. It was not as cold and windy as it had been the previous day but she pulled her jacket tighter as she walked down the steps.

The streets were getting busier and from the skies the Gabians screamed out for breakfast.

She kicked a stone out of the way and looked around. Was someone following her?

What had in the beginning seemed almost like a game had turned into reality and it was starting to scare her. She paused to look in to a shop window whilst figuring out how to lose that unsubstantiated shadow without looking like she had something to hide. In the reflection of the glass she looked for anybody loitering or walking slowly and aimlessly along the street. There was no one obvious, no one that paid any attention especially to her. Still, that didn't mean they weren't there. Oh, God, she was getting paranoid. Was this the way it would be from now on? Always convinced that somebody's watching and that anybody might betray you. She'd turn into Tom and Rémy, scarred by the nature of what they did, and always suspicious.

The Market Square was close by, and at this time in the morning every housewife in Marseille would be there trying to buy some vegetables for their families. It would be as good a place as any to disappear into, and it had the added advantage of being on the way to where she was going. She followed the Boulevard d'Athènes down the hill before turning into the wide allées Léon Gambetta where, just at the turning by the church, a series of grey stone archways opened up. Along the sides of the large square were small shops and boutiques that used to sell everything from flowers and hats to cigars and hardware. Only a handful of them were open now.

The market wasn't as full as she'd hoped. Only a few stalls still had something to sell, their carrots and cabbages pathetically lined up on their tables with women patiently queueing up alongside them. There would be no diving in and disappearing into the crowd here. Instead she increased her speed and crossed the square, her heals clicking along the cobbles. If there had been time and opportunity, she would have stopped to buy some vegetables. There was no food in the house and she knew that Tom was always hungry. She quickly put those thoughts out of her head, if he wanted food he could queue for it himself. She exited through another archway and quickly walked into an alleyway. She stood there for a few minutes, watching the road outside. The sun was trying to break through the clouds above, but in the alleyway where she stood, it was still cold and damp. The only person emerging from the market archways was an old woman carrying a basket of carrots. She threw Anaise an odd glance as she passed, but that was all.

With relief she realised that she was alone and started running up the hill towards Rue Margret and the boarding house where her friend Fleur lived.

The street had survived the bombings well enough and the detached red brick building in the middle of it stood out against the other, once pastel coloured, petite maison de ville.

Fleur had warned her about the landlady's temper and asked her never to visit out of the blue. In this city of shortages she couldn't afford to lose her accommodation. Anaise had spent many a nights there the last few months but they'd always snuck in through Fleur's window or tiptoed up the stairs in the dark. They'd whispered and laughed as if they were children afraid of being caught awake after bedtime. There had been a lot of laughter since they'd met at Christmas. She was always plein de vie, full of life. Since they'd met, Anaise had been full of life too.

A little out of breath from the steep hill, she smiled to herself at the memories. It had been three weeks since they'd last met and she hoped her friend was home. They'd decided to stay apart whilst Em was in town even though Anaise had wanted the two of them to meet. Fleur had insisted that as much as she wanted to meet her sister, this wasn't the time.

The wind blew the thin white curtains from the open windows on the first floor where Fleur was staying. She couldn't climb in through the window like they normally did when they arrived back from whatever bar they'd been to. It was one thing doing so when Fleur was with her and nobody was watching. Now that it was daylight, it didn't seem appropriate, never mind the neighbours would think the boarding house was being burgled. Instead, she walked up the two steps to the front door and knocked loudly.

There was no answer, but Anaise had to see her. Not just because she'd missed her, but also because she might be able to make sense of this mess they all found themselves in. She would make it seem almost unimportant, a small glitch to be fixed.

Maybe the land lady was doing the washing out the back. She turned the door handle and to her surprise it was unlocked. The hallway inside was dark but she knew where she was going. She had made getting in and out of this house without being seen an art. The stairs didn't make a sound and when she got to the first floor landing she saw Fleur's door wide open. Weak sunshine spilt out from her room onto the well-worn red rug that lined the wooden floor of the corridor outside. Her friend was so protective of her privacy that she expected her to stand guard at the door. When she walked in, her mouth fell open in surprise.

The bed had been stripped and all Fleur's belongings were gone. Just empty spaces left where her books on philosophy and art had been, just an uncovered pillow and blanket where the two of them had laid.

'What are you doing in here? I'm not taking new lodgers right now.' The landlady's shrill voice made her jump. Her grey hair was tied back and a crisp white apron was folded in two, doubling up on itself beneath her waist. She stood blocking the doorway as if Anaise might try to escape.

'I'm not looking for a room. I'm looking for Mademoiselle Rousseau.'

The land lady looked at her for a moment with a puzzled look on her face. 'Anaise Laurent?'

'Oui.' Anaise's mind was still racing with possibilities of Fleur's departure to take too much notice of the landlady.

'You don't recognise me? I don't blame you, it was a long time ago now.'

Anaise looked at the old lady again and slowly she recognised her. 'Madam Blanc? From the sweet shop.'

'Oui, I remember you and your sister coming on every Saturday. As different as the sun and the moon you were.'

'Yes, I remember. It was a long time ago, Madam.' Her thoughts returned to the whereabouts of her friend. 'Do you know where Fleur Rousseau is?'

The landlady glance towards the bed and sighed. 'You'd better come with me.'

Anaise followed her down the stairs, past the front door and along the hallway to the kitchen. It smelled of scouring powder, and on the side sat a piece of lard salé, salted bacon, no doubt from the black market. Pushed up against one of the white washed walls was a well-scrubbed pine table and Madam Blanc indicated that she should sit down.

A bottle of Pastis appeared together with two glasses and Anaise accepted the drink with unease, wondering what could have happened that would warrant an alcoholic drink at this time in the morning. Madam Blanc sat down next to her and picked up the bottle. Her rheumatic hands held it steady whilst she poured the anise flavoured liquid into the sparkling clean glasses. She sipped her drink and indicated to Anaise that she should do the same. Anaise wanted to point out that it was not yet ten in the morning but she didn't want to offend the old lady.

'Were you good friends?' Madam Blanc asked.

'Yes. I'd like to think so.' She stopped. 'Why did you say 'were'? Where is she?'

'I'm sorry, I didn't know who to contact,' she paused as if unsure whether to continue. 'She died in her sleep a few days ago. The doctor said it would have been quick and painless, but such a shame. She was only young, her whole life ahead of her. Some official people came and cleared out everything in her room. When they'd gone, it was as if she'd never existed.'

Anaise stared at Madam Blanc without being able to completely take it in. How could she be dead? The land lady was still talking, something about the authorities having to take the body away.

This couldn't be happening. Madam Blanc had it all wrong. It must have been someone else.

'Excuse me, Madam,' she interrupted the landlady's nervous chatter. 'I'm sorry, but there must be a mistake. My friend Fleur isn't dead, she must just have left, gone somewhere else.'

The old lady's shiny blue eyes met Anaise's over the table.

'No ma chéri. The doctor pronounced her dead. There has been no mistake. I am sorry.'

Anaise emptied the glass. 'How did it happen?'

The old lady shrugged her shoulders. 'I don't know. They wouldn't tell me anything. She did look very peaceful though. I don't think she'd been in any pain.'

Anaise looked down at the table and over to the chipped kitchen sink.

'Where did they take her?'

'To be buried I guess. They said they'd let me know about funeral arrangements, but I haven't heard anything yet. She kept herself to herself, but I'd still like to attend her funeral.'

Anaise pulled her chair back and stood up. 'Thank you for the drink, Madam.'

'Mademoiselle, are you alright?'

She nodded before starting to walk towards the front door. She'd just turned the handle when she heard Madam Blanc hurrying down the corridor towards her.

'Wait, just a moment. I found this under her bed when I cleaned.' She handed Anaise a thin notebook. 'I think it's some kind of diary. I would have given it to her relatives, but there doesn't seem to be any. I only had a very quick look to see what it was. I can't seem to make head nor tail of it.' She shrugged her shoulders. 'It seems to be in some sort of code.'

'Why didn't the officials take this too?' Anaise asked.

The landlady shrugged her shoulders. 'I don't know, maybe they didn't find it, or they didn't care.' The old lady moved restlessly from one foot to the other. 'Alright. I had the booklet. I didn't take it on purpose but somehow the day before she died, it ended up in the pocket of my apron. I just forgot to put it back.' She looked suitable embarrassed for what she'd done.

Anaise nodded and put the note book in her pocket. 'I'll let you know if I hear anything about the funeral arrangements.'

Once outside the boarding house, Anaise ran down the hill towards the park and found a bench where she sat down. It was only when she opened the booklet that she realised just how little she knew about Fleur.

~ 3 ~

The next couple of days passed slowly for Tom. He couldn't see friends, he couldn't help out at the church and Anaise had spent most of the time out of the house. She had gone out the previous evening to see a friend and had obviously stayed overnight. Tom worried that she had got into trouble, he worried about the network situation and who could be informing on them. Was everyone else ok? He didn't know and sitting around with nothing to do but wait for Perrault to contact him only made everything worse.

At least the sun had come out, the wind had calmed down and their neighbour, Madam Boule across the street, put out a chair for her invalid husband in front of their house.

Tom was sitting at the window, watching as she helped an unwilling Monsieur Boule outside, and onto the chair. He must have been eighty years old and would obviously rather stay indoors. Never mind what he wanted, Madam helped him outside every morning, weather permitting, and only brought him in at mealtimes. The fresh air would do him good. Other neighbours stopped and said hello to him on their way to the market or work or wherever they were going.

Tom was, for the third day, sitting by the window watching Monsieur Boule 'being put outside', tensely wondering once more where Anaise had spent the night when he heard the back door creak open. He turned around expecting to see Anaise sheepishly grinning back at him, but instead there was Perrault. It was a relief almost, at least now he could put an end to the whole thing. Everybody had had enough time to do what they had to do, and if he was arrested, so be it.

Martin Perrault looked around the messy kitchen and stepped inside.

'Bonjour Alphonse. You look surprised to see me.'

'Only because people normally knock before they enter someone's house.'

'As would I, if I was visiting a friend.' He indicated for Tom to sit down at the table. He was certainly taking liberties, thought Tom, it was his house. Nevertheless, he obliged and Perrault sat down on the chair opposite. His dark eyes settled on Tom's, and he felt the hair on the back of his head stand right up. Enough, he thought. One way or another this had to end.

'Let's cut to the chase. We're not as you put it 'friends'. What do you want me to do?'

Perrault smiled and pulled out a cigarette from a silver case and lit it with a matching lighter. He didn't offer one to Tom.

'You are absolutely correct Alphonse. On Friday, I want you to blow up signal house 2231. You must ensure that this man is inside.'

He put a photograph in front of Tom. It was taken when the subject wasn't looking. He was tall, blond and well built. Tom guessed he was in his mid-thirties and he'd never seen him before.

Perrault continued. 'He should arrive at 16.50 and you must make sure that the explosion takes place exactly ten minutes after his arrival. If he arrives late, you must adjust the timings. There will be another couple of men with him but that can't be helped.' He looked at Tom to make sure he understood. 'These people mean nothing to you. They invaded us. This is surely what you people should be doing. Killing Nazis.'

Tom lit up a cigarette of his own. 'Who is he?'

'His current name is Pierre Lupin. He's a Nazi agent and his real German name is Erik Tag. The Vichy Government is swarming with them, and we try to catch as many as we can, but some are just too clean. We know who he is, but we can't prove it. If you randomly shot ten political aides or members of their staff, at least half of them would be spies,' he paused briefly. 'We can't just kill him ourselves, because if the Germans found out, there would be hell to pay. Now, if you were to kill him as an act of sabotage, we both win.'

Apart from the innocent people caught up in the reprisals Tom wanted to add, instead he exhaled smoke into Perrault's face, making him cough.

'They may be Nazis, but I'm not a 'killer for hire.' You clean up your own mess. There should be no problem for you to get rid of him surely.'

'There are reasons why we can't do it. I'm not going to tell you why, suffice to say that you will do this.'

Tom's eyes narrowed. 'You will have to find someone else.'

Perrault's lips became a red thin line when he realised that Tom meant what he said.

'Well, it's your choice Tom Lancaster. I won't make you do anything you don't want to do. I would strongly recommend you reconsider though.' He threw two photos on the table in front of Tom who had only just realised what Perrault had actually called him. He must have misheard.

When he saw the photos he knew that he hadn't.

One was a shot of Tom in Madrid during the early part of the Spanish Civil War when he'd been there reporting for a Paris paper. How had they got hold of that photo? When he saw the second picture, he knew they had him.

It was a photo of him and Emilie walking hand in hand. It must have been taken just a few days ago. As innocent as you could pretend that was, her husband would see it for what it really was. Perrault was smiling again as he saw the look of surprise and then resignation on Tom's face. He too knew that Tom couldn't get away.

'Keep the photos Tom. I have plenty more of them. I hear Madam Emilie Valois's husband is a good man. One who would not care if his wife was having an affair. Especially an affair with someone he has always hated. Someone who's a well-known Republican. Left wing scum some would say.' He let that hang in the air for a moment or two whilst Tom's brain was racing. Gerard would kill her.

Perrault continued. 'The papers probably wouldn't care about it either. They wouldn't want to push their favourite star of her pedestal just to sell a few more issues.' He took a deep breath. 'As for you, I don't need to tell you what we do with people caught with false papers. I don't think you actually care what happens to yourself, but you do care what happens to Emilie. Possibly even her sister.'

They'd thrown the net over Tom's head and he could see no way of getting out.

'Where is this signalling house?'

Perrault brought out a small well folded map and put it on the table. He was looking to find the spot when the front door opened and Anaise came in.

Perrault looked up with ice cold eyes.

'Leave.'

Thankfully Anaise did not argue, and backed out again. The door closed quietly behind her and Perrault went back to searching for the signalling house Tom was to demolish.

***

Anaise stood watching the door that she'd just shut for a moment. Her heart was thumping in her chest and briefly she wanted to run away. Anywhere. Tom's face had been ashen and he'd seemed smaller somehow. Maybe she should go back in, but what would that achieve? Tom could handle whatever they threw at him. She'd seen him take charge of seemingly impossible situations and pull them through. He'd do that again.

'Are you alright, Anaise?'

The voice came from across the street where Monsieur Boule sat in his normal place. Anaise hurried over to set his mind at rest before the whole street was alerted.

'Yes, thank you. I've just remembered that I forgot something in the cafe.' She smiled as best she could.

'You'd better run along and collect it quickly. Madam Boule tells me there are a lot of thieves in there these days. You shouldn't stay though. It's no place for a young lady now.' He nodded to himself as he confirmed that the world of hooligans and thieves had descended on Marseille. Perhaps he was right. Anaise smiled and agreed with him before hurrying down the street towards the cafe. She didn't want to be outside when, whoever that man was, came out. She'd be happy never to see his cold face again.

There was not a table to be had at the Cafe Deux Amis when Anaise arrived. She managed to find a space by the end of the bar where Monsieur Calotte, the owner, spotted her. The cigarette hanging from the side of his mouth added to the already smoky atmosphere and the noise from the far corner where some kind of meeting had just taken place threatened to give her a headache.

'Coffee?' Monsieur Calotte asked.

Anaise nodded gratefully, wishing it was later in the day so that she could order something stronger. He brought her a small cup and she tried to hand him some change but he held up his hands. 'On the house today.' His eyes fell on her shaking hands as she put the coffee cup to her lips.

'Is everything ok?'

Anaise put the cup down and nodded. 'We've had a bit of trouble recently. Just personal things.' She'd known Monsieur Calotte since she was little and she didn't like to lie to him. He'd been her father's friend, but it was over fifteen years since he'd died and they didn't have much contact now. She came in for a coffee sometimes but he didn't come to her house anymore. He didn't approve of her living on her own before the war and he approved even less of her having Tom as a lodger. It was nice to see a friendly face now though. A friend from before all the secrets and lies. He beckoned her to the back room where they sat down. The room was dark with thick curtains drawn across the large window and boxes of tablecloths, bottles of wine and the occasional one with food stacked along the walls.

'Your barmaid won't thank you for leaving her to serve on her own,' Anaise said.

'She'll be fine for a while.' He looked at her with concern. 'Is Emilie alright?'

She nodded. 'Why shouldn't she be?'

'No reason. You said that it was personal troubles that were on your mind. If it's not her, I assume it's you or that man that lives in your house.'

'It's nothing to do with him or me or anyone else for that matter.' She got up to leave and Calotte took her arm.

'Sit down Anaise - please.'

'I don't want to discuss it. It's really nice of you to care but I know what you're going to say. The same as every time.'

'That just shows that you know that I'm right and your parents, both of them, would have said the same.'

'Can we continue this conversation after the war? If it ever ends and if we're still alive when it does. I have more important things to worry about than what the neighbours think of me having a male lodger.'

'If you're in any trouble I will help you. Whatever it is.' Calotte tried and Anaise gave in and smiled kindly at him.

'It's really nice of you to worry about me, but there's no need. Really.' She squeezed his hand and he sighed whilst shaking his head slowly.

'I should have done more for you girls. And for your mother when she was alive.'

'We're all grown up now,' she paused briefly. 'I'm sorry, but I have to leave. I have to be somewhere.' She opened the door to the bar and Calotte followed her out.

Anaise wanted to be outside in case Tom came looking for her and she could feel Calotte's eyes following her as she left. She tried to brush away the slithering strands of guilt which had started to burrow into her soul. Guilt and shame over who she had become and what she'd done.

~ 4 ~

The clatter of cutlery on plates and loud conversation spilled out onto the quiet street as Tom opened the door to the restaurant. He quickly stepped inside and closed it behind him. Marseille had before the war imported most of its food from other parts of France, now with the Nazis restricting this and keeping most of what was left for themselves, there were severe shortages. Even fishing had been restricted to avoid unlawful exits and entries. Andre's Restaurant always had a good supply of fish though and nobody asked how he got it. He charged enough in ration coupons and cash, but it was always full. The smell of frying fish and cigarette smoke hung in the air.

The waiter, Thierry, would seat him in the far corner where he could sneak into the kitchen easily enough without attracting the attention of fellow diners. He looked harassed by the workload as he came over to escort Tom to his usual table. In a low and seemingly jolly tone he briefly explained his predicament disguised as general chit chat.

Tom had quite easily lost the man following him between his house and the restaurant. Perrault obviously didn't trust him or thought there was more fish from this network to find. Tom didn't know which ones were known to Perrault but he wasn't going to take any chances. He ordered the fish of the day without asking what it was together with a carafe of wine from which he filled up his glass and drained it just as quickly. He was just about to go and see Jérôme when the door opened and his 'shadow' appeared. Thierry must have been stressed because he didn't seat him at one of the side tables facing out towards the street, but at a table only meters away from Tom's. He sighed and poured himself some more wine.

He needed to see Jérôme who worked in the kitchen, but he didn't want to be seen leaving the table now that his shadow had more or less a clear view of him. He could leave and try later, but he didn't have much time, and if Jérôme couldn't help him then he'd have to find someone else, and that could be tricky.

'You're not going to see our friend?' Thierry asked as he brought over the main course.

Tom shook his head and held up his hand as if to say 'no thanks' to more wine. He moved slightly sideways so his face was hidden behind the waiter and out of the 'shadow's' view.

'It's the man in the black coat that is following me. Can you get word to Jérôme that I need to see him, but to be careful,' he whispered

He was a funny chap Thierry, and Tom wasn't sure he was totally trustworthy, but Jérôme had vouched for him.

His 'shadow' hadn't ordered yet and probably wished he hadn't gone in. A meal here wouldn't be expensable. If the little shit would just leave, Tom could get on with it. He only had two days to get everything set up and Jérôme was the only person he knew that would help him now that they were all on red alert. Two days to set something like this up when he didn't even know why he was doing it. He didn't believe Perrault's explanation, but that didn't matter, he had to do it and there was no point trying to get out of it. He couldn't let him show the pictures to Gerard, he just couldn't. He would do this one thing and then ask Anaise to warn Em when she went up to Paris.

Perrault should have at least let him have more time. They didn't have explosives on tap, and the people who had it wouldn't part with any of it because he asked nicely.

'He'll meet you at number thirty-six at ten O'clock.' Thierry rolled his eyes towards Tom's 'shadow'. 'I'll delay him.'

'He won't follow me 'in there' anyway.'

He slapped some money and coupons on the table and walked past his 'shadow' and out the door as if he didn't have a care in the world.

He now had four hours to kill before his meeting and he didn't want to go back home where they could pick him up again. He heard shouting from the restaurant, but didn't stop to see what was happening. Instead he dived into a dark alleyway and zig zagged a few streets before he was sure that he was alone. Then he changed direction, and as dusk fell he walked towards La Canebière.

The main street of the old town leads straight east from Vieux-Port, the old port towards the zoological gardens. He walked past the bustling cafes and restaurants where refugees with something to celebrate gathered of an evening. Some of the smaller cobbled streets running off the main road led steeply to areas where small houses were overcrowded and hotel rooms rented by the hour. Tom walked past it all towards the far end of the street where it was quieter. Even the wind had calmed down, barely shifting the smoke from his cigarette.

From a vaulted doorway opposite L'Église Saint-Vincent-de-Paul, Tom observed the cheese wedge like building in front of him. Wrought iron Parisian balconies ran alongside the upper floors whilst the lower ones had weathered shutters that were for the most part shut.

In that building lived the man Tom was to kill in few days time.

He'd spent a few hours earlier having a coffee at the cafe on the corner hoping to catch a glimpse of him in the flesh. What was really so 'special' about him that the French security services couldn't get rid of him themselves? They could make it look like a resistance attack without having to go to all this trouble.

Here in the southern half of the country, where a French Government was still in charge, such as it was, the relationship between police and the resistance was not as bad as up north. Generally, unless there was a chance of the Germans finding out about it, they would let resistance groups get away with minor punishments. If the Germans did find out, you would not be so lucky, as Vincent and Elise knew. At some point the Germans would want the unoccupied part too. It was only natural for them to grab as much of Europe as possible and they had to be ready when that happened.

Earlier in the day, after Perrault had left, he'd shown the photos to Anaise. She'd told him that only a few days earlier she'd mistaken Pierre for a waiter at the very cafe Tom had spent the afternoon in. She and her friend had laughed when he'd taken offence, and they had still giggled when he'd left the cafe and entered the residential cheese wedged building and not come back out again. Tom could only assume that this was the building he lived in when in Marseille even though he hadn't seen him come or go.

On the other side of the street a couple of gendarmes came around the corner from the church and Tom decided that it was time to move on. He didn't want to draw attention to himself and it was highly unlikely that he'd see 'The Waiter' anyway.

He stepped out of the doorway as the gendarmes crossed the street towards him. Paying them no attention he walked normally up the road and felt their eyes in his back.

'Hey, stop right there.'

Tom's heart did a double turn as he slowed down and casually turned around.

'Papers.' The taller one said and held out his hand, the sleeve of his blue uniform rode up his arm as he did so.

He started feeling around in his pockets for his identification and residence papers. 'I haven't done anything wrong. Is going for a walk a crime these days?'

'Just give me your papers. Quickly now.'

He looked curiously at Tom's face. 'I've seen you before. At the train station, handing out illegal papers.'

Tom had never handed papers out anywhere. They got left in various places or shuffled into letter boxes for people to pick up, he wasn't crazy. The two gendarmes must be bored and he could feel a trip to the station coming along. Never mind what would happen there, he had to meet Jerome in less than an hour.

'You have me confused with someone else. I wouldn't do that.'

'No, I'm never wrong about these things. I have a very good eye for faces and yours is definitely the one that got away.' He grabbed Tom's arm. 'Come on, let's get you to the station and see if you change your mind.'

The shorter of the two took up position on the other side of Tom, but before they had moved more than a few meters, a man stepped out from a doorway and stopped the trio in their tracks. Before the two Gendarmes had a chance to talk he held up a card showing them something Tom couldn't see. Within a minute they had let him go and grumpily disappeared towards the town centre where shouting and gunfire could be heard.

'How did you find me?' Tom asked the short dark haired man.

'You're too predictable. You spent the afternoon here looking at this building and it was a sure bet that this is where I'd find you.'

'Well, that's one to you then.'

'Here's another one.' Before Tom could wonder what he meant, his fist pushed the air out of his lungs and he fell back against an iron railing fence. He tried to catch his breath whilst his 'shadow' went through his pockets until he found his wallet.

'This is for the restaurant. Morceau de merde.' He took the few Francs Tom had in there before throwing the wallet back at him. 'Now just do what you have to do, then go home. I won't be around for the rest of the night and quite frankly I couldn't care less if you ended up beaten black and blue in a cell somewhere, but Mr Perrault does, and you don't want to get on the wrong side of him, believe me.'

He stuffed the money in his pocket and had a quick glance around before disappearing around the corner.

Tom stood up and breathed a sigh of relief before turning around to continue on his way when, out of the doorway came the man Anaise had referred to as 'The Waiter'. The man named Pierre Lupin that Perrault seemed intent on killing. He looked down the street towards the centre where police sirens and shouting could still be heard before striding off in the opposite direction. His dark coat and hat contrasted against his short blond hair and he walked with the arrogance of a man used to being obeyed.

Pierre's height allowed Tom to leave some distance between them as he followed him towards the quiet Le Camas district. He just wanted to see where he was going, get some clue as to why the French Security service couldn't deal with him themselves, but most importantly he wanted something on Perrault. He wasn't sure what, but he knew that he'd need some kind of leverage to get him off his back because this wouldn't be the end, it would go on and on until Perrault got tired of his little game or had no further use for him.

It was dark now and as he turned the corner at the back of the old hospital Tom could no longer see Pierre. He ran along the empty road, hoping to catch up with him around the corner, his footsteps echoing between the foreboding stone buildings that towered above him.

The yellow street lights that used to light up the area had not been lit for many months, making the streets both hazardous and dangerous. The moonlight came and went between the clouds, and the only footsteps heard were his own. Where the bloody hell had he gone? Tom continued to the end of the road before disappointedly turning around and starting to make his way back towards the town centre. This had so far been a rather disappointing evening and he'd have to remember to take more care in future, this was just not good enough. He'd be glad to get back to the lighter streets, but he was disappointed that he'd lost him so quickly.

He'd almost reached the end of the hospital building when suddenly he was grabbed from behind and a knife was pushed to his throat. The sharp blade was millimeters from his carotid artery and he instantly kept still. Blood pumping through his veins was all he could hear and for a moment he thought he was being robbed. Then his assailant spoke.

'Who are you?'

Tom desperately tried to come up with a plausible explanation, but apart from denying everything there was none. His breath came in short bursts as he had to control his breathing to avoid the knife cutting through his neck.

'Look, take what you want. Just let me go.'

'Don't piss me about, why were you following me. I will push this knife through in 5,4,3...'

'Ok, ok. I wanted to see who you were - and why someone wants you dead.' It was no skin of Tom's nose if he knew, in fact he was Tom's enemy's enemy. Something good might come out of it.

The knife loosened somewhat. Not enough for him to move, but at least he could breath. Pierre started laughing, quietly and unpleasantly.

'Ah. I expected better from you Monsieur. Bad surveillance tactics. Make sure you do better on Friday or we will all pay.'

'You know about it?' Tom wanted to turn around but couldn't.

'Just do as you're bloody told.' He let go of Tom who stumbled forwards. 'Now piss off or I really will slit your throat.'

Tom's hands flew up to his neck and he resisted the urge to ask more questions. Instead he turned around and walked down the street, across the road and back towards from where he'd come. Pierre's comments had made things more complicated, but there would be another way out of this.

In the meantime, he only had minutes to get to number thirty-six to meet Jerome.

$$\sim 5 \sim$$

Paris

The horse drawn cab had dropped Emilie off outside the white double fronted town house she shared with her husband Gerard. It had been a long journey and she was tired. Twice she'd had to change trains for no reason and every time there had been checks. Inside her suitcase, written out as pieces of music she had a collection of letters from network members who for one reason or another had de-camped to the un-occupied zone. There were notes on progress, problems and news. When they searched her bags at Dijon station she'd struggled not to stare at the papers, willing the officer to ignore them. In the end he'd paid no special attention to any item in her bags and she had joined the rest of her fellow travellers on the train. When the train reached Gare de Lyon she'd swore never to travel to Marseille by train again.

She walked up the five stone steps to the front door and used her key to unlock it. She turned the lights on in the hallway and her shoes clinked along the polished squares of oak and walnut parquet as she strolled into the dark lounge.

It was well past dinner time and she was not surprised to see that nobody was home. Gerard liked to be out and about, especially these days when the Germans were in charge. From the moment normality left Paris the previous summer and the Germans marched in, he'd plotted and schemed and bowed and scraped to make them notice him. He had also promoted Emilie as never before to make them want his company and his favours. She didn't know what he actually did for them but he was busy one way or another most days of the week.

Even when she was booked to sing the place was filled with Nazis. That was no great surprise, but she sincerely hoped that her old friends, the ones that always came to see her before the occupation, didn't think she enjoyed singing in front of those apes. But of course her best cover was that they did believe just that, that they didn't know that she'd risked her life on a regular basis to rid her country of those blood sucking fleas. It hurt her to know that the people she loved, even though she didn't know them, would think ill of her. She had to keep telling herself that other people suffered more than her and one day it would be over, one day she'd be back on the other side of the Seine, in her small clubs, singing to the people who mattered.

The five arm chandelier that hung from the ceiling flickered a couple of times before light softly filtered down through its dripped ice glass shades. The house felt a bit chilly so she left her coat on and placed her hat on the dark green velvet chair by the door. Her luggage would be there shortly and she decided to wait in the lounge before finding something to eat in the kitchen. First she needed to get the fire started. She walked over to the fireplace and started rummaging around for something to light it with. It had all been prepared and she was still looking when she heard footsteps in the hall. She turned around and saw her maid Louise in the doorway. Her brown hair was tied back and the top of her head covered with a small tissue like white cap made out of the same lace that lined her white apron. Emilie had never seen her wear a smidge of makeup and had on several occasions almost asked if she could apply some lipstick and powder to the girl just to see what she'd look like. Not that she needed make up to improve her looks, she was quite pretty in a countryside way, it was just that every girl should have the opportunity to wear some. What did she know anyway, maybe Louise wore make up and went dancing every minute of her free time.

'Oh, Madam, we did not expect you until Wednesday.' She hurried over to the fireplace to take over from Emilie who took her coat off, sighed and sat herself down on the sofa. How nice that the house wasn't empty.

'I came home earlier than expected.'

Louise looked up at her from the fire which was now starting to take. Its crackles sounding homely and cosy.

'Did you miss Paris?' she asked.

'I did.' Emilie lied. 'I'm not sure what possessed me to visit Marseille at this time of year.' She knew very well why she'd wanted to go. His name was Tom. 'The wind just blows straight through you. Honestly, I don't know how the city still stands.'

'That's a shame Madame. You were so looking forward to it.'

The fire was all done and Louise stood up. 'Is your sister well?'

'She is. She's coming here on Thursday and I thought we'd put her in the large corner room. She'll like that.'

Emilie was looking forward to her sister's visit. Not just because she already missed her, but also because Anaise had not yet seen their new house. The previous house in Montmartre was nice enough and much better than the flat in Saint Germain, but this house was quite fabulous. Five large bedrooms and a painting atelier that ran along the whole loft. Not that anyone of them could paint, but still, it was there if they wanted it. And there was staff. She'd had a cleaner in previous years, but never a maid of her own.

Gerard wouldn't be outdone by her and got himself a man called Jacques to look after his clothes and diary. He didn't really need him and Jacques spent a lot of his time sitting in the kitchen spitting venom at Louise and the cleaning girl. The only one to escape Jacques comments was the chef, Alonde who came in to cook whenever they had guests. He was big and burly after years in the navy before finding his true vocation in cooking and Jacques would never pick a fight with anyone larger than himself.

'I'm looking forward to meeting her. The corner room will be perfect.'

'Do you know where my husband is tonight?' Emilie asked. She wasn't interested in knowing but thought it only polite to ask.

'I don't know Madam, he didn't say. He gave Jacques the night off.'

'Well, you should have the night off too Louise. Go out and enjoy yourself.' She stood up. 'In fact, let's go out together. We can go...' Her sentence was cut short by the sound of the front door opening.

It was probably just as well. She'd gotten excited about going out with a friend but knew that it wasn't really the done thing even in these circumstances. The neighbourhood already looked down on them. What would they think if she went out on the town with her maid? Maybe she didn't care. They were pretending to be people they weren't, they were both of them from humble backgrounds and if it hadn't been for her voice, she'd be the one sweeping and laying fires. Gerard with his ambition for the finer things in life and lack of scruples would have made it anywhere, shadily perhaps and not with a profession he could discuss with their high end neighbours, but all the same, he would live well.

She smiled apologetically at Louise from the sofa just as Gerard walked in and stopped at the door.

'Hello darling,' he said with surprise whilst handing his hat and coat to Louise. 'Don't put them too far away, I'm going out again.' He walked into the room. 'I didn't think you were due back until later this week.'

'My plans changed. I'd forgotten just how dull Marseille can be.'

'I'll remind you when you complain how you miss it next time. Although, I have something quite exciting happening for us.' He looked at his watch. 'We'll talk about that tomorrow. I only came home to change my shirt.' He walked over to Emilie and gave her a kiss. 'I've missed you.'

He left a space for her to reciprocate, but instead she joked. 'Well, you would. I'm very missable.'

There was a brief moment where deep down, almost hidden away, his eyes showed that her comment hurt.

Quickly he kissed her cheek again and left the room to get changed. A few minutes later she heard the door close behind him. She was pleased she wouldn't have to see him this evening and she hoped that he would be too drunk when he got home to make it up the stairs.

She woke up early to find out from Louise that her husband had not come home until early morning. Jacques had helped him to the spare room bed where he was now sleeping, not to be disturbed. Louise continued, in a hushed voice, to complain about Jacques' lack of work.

'He sits around most of the day Madam. I know it's not my place to say so, but could he not be doing something useful?'

Emilie agreed with her, but knew that Gerard wanted him at his beck and call and told Louise to ignore him.

'It just galls me to see him sitting in the kitchen eating, always eating. It's not good for the soul to do nothing Madam.'

'I expect he'll be busy once Monsieur wakes up.' Emilie responded rather more sharply than she'd meant to. What did the girl expect her to do? Jacques wasn't her problem.

'Oui Madam.' Louise went to fetch her coffee and breakfast brioche.

Tom's words came back to her. Food from the Germans. It was true, they were eating better now than they had before the war. Should she throw the food away and just live on bread? That would just be wasteful, and stupid. They would notice, when she thought 'they' she included Gerard, and it would be mad to see it go to waste. If they didn't use it some fascist, French or German, would.

She missed Tom already with every cell in her body. She'd missed him as she walked down the street to the train station with Anaise knowing he was further away from her with every step. This was not a sustainable situation and at some point it would all come crashing down. Either she'd get arrested for what she was doing with the resistance, that was the likely outcome, or Gerard would find out about her and Tom. Neither was something to look forward to, but she'd prefer to face the Germans, knowing that she'd suffer for the good of France rather than her own weakness. She could always pre-empt the situation and leave France as Tom wanted her to. She would love to go to both England and America, but not like this, not running away from her country and friends when they needed her. Maybe the war would be over soon. She finished her breakfast and went out into the morning sunshine. After a long cold winter, spring had finally arrived in Paris.

Dressed in a green spring suit and hat, her heels clicked against the pavement as she walked briskly down the street towards St Germain. That was her old district, where she'd arrived as a fresh seventeen year old, ten years earlier. She'd arrived from Marseille with a promise from one of the club owners to get a regular slot at Le Soleil. Now she'd sang there many times, but when she first arrived, there had been no opportunities waiting for her. There had been no work for her anywhere else either. Luckily enough she'd scraped by doing odd jobs here and there, and her lucky break had come in the form of Mrs Carter, an American lady who had heard her sing in a local bar and taken her under her wing. She'd sang at Mrs Carter's parties and then at several of her friends too. It was at such an event she'd met Gerard and he'd been her agent ever since. At the time he'd not shown any romantic interest in her, but as soon as Tom showed up all that changed. He became moody and possessive. He even went as far as to suggest that it was bad for her career to be involved with a man, any man. When she'd sarcastically said that maybe it would be preferable if she was involved with a woman he'd screamed at her. Emilie was not one to scare easily and maybe that's why she didn't see then what was under his charming calm exterior. He had apologised and nothing more was said of it. When Tom had left for Spain for the second time back in 1937 she would have said yes to anybody who'd asked her to marry him. Standing at Gare de Lyon crying as the train took Tom away, she was determined to get on with her life and not to wait around for him yet again. Then she'd married Gerard, just in time for Tom to return.

She had no idea if they knew about Max and the bookshop but she had to get the notes she'd brought from Marseille to him. To make sure that she wasn't being followed, she changed direction slightly and walked along to Les Halles. The stalls that had once been heaving with produce now looked decidedly thin and sparse. Still, she strolled along between them and mingled with the other customers, and when she reached the end of the line of stalls, she quickly turned and walked up alongside the next line.

Through the gaps in the stalls she searched the path she'd just turned from for anybody following her. At the end of the road she left the market and walked southwest towards the wide Boulevards and somewhere to change out of the eye catching suit she was wearing.

Once out on the wide colonnade lined Rue Rivoli she quickly stepped into the Hotel Hastings where a friend of hers worked. The receptionist looked up as she entered and she threw him a smile before disappearing into the restaurant area. It was still too early for lunch and the only person in there was a waiter laying cutlery on the tables with great accuracy. He paid her no attention and she breezed through towards the staff accommodation at the back of the hotel. On the first floor she knocked on a door and when nobody opened she used her key to enter. She opened the wardrobe and pulled out a brown wool jacket and skirt and replaced her beautiful green suit with that dreary ensemble. Her hair she tied up into a bun and covered it with a hat. As soon as she'd been to see Max she'd get changed again. Quietly she shut the door behind her and left through the side entrance.

She quickly walked back the way she'd come but turned right before Les Halles. The beautiful sunshine glittered on the surface of the Seine as she crossed the bridge over to St Germain.

By the time she reached the bookshop with its worn wooden sign hanging off an iron bar above the door she was pretty sure that she was on her own. The shops on either side on the bookshop were closed and boarded up and on the opposite side of the road flowed the Seine lined with rows of boxes used by market sellers to ply their goods.

The door creaked as she pushed it open and stepped inside, waiting for the owner to appear.

She could hear him moving around in the back and wondered if he'd actually heard her come in. He had progressively become deafer as the years had passed and kept on saying how he wanted to return to New York to meet his grand-daughter again whilst he could still hear her voice. He'd been saying that for many years now and still he'd not gone. His daughter had come to visit him once, but hadn't taken to Paris at all and made him promise to come 'home' soon.

He'd arrived in the twenties together with the lost generation of writers, and now he was the only one of them left in Paris. Everybody knew that he'd never leave his shop, or indeed Paris. Emilie contemplated going into the back room but there were tall piles of books stacked precariously in the way.

The door opened behind her, and as she turned around, a tall dark haired man in his twenties entered. Dressed in well-worn trousers and a jacket with missing buttons, he flashed her a smile. Despite his humble state she found him rather attractive and couldn't help but smile back. When Monsieur Green's white head showed around the corner she hurriedly asked if he had a copy of The Man in The Iron Mask before he had a chance to show that he knew her.

'Oui, Oui, Madam.' He nodded as he understood. 'It is somewhere here.' He indicated towards the stacks of books that were lining the walls and blocking the doorways of the shop. 'As you can see, I am having an inventory with my depleted stock. It may not be as many books as I used to have but it will still take me some time to find your copy. Maybe I can serve this gentleman first?'

'I don't mind.' Emilie said and indicated indifference.

'Thank you Madam.'

The tall man's voice was soft as velvet and spoken with a thick accent that she couldn't place.

'Could you tell me if the Thursday Club still meets here?' He looked at Monsieur Green.

'Ah, are you a writer Monsieur?'

'Well, yes. I try to anyway, and I know that with the war and everything it's probably going to be difficult, but I thought that if I could only meet some other writers they might be able to help me along. I need inspiration.'

'I'm sorry, but the Thursday Club has not been meeting since last June, when the Germans came. There may still be some in the area but most left Paris for the south and have not returned.'

The man nodded and there was a pause before Monsieur Green continued. 'Is there anything else I can help with?'

'No, thank you.' He put his hat back on and turned to Emilie. 'Thank you Madam.'

'I wish you luck Monsieur, with your writing.'

He smiled dishearteningly at them and walked out of the shop.

They both watched the door shut behind him before Monsieur Green smiled at Emilie.

'My dearest girl. You're back home. Paris hasn't been the same without you.' He made his way from behind the counter towards her. 'How was Marseille?'

She smiled back at the old man she knew so well and kissed his cheeks. 'Oh, Max, it's good to see you too. Are you alone?'

She nodded towards his little back room.

'Yes, it's only me here. And now you of course. Is there anything wrong?'

She felt a little paranoid for wanting to check upstairs to make sure that there was nobody there. He hadn't heard her come in so somebody else could easily have gone upstairs. Come on Emilie, why would they. Pull yourself together. Still, she left Max for a moment whilst quickly checking the upstairs part which was empty.

Once back downstairs she locked the front door and led Max into the back room. There she explained to him what had happened in Marseille.

'I won't come back here again unless I absolutely have to. We don't know how much they know, but one thing's for sure, they know about me.'

'Ok, mon Cherie. I will let the others know. You take good care and if you need help, I don't care if anybody notices, you get word to me and I will find a way to help. What can they do? I am an old man.'

'You're a darling sweet man Max, but if I get into trouble you'd do well to steer clear of me. The rest of the group wouldn't appreciate you being the link that gets them executed.' She laughed a little. 'Let's hope it doesn't come to that.' She rooted around her bag and pulled out the sheets of music. 'This is for Andre. He's expecting it.' She handed the notes to him.

Max put the papers under some books and they walked back out into the shop. 'I will get them to him. Now, will you have some coffee with me before you leave?'

'No thank you. I have some things to do before going back home.' She took his old hands in hers and kissed his cheek. 'Take care of yourself Max.' She felt her eyes well up as she realised that it may be a long time before she saw her old friend again.

'You too my girl. It won't be long before all is back to normal. You'll see.'

'I hope you're right Max, I hope you're right.'

She wandered around Paris aimlessly for a while after she left the bookshop. She didn't have anywhere in particular to go, but wanted a little time on her own. Gerard would be awake by now, wondering why she wasn't there, and she knew she should go back home. Still, she lingered by the river. Standing on the left side of the Seine, looking up at Notre Dame, it could have been 1939 again. From this angle there were no signs of war and the streets and cafes at lunchtime were full of people. It all seemed so normal. Ordinary people who'd hidden their initial fear of the Nazis behind relief that they were still ok and determined to live as they always had. The people who couldn't hide it, stayed away, out of sight, hoping they would be out of mind. She walked a little further along the river, stopped for a coffee at a quiet cafe and read a paper whilst delaying walking back home a little longer.

She smiled at a couple of young men that recognised her but were too shy to say anything. She could hear them talking excitedly as they passed.

It was time to go home and she reluctantly started walking back up the cobbled street. The two young men who'd smiled at her earlier were now standing with the green grocer who was whispering in their ears. All three of them looked towards her, and as she passed, the two men spat at her and mumbled something she couldn't hear.

Expecting back up from the green grocer she indignantly asked what they thought they were doing.

There was no response from either of them.

'Well, you apologise now.' Emilie insisted, again looking to the green grocer for support. He stood off to one side with his arms folded in front of him whilst one of the young men came within an inch of her face.

'Go back to your Nazis, whore,' he said menacingly. She felt his breath on her face but she refused to move even though her heart was racing and she felt faint. The words had jolted through her like an electric shock but she'd be damned if she let them get away with it.

The other one came up behind her and knocked her hat off.

'Yeah, run to Germany whilst you still can. We know all about you.'

She'd been warned about this, but somehow thought it wouldn't happen to her. For the first time she felt scared. Really scared, and she couldn't tell them that she was on their side. These were her old neighbours, the people for whom she'd travelled up from Marseille worried sick that someone would realise what the music sheets actually were. They were on the same side and yet she couldn't tell them. She stepped aside to pick up her hat when one of them grabbed her arm and twisted it up her back making her scream out.

'Let me go. We'll say no more about it.' She fought back the tears that were threatening to come pouring out.

'You remember this; when your friends have left, we will get justice, and you and your fascist traitors will get what's coming to you. Do you hear me?'

The younger one pushed her arm up further, until once again she screamed out, and he let go. He picked up her hat from the pavement and pressed it down hard on her head.

She bit her lips together and held up her head as she started walking away. Before she reached the street corner she turned around against her better judgement to see them still looking at her with big grins on their faces.

'You shouldn't judge people you don't know,' she shouted at them before turning around the corner and started running.

Tears blurred her vision, but there were no shouts echoing down the street behind her, no running footsteps following her and it was two blocks before she realised she was going the wrong direction. She must have looked distressed because people walking past stared at her. Now convinced that they all hated her, she ran into an alleyway just to get away from their stares. She stopped there and dried her now unattractively blood shot eyes and eased her breathing. 'Calm now, Em. One day they'll know the truth.'

She knew that day wouldn't be 'soon' at all. France had willingly given away its freedom and it would take a lot of people a lot of fighting and sacrifice to get it back. One day they would though. One day.

It was afternoon by the time she arrived back home. Gerard's voice boomed from the sitting room and she could tell by the sound of his voice that they had company.

Her eyes were still red rimmed from her ordeal and all she wanted was some strong coffee and sugary cake in silence.

This was not to be. No sooner had she shut the front door before Gerard appeared in the hallway. He looked her up and down before smiling. 'You look awful my dear. What are you wearing?' His voice low so that nobody else would hear. 'Go get changed and then join us. And for God's sake, do something about your face.'

'I'm not feeling very well Gerard. I'm going to bed.'

'You'll have to put on a brave face darling. Sturmbannführer Kluger has waited here for over an hour just to meet you. Now, get changed and be back down here in five minutes.'

He went back to his guest and Em felt terribly lonely as she quietly went upstairs to get changed.

$$\sim 6 \sim$$

Gerard slowly opened his eyes and stared up at the crisp white ceiling. The spider in the corner was still there, and for some reason he hadn't been able to concentrate at the task in hand because of it. Lilou's hair tickled his stomach as she made her way back up from her unsuccessful mission. This wasn't his fault, he'd never had this happen before, she must be losing her touch.

What if their special customers found the same thing? Too much was running on this, he had to deliver what they wanted. There were plenty of others who would be only too happy to supply what he sold.

Lilou was too experienced to show any embarrassing concern for what hadn't happened and sat herself up and lit a cigarette which she quietly offered to him.

Ignoring her, he tore his gaze away from the ceiling and got up. The floorboards were draughty and cold against his feet. He gathered up his clothes and got dressed without meeting Lilou's eyes which he knew followed him around the room.

'Get dressed Lil. I'm not paying you for lazing around.'

'Where's Jacques?' She asked and pulled the sheet further up. 'We need to get set up.'

Still wrapped up in his own thoughts he ignored her once again. The three of them had been a team for a long time, but she must know that her services wouldn't last forever. That was the trade she was in, the route she had chosen.

He'd find someone else, someone who could do what she used to be able to, someone younger and less.... well... familiar. It was a shame because she was so loyal and the two of them together with Jacques had set the whole business up from scratch. All three of them bringing their special skills to the pot, all in it to make a lot of money and it was sad that he couldn't let her enjoy it. Right now, there was too much at stake.

Finally he looked at her with unblinking eyes.

'Everything is going ahead as planned. Jacques will be at the flat in Rue Diermont at 6pm. That leaves you over an hour to set it all up.'

He knew she wasn't stupid and he didn't want to alert her that something was wrong. 'It will all be fine Lilou. You're still the best there is.' He bent over the edge of the bed and kissed her. 'I'll see you on Friday.'

She nodded, but he'd already left the room.

For a few minutes she sat where she was, leaned up against the wooden bed head and ran through every possible reason why nothing in their relationship would have changed. There was only one reason and that was his words which she knew not to trust. She knew him better than he knew himself and he couldn't hide his thoughts from her. For a few weeks now she'd known there were changes ahead, and that none of them included her. She'd be damned though if she'd let him get the better of her, she knew where his secrets were buried.

Over the years she had tried to save some of the money coming her way but there was always something she needed, or more often than not, just wanted, because she could. Now she wished she'd saved some of it. She was only twenty eight, she could start again somewhere else. Coco Chanel had apparently started by selling hats, shop bought boating ones that she tied ribbons and things to and look at her now, set up quite nicely at the Ritz. She had style, everybody said so. A new career for a new life.

Feeling positive and excited about the future she got up and dressed quickly. She brushed her fair hair back and tied it into a high chignon and put some colour on her lips. If he wanted her gone she'd quite happily go, but he'd have to pay. She'd need a lot of it to set herself up.

Once dressed and made up, she walked out of the house towards Rue Diermont.

At six thirty Jacques turned up at the house where Lilou had set everything up for what she believed to be her last assignment. The house was situated in a side road of a central smart area that their influential clients didn't mind visiting. The houses on either side were un-occupied and the windows covered with heavy curtains to keep any noise well inside its walls.

The camera was in place, the house smelled clean and she was about to get changed into her work clothes when Jacques called her downstairs. How she disliked the man, he was so coarse. A street hooligan and Gerard had chosen to have him in his house. In the lounge she found Jacques standing by the window with his hands in his pockets. His brown hair was in need of a cut and his shifty eyes settling on hers as she entered.

'What is it? I need to change.' She glanced up at the grandfather clock.

His wide lips curled into a smile. 'I can't get the fire to light. The house is quite chilly and you got it going last time.'

There were some twigs scattered in the grate and Lil sighed. She knew he just couldn't be bothered to do it and it annoyed her immensely. She's the one who does all the dirty work and all she gets in return is the smallest amount of money and a lot of disrespect. She's the one who had made them rich.

She gathered the sticks and put them back where they were supposed to be and was just about to light a match when she noticed Jacques shadow move behind her. Some instinct made her stand up and the fire poker that would have hit her head if she'd stayed where she was now whacked her thigh and she screamed out from the pain. Jacques threw the poker to one side and grabbed her throat with the hook of his arm. He pulled her up and tried to squeeze her throat with his arm but it wasn't successful and he had to let go to get a better grip.

Lilou gasped before taking the opportunity to turn around. She threw her knee upwards, making Jacques double over before quickly moving towards the poker. It was almost within her grasp when Jacques grabbed her feet and she fell flat on her face.

'You bitch. I was going to make it quick for old times' sake but you've bloody well lost that chance now.' He grabbed hold of her hair and started to drag her along up the stairs. Lilou screamed for all she was worth even though she knew the house had been chosen especially because nobody cared about what went on in there. She grabbed hold of a banister spindle which broke loose and she used it to hit the arm Jacques used to drag her along. He turned around and she scrambled up onto her feet and whacked the piece of wood over his head. It must have dazed him because his grip relaxed enough for Lilou to slip back down the stairs and grab the only weapon she could find, the poker.

'Put it down Lil.' He held his hands up in front of him as he walked back into the lounge. 'We can put this behind us. I won't let Gerard know you're still alive. Ok? You can just leave quietly.'

'This was Gerard's idea?' She stood with the poker ready to strike.

'Of course. It wasn't mine. We've worked together for years you and I. Maybe I was a little harsh.' He walked a little towards her. 'You know too much about his affairs. That's the danger of being good at your kind of work. People just tend to trust you with all their little secrets.'

He was close enough to grab the poker when she hit. 'Take that you bastard.' The blow hit the side of his face, the force of it sent him out cold onto the wooden floor.

His face was bleeding where he lay and she resisted the urge to hit him again.

'Someone like you won't get the better of me,' she said as she left the room to quickly clean herself up. Thank God that she'd been at least a little prepared.

~ 7 ~

The station clock struck nine and Anaise shifted uncomfortably on the hard wooden bench. With less than an hour until the curfew set in, people were rushing to and from their trains. Right in front of her, above the exit gate of Gare d'Lyon, a large red swastika hung unfurled from the ceiling and nearly reached the top of the entrance hall doors. They didn't want you to forget that they were there, that it was their city now and it sent shivers down her spine every time she looked up at it. There were plenty of German soldiers in their green-grey uniforms, making their presence known. Their paths were always clear, as people afraid that their thoughts would show in their eyes, moved away. The population of Paris had already had ten months to get used to seeing foreign soldiers on their streets, but it hit newcomers like a sledgehammer

Anaise pulled her small bag closer and looked down as a couple of soldiers walked past. She briefly felt their eyes on her person. Everything that was evil in the world was here, here in this station and she assumed that the rest of Paris was the same. An urge to get back home to Marseille, even with all the trouble they were having there, suddenly washed over her. Turn and run away; but she couldn't. None of them could.

There was still no sign of Emilie and it worried her. She'd promised to be there waiting for her when she arrived and that had been over an hour ago.

The evening chill started seeping through her grey woolen travel suit and she felt alone and uncomfortable sitting there like a stranger in her own country. She couldn't just wait forever and hope that Emilie would turn up. For all she knew, she might not have made it back to Paris. She quickly put those thoughts out of her mind, picked up her bag and went in search of a taxi. Outside the station it was dark and a few spits of rain had made the horse drawn cabs scarce. In the end she found herself in an improvised carriage pulled along by two bikes. Darkness had fallen and the streets were almost empty as they approached the upmarket residential area where her sister lived. On the way they had nearly been hit by a large horse and carriage and the cobbles along the smaller streets had shaken loose the bar that connected the carriage to the bikes that pulled it. It must have happened regularly because the man and woman who rode the pulling bikes fixed it in moments. Once the bar was secured the man smiled at her and got back on his bike.

When they arrived at Em's house it was in darkness and there was nobody home. There was only one place she could think of going to ensure she would be indoors before the curfew and she was pretty sure she wouldn't be welcomed with open arms.

***

'You have a nerve showing up here.'

The young unnaturally blond woman had already shut the door on Anaise once. Her bright red lips had already spouted obscenities through the door and one neighbour had shouted down the stairs at her to be quiet.

'Ballou, I'm sorry. Can I come in?'

'Why should I let you do anything after the way you treated me?'

'Because we were friends and I'm sorry I left without telling you.'

'You have nowhere else to go, have you?' She raised her groomed eyebrows as Anaise agreed that she didn't. Silence settled heavy over the dimly lit hallway whilst Ballou decided what to do.

'Well, you'd better come in then. Don't expect niceties though.'

Anaise moved past Ballou into the small lounge and put her bag next to the faded blue velvet sofa. 'Thanks. You won't even notice I'm here.'

'The hell I won't. I'm off out shortly.'

'At this time? There's a curfew isn't there?'

Ballou laughed. 'You're such a country girl. The club around the corner stays open through the night and when it's time to go home, the curfew is lifted.'

'Oh.' Anaise was pleased that she was going out and leaving her alone to rest.

Ballou's face softened a little. 'You look tired. There's ersatz coffee in the kitchenette if you want it. I'm not making it for you though.' She tried to sound harsh but the anger had mostly gone.

'I'm alright. It's been a long day. I'm really grateful that you're letting me stay the night. I'll be out of here first thing in the morning.'

Ballou nodded. 'Why don't you come out with me. You will love the Zous. It's all swing and full of Zazous. It's where they got the name from see. I'm still mad at you, but I can't leave you here on your own.'

'I'm fine here, really. A few hours sleep is all I need.'

'No. I insist you come along. It's the least you can do to start making up for leaving me like that.'

Backed into a corner Anaise reluctantly agreed. Maybe some music and a few drinks would be what she needed.

***

'I can't believe you've done this to me.' Emilie hissed through a sweet smile. 'We're stuck here all night now.'

'I swear I didn't know it would over-run. How could I have?'

'What about Anaise? I should at least have been at the house when she arrived?'

'Jacques will have looked after her and she's been in Paris before.'

'I know, but not since last summer.'

She had to swallow what she was about to say as Sturmbannführer Kluger walked towards them. It was after all the German officer's birthday party and Emilie widened her smile as he approached them. 'Happy birthday Sturmbannführer.'

'That was lovely. Thank you very much for the good wishes.'

She'd almost choked on the words as she'd congratulated him on stage and sung happy birthday in German. For a brief moment she'd seen the faces of the two youths and the green grocer before her, their contemptuous faces judging her. This was her battleground though and she had to snake her way in to be able to help. She was very aware that if they knew what she did they would instantly deport her into night and fog. Her heart wouldn't stop beating out of her chest every time she was near them. She must be a very good actress because nobody ever seemed to notice.

'I'm glad you liked it.'

'Yes, your German is quite good and I have a proposition for you. One I think you will like very much. Come, let's sit down. There are people I'd like to introduce you to.'

He led the way to a large round table with a handful of officers and some fashionably dressed women. None of whom Emilie knew, but they all stood up and clapped as she approached. She wasn't sure if it was for her or the birthday Nazi. The table was full but they managed to squeeze a couple of chairs in for her and Gerard. Emilie put her professional face on and pretended they were just normal people. Their uniforms fancy dress.

'Madam Valois, I'm Oberleutnant Joachim Gerber, a great admirer of yours.' The young officer on her right held up his glass to her and she lifted her own. Her eyes narrowed slightly as she tried to remember where she'd seen him before.

'Thank you. That's very kind.' She was just about to ask him if they'd met before when the Sturmbannführer's voice boomed across the table.

'Gerber, no toast without the rest of us. Here's to Madam Valois.'

Everybody stood up and lifted their glasses to her, to Kluger's birthday and to Germany. Then Sturmbannführer Kluger looked over to Emilie and smiled. He held his right hand up to quiet the table before speaking. 'I am honoured to be in charge of the French contribution to the Victory Festival in Berlin. I have spent some time reviewing performances in Paris.' Everybody laughed at this apart from Emilie who could see where it was leading to. 'Chances to perform before the Fuhrer come but rarely and I would like to offer it to... Madam Valois.'

Everybody's faces turned towards Emilie who could do nothing but gracefully accept the offer. She had no intention of going. Gerard could come up with an excuse in a few days.

'I am truly honored. Thank you very much.'

They sat back down and the conversation around the table droned on until the heat and smoke made her feel faint. She excused herself and left the restaurant area. Remembering that this club had a balcony on the first floor she walked up a set of stairs and through a large rectangular room decorated in a green and gold baroque style. The balcony doors opened up easily and the fresh night air filled her lungs.

She'd only been there a minute when the doors opened and Oberleutnant Gerber came out and stood next to her looking out over the wide dark Boulevard below.

'Are you alright Madam?'

'I just needed some air. It was very smoky down there that's all.'

The curtains fluttered slightly in the breeze, throwing shadows across their faces. She looked at him for a moment before shaking her head. 'You look very much like someone I met the other day. Almost spookily so.'

He turned towards her. 'I recognised you the moment I saw you in the shop. The Man In The Iron Mask wasn't it?'

It took her by surprise and he must have noticed it because he laughed.

'Can we keep this between ourselves? I'd probably be court martialed if they knew that I, very occasionally, roam around Paris in civilian clothes.'

Emilie laughed with relief. He hadn't been spying on her. 'Your secret is safe with me, but why...?'

His dark eyes shimmered with mischief and strange kind of innocence she'd not expected to see in a German officer.

'Well, I've always dreamed of going to Paris. To walk in the steps of writers like Fitzgerald and Hemingway and write my own stories here. I can't do that in uniform.' He paused to light a cigarette. 'You must think I'm mad?'

'Maybe a little.' She turned back towards the iron balustrade. 'Why American writers? Why not French or German?'

'My parents met them and spent time with them when they were here in the twenties. I grew up with their memories and stories.' He looked at her. 'I'm sorry, I've been talking too much. Are you still feeling unwell?'

'No. I just find these long nights rather tiring I'm afraid.'

'Would you like me to arrange for someone to take you home?'

She declined his offer as Gerard wouldn't take too kindly to it and oddly enough she found herself enjoying Gerber's company.

'How are you finding Paris?' She asked as neutrally as she could.

'I am absolutely in love with it. I'd never been outside Germany before the war and now I've been all over the place.'

'That's a shame. Most places are nicer seen in their natural state.' She regretted her words as soon as they came out. She really didn't know him well enough.

'Well, as I mentioned before, my mother and father lived here for a little while in the twenties and they told me everything about it. The city of romance. In fact, my uncle has been trying hard to re-educate me on this subject and several others.'

'Where is your uncle?'

'He's downstairs. It's Sturmbannführer Kluger. My father died when I was young and my mother and I had to move in with him and his wife. He's a good man, but very different from my father. And from me. He used to call me a dreamer, still does, but how anyone can be a dreamer in this war is beyond me. All I've seen is nightmares.'

There were a few moments of silence where they both looked out over a sleeping Paris.

'I'm not cut out for this soldiering, you know. The plans I had all changed too. I trained to be a veterinarian and I could have used those skills in the army, but my uncle wanted me to rise in the ranks quickly, so here I am. - I'm not sure why I'm telling you all this.'

He seemed so young, his dark hair showing beneath his grey cap and his eyes seemed so normal, not the eyes of the monsters that had invaded them. Just a normal boy far from home whose life had been turned upside down.

'Maybe if there had been no war we could have been friends. Try not to let all this change you. Be strong and get through it like the rest of us.'

They stood facing each other and she took his hands in hers like a big sister would.

When his hands softly squeezed hers back, the atmosphere changed. For a few seconds the very air around them was charged with unexpected emotions and suddenly she found it hard to breath.

Then the full lights in the baroque room came on and they both turned to see Kluger and Gerard looking out at what must have seemed like an intimate moment. She let go of Gerber's hands as if they suddenly burnt her.

Kluger opened the balcony doors and waved them back in.

'You'll catch a chill out there. We came to find you Madam to let you know that we're having another dinner downstairs and wondered if you wanted to join us.'

She went back into the room where her husband was still standing by the door. His lips a hard thin line and his eyes narrow. He moved from the door way to let her past only when Kluger walked towards him.

As she walked ahead of them all down the stairs she could feel Gerard's stare burning into her back.

~ 8 ~

Mountains of Vaucluse - East of Avignon, France

Pierre Lupin was late. As the sun started to set over the hillside, Tom scrambled up from where he'd been lying and lent his back against a wind bent tree.

'I'm getting too old for this kind of stuff.' He stretched his arms and legs out in front of him to ease the aches from tensely lying on the damp ground for a couple of hours.

Jérôme laughed and handed him a cigarette. 'You wouldn't see my father spending hours in the wet undergrowth. It's for a good cause though, eh?'

'I'm not that old.' Tom said defensively, whilst feeling every minute of his twenty nine years.

'Come on. You're a lot older than me.'

'Don't remind me. I should have left you in Marseille on your mother's knee.'

Jérôme stubbed out his cigarette on a mud patch. They were well hidden behind a few shrubs just up the hillside from where the disused signalling house was. Dark storm clouds threw shadows over the mountains in the distance and they were both keen to get it all over and done with. The explosives had been placed earlier and the plunger was right next to them, just waiting to be pressed. The only problem was; there was nobody to blow up.

'I think we should head back. It'll be trouble getting home if the car gets caught in the mud. Those clouds look stormy and it's not like it's one of our operations.'

Tom wanted nothing more than to leave this awful mountain, but couldn't. He had to stay and finish it. The kid should get home though.

'Take the car and go back. There's no point in both of us getting stuck here.'

'I'm not leaving a friend. How would you get back?'

'Don't worry about that. I've always gotten myself back home. The thing is that if you don't get back tonight your family will have a search party out for you. We don't want anybody to know about this. Especially Remy and that gang because I shouldn't have asked you to come.' Tom knew very well that he shouldn't have taken Jérôme along, but even though he was only eighteen he was the best explosives man in Marseille. And for some reason he looked up to Tom. Maybe it was because his uncle had fought and died in Spain back in '38, and maybe he felt a bond between them because Tom had been there too.

Mulling it over for a while, Jérôme finally agreed to return to Marseille.

As soon as Tom heard the car start on the other side of the hill he pulled his coat up and settled in for a long and wet wait. It wasn't long though before he noticed a vehicle approaching from the south. It drove down the white road from the hillside, past Tom's hiding place and pulled up outside the house. Between dark clouds the late afternoon light flickered onto the hills and he watched Pierre, dressed in a smart grey suit, leave the car together with two Germans in officers uniforms. Not something you saw very often down here in the un-occupied zone where Germans mainly wore suits

The driver, who had opened the car doors for the officers, ran ahead up the slight slope of the overgrown signalling house garden to open the front door. The house was small and with a ticket office on the side for when somebody wanted to travel from that station. Tom had no idea who would, there were no people living nearby. Maybe that's why the rail extension had never been finished.

The four Germans entered the house and Tom looked at his watch. Ten minutes and it would all be over. He wasn't stupid enough to think they wouldn't want more from him once this was finished, but he'd deal with that later.

Five minutes had slowly passed by when the door opened and the driver came out. Were they leaving? His hand tightened over the plunger and he got ready to detonate the explosives early. They would still be killed if they were close to the house. To his relief the driver closed the door behind him and went back down the path to the parked car. Moments later he drove away.

Tom looked once again at his watch; three minutes left. He toyed with the idea of detonating early. What difference would a few minutes make? But he didn't. The car had disappeared up the road from where it had come and Tom wondered what they were doing in there. They were obviously planning to stay for a while. Maybe they'd sent the driver off to fetch something. If he came back too soon and raised the alarm Tom would have to be quick about getting away, especially now that he no longer had the car.

It was only seconds to go and Tom took a deep breath before pressing down the plunger.

The explosion echoed around the hill sides before absolute silence settled back in. He slid down to the road and ran up to the house. A few small fires were burning here and there inside and they were all visible from the large hole made in the wall by the explosion.

He had to check and make sure Pierre was dead. That was the deal. He also wanted to see if there was anything useful in there that had survived the blast. The front door hung on its hinges and Tom cautiously went in with his hand tightly gripped around his revolver. His eyes darted quickly around the square room; there was no sign of life anywhere. The beams were still intact, but the wooden planks on top of them had broken clean off in most places. Through the hole in the wall, he could see all the way up the hill where he'd hidden only minutes ago. The two German officers were slumped against the far end wall and he walked up to them. He could only tell it was them from their uniforms, their faces were both unrecognisable. Normally he would have gone through their pockets for any useful items or information but they were too messy and he didn't have the time. He took another look around the room. Where was Pierre? The blast could have taken him along and dumped him outside but Tom was sure he would have seen him if he was there. He quickly walked back outside and started moving the debris from the blast, he looked around the other side and still there was no sign of him. A slight panic rose from his stomach as he rushed back in. He was running out of time. The blast would have been heard for some distance and it wouldn't take long for the police or military to arrive. The smoke from the smoldering fires made his eyes sting and he made one last attempt at finding him amongst the scattered rubble and wood indoors. Suddenly he heard a noise from where the table had landed. With the gun stretched out in front of him he walked over. Unless it was a very lucky animal it meant that Pierre was alive and he'd have to finish him off. He pushed the table to one side and there he was. His uniform was covered in blood, but he was conscious. Half sitting up against the wall, his clear blue eyes looked challenging at Tom.

'Go on then. Shoot.' His voice was weak and croaky but what caught Tom's attention game that he spoke English. 'Do what Perrault asked. I knew that bastard would double cross me.'

'What?'

'You know who I am. And I know who you are. It was only forty eight hours ago.'

Tom saw his brief glance at the gun and knew he calculated his chance of success in stealing it. Tom backed away. He should just shoot him. Quickly because there wasn't much time. He hesitated because he'd always found it difficult pulling the trigger face to face, and also there was something wrong with the whole thing. He'd known it from the start but now, the man that had told him to go ahead and do it, says it's a setup.

'I do know who you are. Get up.' Tom indicated with the gun. Pierre rose slowly, grabbing hold of the overturned table in front of him with one hand and the wall behind him with the other. Tom had on a spur of the moment decided to take him with him. Away from the house where soon there would be any number of people arriving. He wanted to know why the whole thing had been set up and what Pierre had expected.

It would be his one chance of getting something on Perrault, to keep him away from Emilie. He pushed Pierre forward out of the house and towards the path he had come down with Jerome earlier. He didn't know this area but he intended to take him up into the hills and find out what he knew and then shoot him. Surely it wouldn't matter where or when he was killed.

Pierre walked up the path slowly, holding one hand up to the wound on his head to stop the blood trickling down but it didn't work and his blond hair was sticky red in places. Tom picked up the detonator from the hiding place and as they walked up the hill he could see headlights coming down the hill towards the house. Moments later the large storm clouds exploded above them with a flash of lightning crossing the dark sky and the heavens opened up. Within seconds they were both soaked and the hillside they were clambering up became slippery. Before the house was out of sight Tom turned around and saw that the two cars had reached it. A couple of police men had left their vehicle and were looking around for signs of the perpetrators whilst the plain clothes men headed for the house.

Until they reached the trees on top of the hill, Tom and Pierre would be easily spotted. Pierre moved slower and slower and Tom could hear his raspy breathing through the rain.

'Come on, move.' Tom tried to pull him along when a shot suddenly echoed around them. The two policemen had started scrambling up the hillside in pursuit. Tom pushed Pierre to the ground and aimed his gun at them. Water dripped down his face and obstructed the view. His first shot went wide and he tried again, this time hitting one of them. The injured policeman fell against his colleague and then onto the ground. The civilian shouted something at them and the policeman Tom had hit, leaned heavily against the other one as they tried to get down to the car. Tom gave a sigh of relief. He'd only hit his leg and they weren't going to take another chance. No doubt they were going for back up, but it gave Tom enough time to get away.

He only had one more bullet and he'd need that for the bloody Nazi in front of him. Maybe he wouldn't, he was more dead than alive and Tom looked for somewhere to stop. He needed the information quickly and Pierre looked like he didn't have long.

They'd reached the trees on the top and sat down under an oak tree. It was relatively dry, but not an ideal place to shelter during a thunderstorm. Tom decided to take the risk.

Pierre's eyes closed as he leaned back against the tree trunk. 'You're English.' It was a statement.

'It doesn't matter where I'm from,' Tom replied and sat himself down next to him. 'What matters is the fact that you will die if you don't get medical attention quickly.' He lit a cigarette and blew the smoke into Pierre's face. 'It doesn't matter to me whether you live or die. It does matter to someone else though. I will help you get down to the road again if you tell me why Perrault wants you dead. Why this whole charade was set up.'

Pierre was quiet for a moment before responding. 'We both know I won't make it anywhere.' He laughed and started coughing. 'Ironic that I should end up killed by an Englishman.'

'Two days ago you told me to go ahead with it. What's changed?'

'You were supposed to wait 20 minutes after I went in. I had to have enough time to drug the two Germans that were with me. Then I would have hidden in the basement, safe and sound. The driver would have confirmed that I was in there and everyone would have thought I was blown to pieces. As it turns out, I nearly was.'

'Ten minutes, I was told ten minutes.'

'That's because Perrault actually wanted me dead. I have been blackmailing him for some time and I knew he'd try to get rid of me.' He turned his head towards Tom. 'We're on the same side you and I. At least I hope we are.'

'I doubt that very much.'

'Shut up and listen. I've no choice but to ask for your help. This is more important than any small-time crap you do. This could end up costing us the war,' he paused and it took him a few moments to continue. 'They have to be certain that I'm dead, if they believe that I'm still alive the information I have is useless. They will guess what's happened, that I've gone over to the allied side or even worse, the truth, that I've been a spy all along.'

Tom listened with interest, not knowing whether to believe him or not. It did all make sense.

'Why couldn't you just send whatever it is through the normal channels?'

Pierre tried once again to laugh. 'Normal channels are what you have. I'm alone, any contact I've had with London has been sent or transmitted by myself but that's no longer safe. The information I've sent over the years would be useless if I was caught or exposed. Anyway, the London line's not safe. It's all in the film.'

Pierre didn't have long left but he seemed determined to hand over whatever it was he had to Tom.

'My real name is Erik Tag and in my pocket you will find a roll of film. You have to deliver this to Charles Johnson at CJ Films. Nobody else do you understand. Nobody else can even know about it. Or me.'

Tom nodded and lit another cigarette as Erik told him about the escape route he'd set up to get him out of France fast.

'Don't fail me Tom. I've sacrificed my life for this.' He managed to use his right arm to get the roll of film from his pocket and handed it to Tom. There was a thick scar travelling up from his little finger to the base of his arm. 'Hunting accident when I was younger.' Erik explained as he noticed Tom's stare. He wasn't thinking about the scar, he was deciding how to handle this.

Tom was now sure that Pierre, or Erik, was who he said he was, but he was still not too keen to go back to London. He had business here to sort out, he had to get rid of Perrault to start and he mentioned it to Erik.

'This is more important. More important than any of us. Go to London, deliver the film. I could order you to do this but I think you will do it anyway because you know it's the right thing to do.'

Tom sat quietly for a little while, trying to come up with an alternative plan. He knew Emilie wouldn't leave Paris.

He couldn't even send her a warning now that they were all on red alert. On the other hand, what if this information could have an impact on the war. Britain needed all the help it could get and Tom didn't want to be the person who could have shortened the war, but didn't.

Pierre noticed his reluctance and continued. 'Haven't you been listening to me? There's no other option. This takes priority.' His words were coming out blurred. 'I was stationed in Germany for seven years you know. Seven years. I'm not even sure who I actually am anymore.' He went quiet and Tom thought he'd died when suddenly he started talking. 'Always thought I'd make it back to London. No place like it. Piccadilly and Hyde Park.' He opened his eyes briefly. 'Promise me to have tea at Lyon's when you get there. And scones, thick with cream and jam.' His eyes closed again and Tom felt for his pulse. It was very weak and he needed to get away.

'I'm really sorry old man.' He went through Erik's pockets to make sure they contained nothing incriminating. What a waste of a life. If only he'd known, if only Erik had told him back in Marseille then Tom could have helped him find another body to take his place and he could have brought the film back himself. With a last glance, Tom left his body under the tree and started making his way back to Marseille and the boat that would take him to London.

~ 9 ~

Paris

The night had been a strain after they re-joined the party downstairs. Gerard had stayed close to her but not spoken more than two words as the hours slowly went by. Once they were back at the house she tried to act normally even though she knew he was angry. All she wanted to do was to go to bed, but there was no sign of Anaise? Maybe the train hadn't arrived. That wouldn't be unusual.

'Who did you send to pick up my sister?' she asked Gerard.

'Jacques, why?'

'Well, she's not here.'

'The train will have been delayed. It happens. She'll be here soon.'

'Are you sure Jacques went to the station?'

'I asked him to so I can't see why he wouldn't have.'

'Where is he?' Em got up from her chair and walked towards the door.

'I don't know.'

'How convenient. Are you sure you actually asked him? I know you didn't want her to stay.'

'Are you calling me a liar?'

'No. I'm sorry. It's been such a long night.'

'You don't sound sorry.' He got up from his chair and walked slowly towards her. 'You have everything you could possibly want and still you're not happy. I won't have you make a fool of me Madam. Kluger must have thought exactly what I thought when we entered that room.'

Emilie had backed out of the lounge towards the stairs. She recognised the intense look in his eyes and wished she'd just gone to bed when they got home.

She turned towards the stairs and started walking up them slowly even though she wanted to run. 'Sober up Gerard. And get some sleep. I'll talk to you this afternoon.'

She'd almost reached the top of the stairs when she could hear him coming up behind her. There was nobody else in the house and there wasn't enough time to reach the bedroom and lock the door. She stumbled across the threshold when he got hold of her hair and pulled her back.

'You fucking useless whore. Do you have any idea how hard I work to keep us here? In this house, away from the riff raff on the streets where you belong. Out there with the other tarts.'

'Please Gerard, you're hurting me. Nothing happened on that balcony. I'm married to you.'

'Yes you are but you seem to forget it regularly. One of these days...'

'Let go of me.' She tried to turn around but his grip on her arms was too strong. She needed to calm him down so she stopped fighting back. 'You're just tired darling. Let's have some rest and when we wake up...'

His hand whacked the back of her head and her face went sideways into the blue rose wall paper. It took her by surprise and a burning sensation spread from her cheek to the rest of her face. Through the echoing noise in her head she could hear the staff door opening and the cleaning lady arriving. Briefly Gerard let go of her but his anger hadn't subsided.

'Get in there.' He pointed to his study.

Her head still hurt and because she didn't want any of the staff to see what had happened she did as he asked.

***

Loud voices outside the window woke her up. Normal noise, noise from her childhood. Wooden wheelbarrows on cobbled stones, traders conversing loudly, swapping gossip before trying to sell their meagre goods. Her eyes were blurry when she opened them. Hell, last night came back in a flash. Yes, I'll have another drink. If I drink enough maybe my life will be back to normal. She remembered holding back the tears over Fleur even though she'd read the diary, she'd chatted to Ballou and her friends in the corner of Zous, the club. How small the world really was. How they'd all changed, how the world had altered, but a few drinks and some music made it all seem so normal. On the surface everyone was acting normally, as the night went on, as people got drunk the talk changed. Most of them were dancing to a band covering Django Rheinhardt songs but at a few tables, Anaise's included, small gangs were leaning into each other, making sure there were no eavesdroppers.

She'd been pleased to see Christophe there. They'd got on really well when she'd been in Paris the last time, well enough for him to make a move on her which was obviously turned down. He'd been good about it though and now he was part of Em's gang here in Paris. She had been tempted to ask if he'd heard anything from her these last days, but she hadn't in the end.

It must have been well past three in the morning when she and Ballou sneaked out. The lights on the streets were off and they tiptoed around the corner and up into her flat through a hidden back door. It had been a nice ending to an awful day.

She couldn't stay in bed any longer. Even though her head felt thick with last night's drink she lifted it off the pillow and looked down on Ballou's fair hair showing just above the duvet edge. She needed coffee so she sat up and put her feet on the large worn rug that covered most of the floorboards. The chill made her instantly want to crawl back under the cover but she couldn't; she had to see Em. At some point somebody had tried to decorate the flat. One wall of brightly coloured flowers contrasted with the other three in faded brown. She wondered who'd done that. Ballou wasn't the decorating kind. Who'd lasted less than a wall?

She walked into the kitchen and filled a saucepan with water for the coffee, but the gas cooker didn't work. After a few tries she gave up and looked around for something else to use. There were a few unwashed dishes in the small sink and some stockings hanging from a chair. In the corner she noticed a paraffin light with a jar of replacement coffee next to it. That must be what she used. Ten minutes later she had two coffees to bring into the bedroom. Ballou was still sleeping soundly and Anaise could easily have left her there with a note. After the last time though she didn't think that her friend would take it too kindly.

She put down the cups on the bed side table and opened the shutters. Even the increased noise of the market traders and shop keepers didn't wake up Ballou.

'Wake up. Come on, I have to go.'

Her friend appeared from under the duvet. 'What time is it?' Her voice was weak with the excesses of the previous night.

'It's just gone half past seven.'

There was no response to this so she repeated it a bit louder. 'I have to go Ballou. I have to see Em.'

'Can you hand me the headache powder on the side there. I don't know why the drinks last night affected me so.'

Anaise handed her the powder and her friend sat up. Her back leaning against the wooden ornate bed that she remembered from years back, the bed Ballou had seen and just had to have. It had taken five of them to get it up the stairs and into her flat.

She poured some of the powder into her cooling coffee before sipping it.

'You look ready to leave.'

Anaise nodded and stroked her hair. 'But I will come back. I won't leave Paris again without saying goodbye.'

'If you say so.'

'I do. I have to go and see Emilie, I'm worried about her. I might be back here sooner than you think.'

'Ok.' Ballou handed her the empty cup and closed her eyes. 'There's a spare key in the top drawer. I have to get some more sleep chéri.'

'I'll see you later then.' Anaise picked up her bag and left her friend to recover.

The walk that should only have taken thirty minutes took her almost two hours as she got lost several times. Emilie's new house was in an area she'd only ever visited once and that had been the previous night. She finally found it and the girl who opened the door informed her that her sister was still asleep. She was a sweet enough girl who convinced her to have coffee, proper coffee, and brioche whilst her sister slept for a little longer. After half an hour she'd had enough. When did Em get quite so rude? She'd travelled a long way to get there, nobody had been to the station to meet her and now she was just sitting there look-ing at the wall getting angry.

She went out into the hallway and looked for the maid.

'Hello.'

Louise came up from the downstairs kitchen.

'Oui Mademoiselle.'

'I'm going to wake my sister. Which room is she in?'

Louise wringed her hands and looked pleadingly at Anaise.

'Please leave her to sleep for a little longer. She's not well.'

'Why didn't you say so? What's wrong with her?' Anaise started up the stairs with Louise, trying to persuade her not to, following closely behind.

'She just really needs her sleep.'

Anaise opened two doors before she found the one that her sister was sleeping in. The shutters were closed and Anaise marched up and opened them to let the outside light in.

'Emilie, wake up you lazy girl.'

Her eyes opened and a smile found its way to her lips.

'Where have you been?' She sat up and dark purple bruises showed on her arms.

'My God. What happened to you?'

Emilie pulled the duvet up to cover them and turned her face towards the wall to hide the mark on her cheek.

'Nothing. There was some fighting at the club last night and I got caught up in it. I'm fine now.'

Anaise shook her head slowly and her eyes narrowed.

'It's him, isn't it?' She'd seen his temper before.

Emilie stayed quiet, sunk back into the bed and closed her eyes.

Anaise looked over to where Louise was standing by the door. Knocking the chair she was sitting in over, she charged down the hall opening doors until she found the one with Emilie's husband sleeping in. He was stretched out on a sofa, fully dressed. The rest of the room was in disarray. A chest of drawers had been pushed over and broken porcelain was scattered on the floor. If Anaise needed any more proof that he was the reason her sister was black and blue, this was it.

Even the racket she was making hadn't woken him up but the slap she landed on his cheek did. He quickly recovered from the shock and looked up.

'What the...'

'Don't you ever touch her again you filthy salaud.' She restrained herself and turned to leave when Gerard leaped out of bed and furiously grabbed hold of her. Anaise screamed out more in surprise than from any pain inflicted.

'I'm going to let this go for now but you'd better stay out of my way,' he said brusquely.

She tried to get out of his grip whilst still shouting insults at him. She just couldn't stop. All the tension over the last week came out in the form of hate for this man.

When he noticed his wife and maid in the doorway he let her go. Anaise turned around and kicked his leg and in return she got a slap that sent her sideways. She tripped over the overturned chest of drawers and landed on top of it.

Gerard glared down at her. 'I'm going out. When I get back you'd better make sure you're not around. Find yourself some hole to stay in and don't even think about seeing Emilie. If you do, I will make sure you're arrested and sent to oblivion, and don't think that I won't.' He kicked a broken vase and pushed past the two women at the door.

As soon as he'd left, they went over to Anaise who was burning from embarrassment more than pain. She got back to her feet and noticed a small cut on her leg where it had hit the side of the chest of drawers.

'You have to come away Em. You can't stay here.'

They all heard the front door shut loudly.

'Let's go downstairs.' Emilie said and led the way to the kitchen. Somehow it was the more homely place and that was what was needed.

Louise fixed them some coffee before leaving them alone at the table. Anaise lit a cigarette from the packet she found on the table and blew out the smoke slowly. She only smoked occasionally and now that they were difficult to get hold of she was pleased about it.

'So, has he done it before?'

'Not like this,' she paused. 'I will leave him you know. Once things settle down I'll go. I can't leave Paris yet, not just yet.'

'You have to leave now. Who knows what he will do next time. And there always is a next time.'

'Can we change the subject? Did you just arrive?'

'No. I stayed with a friend last night. Now I understand why you weren't there to meet me.'

'I got stuck in this club and couldn't get out. Jacques, Gerard's little helper was supposed to pick you up, but I guess he didn't.'

'No. It's fine though. Actually it made me have to deal with something that had bothered me for a long time.'

'What?'

'Just repairing a friendship from last time.'

'I'm sorry I wasn't there. How is Tom?' She whispered his name.

Anasie briefly explained what Perrault wanted him to do. 'He was just going to do the deed when I left. I guess it must have been done by now.'

'So, what happens now? It won't be the end of it.'

Anaise looked around the kitchen and around the hall-way outside before getting the photos out of her purse.

'They know who he is and they know about the two of you.'

Em stared at the pictures on the table. 'And they will use it to blackmail him into doing other stuff for them. Maybe us too?'

'Who knows Em? We do need to make some exit plans and they can't wait until the war is over. What good will we be to anyone here. We can't do any good and if we're arrested we might incriminate others. And you can't stay in this house another day.'

'I'm going to get dressed and then we'll go out. I can't think here.' She picked up the photos from the table. 'Can I keep these?'

'Of course, but be careful.'

'I'm always careful. Every minute of every day I'm on full alert.' She stood up. 'This town is like a murky old lake covered in a paper thin layer of ice. It sparkles and glitters but step too hard and that dirty water will drag you down and show you what it's really like. On the surface, apart from the soldiers and the flags Paris seems like a normal place, but it isn't. You've got to remember that. I know you think I'm a little shallow and too concerned with my career and maybe I am, but I'm not stupid.'

'I know that,' Anaise said, surprised at her sister's outburst.

'He won't be the one to drag me away from Paris you know. I've worked hard for all of this, and I'll be damned if I let him be the reason I leave.'

'You'll be back once the Germans are out and until then you can have a career anywhere.'

'He's only like this when he's drunk.'

'No he's not and you know it. It might make him worse but he's got a mean streak and you're getting the brunt of it.'

Silence settled over the kitchen for a few moments before Emilie stood up.

'I'll be back down in five minutes.' She picked up the photos and went upstairs to get dressed.

Anaise picked up the picture of 'The Waiter' and put it back in her bag. Her head throbbed where Gerard had hit it and she couldn't wait to get out into the sunshine.

~ 10 ~

Small lumps of damp crumbly mud fell onto the brown kitchen tiles as Tom unwrapped his Baby Browning. It had been hidden in the garden for the last six months together with a fresh set of identification papers and some emergency money. The rough winter weather didn't seem to have done them any harm. He thoroughly cleaned the protective grease off the gun and put it on the table next to the metal pipe that had hidden it. Now he just needed to find the bullets and the identity papers. The money he had already stuffed down his trouser pockets.

The house was dark and silent. The shutters were closed and the previous night's thunder storm had forced rain in through one of the windows and there was now a water puddle below it adding to the sense of abandonment.

The journey back to Marseille had taken him longer than expected. He'd tried to stay out of sight, but he had a boat to catch that very night, so in the end he'd caught a lift for the last bit of the journey. Luck had been on his side and a flimsy excuse had been accepted without questioning by the opinionated driver. His constant talking had at least

114

let Tom think about what lay ahead. He would leave a message for Emilie with Father Michel. He'd let her know that he'd left France and that he'd be back as soon as he could, Anaise would tell her the rest.

The old wooden staircase creaked as he took the steps two at the time. He wanted to change into some dry clean clothes before setting off for the church, but he'd only reached the top step when he heard the front door being gently pushed open. The cloth that the gun had been wrapped in was still on the table, covered in grease and would not be mistaken for anything else. Tom cursed quietly when he realised that the gun was next to it and his wet footsteps would show that he'd only recently been there. Now, it could be a friend or a neighbour but he wasn't willing to take that chance. Besides, they would have knocked first. It only took him a few seconds to quietly dash across the landing and into his room. Ever since he had arrived, he'd been planning escape routes from every room in the house and now he was glad he had. The window eased open slowly and quietly, the next door neighbour's neglected wooden shutters were still closed. He grabbed a clean jacket that hung on a chair and as he stepped out onto the ledge he could hear the stairs creaking. He grabbed hold of the wooden trellis that in summer held up heavy branches of Wisteria but which now only had some sticks left over from the previous year. As strong as it seemed it couldn't hold his weight and he had to jump the last meter, landing with a quiet thump across the road from Monsieur Boule. There was a glint of amusement in the old man's eyes. His head moved slowly towards Tom's front door indicating that he should not exit that way. Tom nodded a thank you and with his heart beating hard he slunk down one of the back alleys towards the church.

Two blocks away there was a march by The Legion des Anciens Combattants and the chants Viva La France and La France aux Francais echoed muddily through the air. They were the old guard, the ones that had fought in the first war, the ones that put their trust utterly in Petain and wanted peace with Germany. It didn't seem very patriotic to Tom, to give up your country without a fight. Well, the Germans had taken over the North and the situation wouldn't change because he wished it to. He didn't know if an order for his arrest had been issued or if this was Perrault's own operation. All the same, it would be silly to assume that they weren't all out to get him, easier to survive if you were on your guard. Keeping his head down and keeping to the shadows, he walked briskly past the backs of houses and it occurred to him that this had been his life for too long. One way or another he'd been on the run since July '36. First from the fascists in Spain, then from himself and now from... well, almost everyone. What would it be like to be carefree and happy again, not having a past of bloody scars and broken lives? The world could never be the same again, not after all of this, not for anyone.

He hoped Father Michel was at home and alone because he was the only one he could leave a message with, the only one who could let Emilie know what had happened. A few minutes later the church tower came into view, and after making sure that there was nobody following him, he snuck around the back and into the empty kitchen.

It had been several days since his last visit and it would seem that Madam Ecout had still not returned. The flowers on the table were still there but the water must have run out and they had dried up and died. There were two more rooms on the ground floor and he could hear voices coming from one of them. Father Michel was talking to someone; a woman, and suddenly they both came out. She'd been crying and hurried out through the front door without noticing Tom. A few moments later, Father Michel came out and when he saw Tom he smiled sadly.

'Poor woman. Her son has just died,' he said tiredly and sat down at the table where Tom joined him. 'He'd been ill for a while but their meagre diet didn't give him a chance to recover.'

'I'm sorry for her,' Tom was sorry but he didn't have much time. 'I need to talk to you. It's important.'

He explained that he had to leave for London immediately. He didn't tell him the reason for his sudden departure and Father Michel didn't ask. The message he needed Father Michel to send told Emilie that everything had gone wrong and that he had to leave for London. He didn't tell her to leave France even though he wanted to, but he'd drilled Anaise before she left to that effect, and if anyone could influence Em, her sister could.

'I will get the message to her, of course I will.' He tapped his fingers on the table and looked at the dead flowers before returning his gaze to Tom. 'Will you take Sophia with you?'

Tom shook his head, surprised that Father Michel would ask. 'I can't. The boat is only expecting one person and it's too risky.'

'What's not risky these days? If she stays here after you've gone, her chances of getting out have all but vanished. With no papers she's a target on the streets and anyone who could guide her over the mountains would want money.' He put his wrinkled hand over Tom's on the table. 'Please.'

With everything else that had happened, Tom didn't need this pressure, but in the end he agreed to take her along. If there was room for one on the boat then he was sure they'd take two, if not, then he'd sort something out. He'd always found it difficult saying no to Father Michel, an old man, who in his own way risked everything to make the world a better place again. The kind of Priest this world needed more of.

~ 11 ~

Father Michel closed the door behind Tom and Sophia and sighed. One more saved. One less life taken. He went over to the table and picked up the ceramic jug holding the dead flowers. He should have put them in the rubbish days ago, but there was always something more important to do. And tomorrow Madam Ecout would be back, and there were funerals and weddings and confessionals to keep him busy. He had every faith in Tom; Sophia would be safe with him. He quickly wrote down Tom's message and put it under the third row of seats as usual before making his way back to the house.

He closed his eyes and prayed for Sophia's parents safe return and the easing of pain for everyone. It couldn't last much longer, God would surely see to that.

A knock on the door jolted him back from his prayers and he made the sign of the cross before opening it. A tall dark man stood outside with a worried look on his face.

'Yes, how can I help you?' Father Michel said kindly. The man looked harassed and out of breath from running.

'My brother is dying, Father. He needs the last rites straight away.' The accent was not from Marseille, but that was no surprise as the city was crowded with refugees.

Father Michel stepped outside. 'Where is he?'

'In Rue de Malon, up there.' The tall man pointed north. 'He was stabbed and he's bleeding. We have to hurry.' The tall man led the way through the church yard and up a quiet residential street.

The old priest hurried along after him as best he could, hoping that they would be in time.

'He's over there.' The tall man pointed towards a brick doorway and Father Michel hurried up ahead.

When he got there, the doorway was empty and he turned around.

'There's nobody here.'

The short man looked around. 'No, there isn't.' Within seconds he had produced the Baby Browning he'd found earlier on the kitchen table in Tom's house and pointed it at the Priest's surprised face. 'I'm sorry, I really am.'

'I don't understand.' Father Michel said, but he did. He understood only too well. It was the end for him and the only consolation was that Sophia had gotten away. He took a deep shaking breath and surprised himself by feeling fear. He was a Priest, he knew death was not the end, but still, his mouth had gone dry and his hands shook when he touched the cross hanging around his neck.

'There's nothing for you to understand. You were helping the wrong side that's all. If there was any way I could change this, I would.'

Father Michel would not have heard the last word of that sentence as a bullet from the Browning took his life.

The man that had earlier followed Tom was sincere in his wish that it could have been different. His duty had just cost him another part of his soul.

***

The dark blue Mediterranean Sea came in gentle waves, brushing the grey rocks that divided the long pebbly beach west of Marseille. It was quiet and dark until the large mottled moon appeared from above the high clouds and lit up the landscape.

Tom looked at the girl sitting next to him on the rocks and wondered how Father Michel had convinced him to take her along. Sitting with her back straight and alert, she jumped at every sound that varied from the waves lapping over the rocks and pebbles. After what she'd been through he couldn't really blame her. They had been sitting in the same place for a couple of hours and soon it would be light. There was no way of telling if they were even in the right place and soon they would have to leave and then what would they do? He hadn't slept for a couple of days and constantly felt himself nodding off only to jerk awake for some reason or other.

He'd calculated that he'd be in London within a week, hand over the message and once he found out what it revealed about Perrault he would make sure they parachuted him back into France. Ten days at the most before he could go to Paris and take Emile and Anaise away somewhere safe. They'd all done their bit and he felt tired. Tired of everything.

He was thinking of this when Sophia nudged him and pointed to the far side of the beach where there was movement. At first Tom thought it might be their pick up, but it only took a few seconds before they could hear dogs barking and the Gendarmes shouting. Their flashlights cut through the semi darkness towards their hiding place. The shouts indicated that they were after someone else, but there was no way for Tom and Sophia to explain their presence on the beach in the middle of the night.

'Come on. There'll be no boat tonight.' Tom grabbed Sophia's hand and pulled her up. The flashlights were getting closer. 'Maybe it's the boat they're after. If it was us, they wouldn't make so much noise, but we'd better get out of here before they see us.'

'Where are we going?'

'I don't know,' he answered a little more abruptly than he wanted. He knew it was a bad idea to have someone else along. If it was just him, he would be able to get away quickly.

They slid down the rock on the west side and started running, hunched down, alongside the outer edge of the beach. At any time the moon could come out and show them to the world. The banks alongside the beach were steep, and normally you'd enter and exit through tunnels that were dotted here and there. There were no tunnels nearby though, and having put some distance between themselves and the dogs they stopped to climb up the grass covered bank. Tom put his hands together and lifted Sophia up so that she could get a foot hold before climbing over.

'Come on. Quickly.' He hurried her along and she stepped into his hands before launching herself upwards. The foot she tried to get a grip with twisted and she screamed out. Not loudly, and not for long, but there was no doubt that the Gendarmes down the beach would have heard it.

She slid down onto the pebbles and seemed more worried about anybody hearing them than with her ankle.

'I'm sorry. Don't leave me here.'

He helped her back up and they both heard the dogs getting closer, their barking increasing as they pulled their leads.

'Can you move?'

Tom leaned down and tried to see what the damage was.

'I will. Just give me a second.'

'No point in trying the bank again,' he said looking around for another way to get out.

The beach stretched out in front of them, offering no escape until one of the tunnels materialised and God knew where that would be.

'Yes, there is. Do it again and I'll pull you up.'

'Are you sure you can do it?' he whispered and she nodded.

Holding on to some patches of long grass whilst putting her good foot in Tom's hands once more, she climbed up slowly before turning around. One of her hands holding onto a large shrub whilst the other one was held out for Tom to hold onto.

Tom managed to pull himself up with the help of Sophia and it was only when they were both safely up that they realised that the beach was silent. There were no dogs barking or orders shouted. They would have heard them, of that there was no doubt. They must have seen where they were going and taken a short cut somewhere.

The top of the bank was broad but they needed to get down on the other side. Towards the east you could make out Marseille, surrounded by grey limestone mountains and the sea, and Tom knew they couldn't go back there. They slid down the bank to the other side where wetland and fields stretched out in front of them, only interrupted by the occasional farmhouse and windswept shrub.

'How's your foot?' he asked.

'It's not so bad, it's getting better.'

Tom knew she was lying, but it didn't matter, they had no choice but to move forwards, away from this location and towards somewhere safe with a telephone.

Only moments later they could hear the sound of approaching vehicles. The headlights of two cars were coming towards them and there were no obvious hiding places. It was still dark however and they ran off the road and lay down flat on the ground, blending into the low landscape. As long as the cars didn't stop right there, they would be ok. The night time dew started soaking into their clothes and Tom's heart beat so hard he could feel his whole body moving with it. The cars slowed down where they knew Tom and Sophia had climbed over the bank, but then drove on. They obviously thought they would have gotten further away than they actually had. When they realised their error they would be back.

Once it was safe to move, Tom helped Sophia up and they started walking across the fields, away from Marseille, away from the Gendarmes, away from the ship that had never arrived.

***

Tom put the telephone receiver back on its base and thanked the seemingly uninterested barman. Several times during the brief and seemingly jolly conversation he'd had with his friend Marcel's wife he'd noticed the barman glancing over. Interested no doubt as to why two strangers had arrived by foot into the small village. Apart from the barman, whose name was Monsieur Trouit, the bar was empty, but Tom had still kept the conversation in code and hoped that Madeleine had understood what he meant. He did worry that even if she managed to get hold of Marcel immediately, it would still take him a good two hours to drive there. As they were now stuck in this little village for a while, they needed a cover story. He hoped the barman had heard enough of the phone call not to alert anybody to their presence.

'Monsieur Trouit, our car broke down a few kilometers from here and we're waiting for a friend to pick us up. Would you have somewhere where my sister and I could wash and have a rest until he arrives?'

The well rounded barman tweaked his large ginger moustache and shook his head. 'We're only a small village cafe. No rooms to let I'm afraid.' He looked out of the window towards the table where Sophia was sitting in the morning sunshine. Her eyes down and her coffee untouched. 'You can wash upstairs in my room if you wish. There is water and soap.'

'Thank you monsieur. My sister isn't well and I thought a few days away from the city would do her good.'

They both looked over to where she was sitting and feeling their eyes on her, she looked back.

'She misses our father. He's in a camp up north. It's all been too much for her these last few months.'

'Ah, we're missing many men here too. At least there is peace now, eh?' The barman smiled encouragingly. 'It will all get better from now on. Pétain will make sure of that.'

Almost choking on his reply, Tom agreed.

Having secured the sympathy of Monsieur Trouit, Tom collected Sophia and together with the barman they went upstairs.

There was only one room with a wash stand in the corner and as soon as there was enough water for them both to wash, the barman went back downstairs.

'What's happening now?' Sophie asked still standing rigidly in the corner by the door. 'What did your friend say?'

'Shhh!' Tom urged and put his finger to his face and walked over to her. 'You have to speak quietly.' He quickly explained what he'd told the barman. 'We'll get a lift soon. My friend wasn't in, but I left a message.'

'Can you try him again? What if he doesn't get it?'

'He'll get it.'

'Maybe we'd be better off in the countryside.'

'Stop it Sophia. Everything will be fine. I promise.'

She was silent for a moment and then she went across the room to the wash stand.

Tom stood still in the corner, his eyes fixed on a spot on the floor as he remembered saying those words to someone else, a long time ago, on a street in Madrid. If he closed his eyes he could almost be there now. Right there, with her, holding her, promising her that all would be ok again. That Franco would never take Madrid. See how that turned out.

He needed a few minutes on his own. 'I'll see you downstairs when you're done.'

Without waiting for a reply he shut the door behind him and went downstairs to see if the barman had a proper drink.

It was late in the afternoon by the time he saw Marcel's car approach the cafe. Sophia must have fallen asleep upstairs because she'd not appeared in the bar and he hoped the barman didn't mind. He could very easily have finished the bottle of wine the barman had produced for an extortionate number of Francs, but he'd only had a couple of glasses and then gone for a short walk around the almost deserted village. When he'd returned to the cafe, there had been an old couple there who'd offered a bed for the night if their friend didn't show up. As the hours went by he wished he hadn't declined their offer.

Taking the stairs two at the time he knocked on the door before opening it. Sophia was curled up on the bed, breathing jerkily. Her closed eyes moved rapidly from side to side as if she was struggling to wake up.

'Sophia. Wake up,' he said gently feeling a little guilty over his abrupt departure earlier. 'Our lift is here.' He shook her shoulder and she jumped awake. It took her a few moments to remember where she was and then she sat up. 'I'll be down in just a minute.'

Tom went back downstairs just as Marcel walked into the cafe. When he saw Tom, a big grin appeared in his now bearded face.

'Ah, mon ami.' He embraced his friend and noticing the barman, he commiserated about their bad luck with the car. They sat down and Tom poured them both a drink from the wine bottle. Once the barman realised Marcel wasn't going to order anything he went to the back room.

'Am I glad to see you,' Tom said and lit a cigarette. 'Can you give us a lift to one of the crossing points?'

Marcel's eyes narrowed. 'I won't ask what's happened, but now is not the best of times to cross.'

'We have no choice. If you have a better way to get to London quickly then please tell me.'

'You've got papers. Why not just use the official borders into Spain?'

'For one, I'm not a friend of Spain as you know, and two; the girl who's with me has no papers at all. None of us have exit visas, so we need to sneak over.'

Marcel sighed. 'Who is she?'

Tom smiled and briefly explained about Sophia.

'We can get her papers in Perpignan, but it'll take a few days,' Marcel said. 'Good papers, and as it's you, we can get you exit visas too. They'll catch on to those visas soon enough, but for now it's all working beautifully,' he grinned.

'Thanks, but we haven't got the time. If we can get into Portugal I can probably get her papers from Lisbon.'

'You could leave her with us. We'll get her out in good time.'

'No. I need to make sure she's safe. I promised to get her to London, she's a nervous wreck as it is.'

Marcel shook his head. 'You're a fool to yourself. But then again, I already knew that. I still think you should take the official roads. It won't take long to get the papers for her, and if you don't, you're going to get into trouble in Spain and in Portugal. How are you going to get her to Britain if she has no papers?'

Tom had to agree that Marcel was right. It might be a slight delay on this side, but it would make it easier on the other side.

'How quickly can you get them?'

Marcel thought for a moment. 'Madeleine has a spare set for herself. If I tell her it's for you, well, your friend, she'll probably let you have them. That would be the quickest way.'

They agreed that Tom and Sophia should stay in a safehouse in Perpignan for a couple of nights whilst Marcel organised their papers and visas. A minute later they both heard the door upstairs open and Sophia came down the stairs. Within two minutes they were in the car heading towards the safe house in Perpignan.

~ 12 ~

Paris

The boy made a mistake on his final piece of music. His fingers slipped briefly to the wrong key at the end of Moonlight Sonata but the rest had been perfect and his mother started the applause. The boy could not have been more than thirteen and showed a lot of promise which his mother was intent on taking advantage of.

Emilie was sure that this whole salon open house was just a way for her to show him off. Still, it had been pleasant to listen to. The boy's mother, Madam Sager, now thanked everyone for coming to her little afternoon salon party. There must have been at least fifty people drinking endless cups of tea or cocktails in her large salon whilst chatting endlessly about art and gossip as if Paris was as it always had been.

'Ghastly, isn't it?' Mrs Carter's American accent was still dominating her French and Emilie liked it. They'd known each other for years, ever since Mrs Carter had helped her out in the beginning of her career. Even though they didn't see much of each other nowadays, when they did meet, it was like they'd been discussing the hat selection at Lafayette only the day before. Now she was working her way through the cocktail selection with vigour and their hostess threw worrying glances towards her frequently.

'Do you mean the music or our hostess?' Emilie whispered conspiratorially.

'Oh, God, both. The poor boy can't help it of course, but really.'

They both laughed. Mrs Carter touched the bruise on Em's cheek with her finger. She didn't need to say anything, she knew what had happened.

'I noticed that husband of yours left just in time.'

'Yes, he had some business to take care of. Honestly, he doesn't like these things.'

'Well, he wouldn't darling. Too many decent people around for his liking.'

'Madam Carter, you know you shouldn't say things like that.' She smiled inwardly. Gerard had left to see Kluger, to let him know that she wouldn't be able to go to Berlin. He had been very unhappy about it, but she'd told him that she'd do it herself if he didn't. After a lot of arguing he'd reluctantly agreed to do it. He'd been sober then.

'I am sorry honey, but I find it very difficult to lie. Well, in some cases anyway.' She finished her martini and grabbed hold of another from a passing waiter. 'Look at them all here. German officers socialising with the Parisian set and fascist writers.'

'Shh, they'll hear you.' Emilie leaned down towards Mrs Carter's ears.

'Oh, I'm too old to care if they do honey. My first husband died in northern France in '17 and I never thought I'd have a drink in the same room as any German ever again. Yet here I am, but in my defense I didn't realise they would be here acting as if nothing was wrong.'

'No, but we'd better not discuss it here and now.'

'You're probably right.' She paused and took Emilie's hand in hers. 'There are some rather awful rumours going around about you and them my girl.' She nodded over towards a couple of Germans. 'I always stick up for you whenever anyone mentions it but it might be an idea to stay away from them. They will leave one day, and never mind if there is truth in the rumours or not, you will still be here. You might pay a high price for your actions.'

Emilie's eyes glazed over as she remembered the two boys and the green grocer. What could she do though? Her skin had to grow thicker, she couldn't let this upset her.

'It's not true you know. None of it. None of it.' She so wanted to tell her the truth but again knew she couldn't. Another person to think badly of her.

'Of course it's not. All I'm saying is that you should perhaps keep a little distance.' She lit a cigarette. 'Who's that girl standing in the doorway looking lost?'

Emilie looked over and waved to Anaise. She wore one of Emilie's many dresses which was a touch too short, but the purple silk suited her dark hair. Anaise walked across the room towards the two women whilst throwing glances at the variety of guests.

'Well, isn't this a charming party,' she said as she reached them.

'Anaise, this is Madam Carter. Madam Carter, this is my sister. I can't believe you two haven't met yet.' Emilie was immensely pleased that a change of conversation had arrived along with her sister.

'I would never have thought you two were sisters.' Madam Carter's eyes darted between the two of them. 'You are so different.'

'So were our parents Madam.' Anaise smiled a little uneasily and Madam Carter laughed.

A few minutes of small talk later, Madam Carter quietly announced she couldn't stand being in the same room as 'these people' any longer. She extended an invitation to Anaise to come and see her before asking Emilie to help her find a taxi.

Once Mrs Carter had been safely put in a cab, Emilie walked back upstairs to the salon. It was at that moment she decided that it would probably be best for her to leave Paris. This wasn't doing her career any good, all that she'd worked for so hard over the years, sacrificed so much for would slip from her fingers no matter what she did. She ached for Tom and there had been no news coming through from Marseille. She didn't know if it had gone to plan or if he was languishing in some hellhole prison.

She stopped on the steps for a moment and lit a cigarette. The smoke curled up towards the sparking chandelier where it remained suspended in the air curling itself around the lights. It would take a little while to get the papers done for their escape and in the meantime she'd double her efforts in finding out information from any Germans she came across. That way she'd have something to bring with her to England, something that would prove her worth to Tom.

She walked towards her sister who was standing in the same place as when she'd left, but she wasn't alone. Oberleutnant Joachim Gerber was standing next to her, having a rather one sided conversation. His face lit up when Emilie arrived.

'Madam Valois, how nice to see you again.'

'And you ,Oberleutnant Gerber. I see you have met my sister already.' Emilie said and thanked God that Gerard had left.

'Yes. I'm afraid I've been taking up her time ever since you left with the older lady.' He didn't want to make anybody uncomfortable, but she'd been on his mind every hour since their meeting at the club. Her pale skin, fair hair and stunning blue eyes was in front of his every time he closed them. He didn't kid himself that anything would ever happen between them, but he couldn't help himself. There had been a moment on that balcony when he'd thought that anything was possible, a moment when he'd felt Paris. He just wanted to spend a little time with her, make her laugh and listen to her sing.

'I don't see your uncle here, Oberleutnant.'

'He's too busy at the moment. Some big operation he's assisting with. And of course he's putting together the French part of the Victory Concert. You must be looking forward to it.'

'I would be if I was going, but it's not possible for me to leave Paris as the moment.'

'Oh, but I thought it had already been settled.'

'No, my husband has told your uncle. He can easily find someone else,' she said more harshly than she'd intended. She rubbed her temples and started excusing herself when she noticed Gerber's eyes on a bruised part of her arm where her sleeve had ridden up. She quickly pulled her sleeve down and made sure she kept her bruised cheek away from him.

'I am sorry, but I have a headache coming on.' She smiled at his concerned eyes. 'I must have had too much champagne.'

Anaise put her drink down. 'I'll get our coats Em.' She glanced at Gerber. 'I'll be back in just a tick.'

Once she'd gone, Gerber lightly touched Em's arm. 'I hope it passes quickly. I find a little rest does the trick.'

'I'm sure it will. There always seems to be something wrong with me when we meet.'

He smiled. 'I have to ask if you could find the time to have lunch with me.'

His request took her by surprise and she knew she should say no. If Gerard found out he'd go mad, but she found herself wanting to meet him again. There was also the possibility of finding out more about the big operation Sturmbannführer Kluger was busy with.

'That would be nice. I'm not sure how much my husband would appreciate it though.'

'Let's not tell him. I promise you I will be the perfect gentleman.'

She couldn't help smiling. He was a few years younger than her, and a German, but she was sure that he was a gentleman.

The details were settled before Anaise showed up with the coats. Half an hour later the two girls were sitting in a smoky bar drinking gin whilst a man played the piano in the corner.

'Bloody hell, I thought my heart would bounce out of my chest when he started talking to me. A German for God's sake.' She drained her glass.

'He's alright, not like the others. Still a German though, that's the trouble.'

'How do you know him?'

Emilie explained about their meeting in the bookshop and on the balcony. Anaise looked her in the eye with a serious look. 'Don't think well of him Em. He's the one killing our families and friends, the one that would have you arrested in a moment if he knew what you were up to.'

'I know. It's just he mentioned something about a big operation and I thought I should find out more.'

'He's not going to tell you anything. Keep away from him Em and have another gin.' She smiled now. 'It really is a girl's best friend you know.'

The gin warmed Emilie's throat and they ordered more. There were still some hours before curfew and this was one of her old bars. After several more drinks and a resisted urge to get up and sing with the piano player like she would have done in the olden days, she stayed sitting on her bar chair, afraid that someone might recognise her again.

'I've made up my mind, I want to leave Paris.' Emilie leaned over towards Anaise.

'I knew you would. I've got some guys organising the paperwork and we should have them in a week or so.'

'You didn't know I'd leave.'

'Yes, I did. Because to stay would just be pure stupidity. I'll try again to get some information on what's happening down south and with Tom first thing in the morning. It's all been quiet as a grave so far. Excuse the expression.'

'My Tom, where is he do you think?'

'Don't know. We have to assume he's in the house as usual. I guess it would be difficult for you to get another pass back home. If not, we can leave through the usual route from there.'

'Not now. Gerard would wonder why. Anyway, I can't leave for at least a week.'

'Why? Don't tell me you have some club arrangement.'

'No. I just have some things to do that's all.' Emilie knew then that she would never tell Anaise about the lunch with Joachim.

'We'll discuss this tomorrow.'

'I'm the older sister. I make the decisions. That's the rule.'

~ 13 ~

'I hope you don't mind meeting here.' Oberleutnant Gerber looked around the small hotel restaurant on the outskirts of the Latin Quarter. It was clean, and he didn't want anyone seeing them having lunch, especially not her husband.

'It's charming. I used to live not far from here when I first arrived in Paris. Down at the square. On a Sunday, there was music and dancing and singing. Always a day for living.' She raised her eyebrows and looked at his attire. He wore the same clothes he'd worn in the bookshop. 'How do you get away with dressing like that?'

He laughed as the food arrived. 'My uniform is in the bag underneath the table. I changed in a cafe on the way here.'

Emilie shook her head and smiled. 'I know you want to see the real Paris, but is it really worth the risk of being caught?'

He paused a moment before answering. 'Yes, I think so. I wanted you to see me as a normal person. Someone you might be friends with, not as part of the occupying force.

140

Silly I know. I think I would be in quite a lot of trouble if I was stopped for papers.'

His dark hair was combed back but a couple of strands had found their way out and bounced over his forehead as he moved. His brown eyes were full of mischief, wanting to find the Parisian romance his mother and father had told him about. He wanted the Paris before the war and she knew that he wanted her.

'The food isn't bad, is it?'

'It's awful,' she replied and took a bite of the over-cooked small piece of fish on her plate. 'You should go to Pascal's, they'll still cook you a fabulous meal in the middle of all the troubles and shortages.'

'I've been there, but I always think that it's the company that makes the meal.'

'You're making me blush... What do I call you now?'

'Joachim, please.'

She paused for a moment. 'Alright, only for this meal, whilst you're out of uniform.'

Silence settled over the table and the waiter brought another bottle of wine.

'So are you from Paris?' he asked and filled their glasses with gold coloured wine.

She shook her head. 'No, I was born in Marseille. I visit so rarely now that if it wasn't for my sister living there I'd hardly ever go back.'

'I'm the same. The last time I was in Stolpen was at my father's funeral. My mother went back a few times to look after his grave but the train fares were so expensive she had to stop going.

'That's very sad. Promise me you'll take her there when you go home on leave.'

'I promise. There's not a lot of home leave on the cards at the moment though.'

'Is that because of the big operation you mentioned the other day?'

For an instant he looked taken aback by her comment. 'No it's not.'

'I'm sorry, it's just that you said your uncle was tied up with something and I thought he'd want your help with it.'

'Don't be sorry. I shouldn't have mentioned it at all.'

His eyes held hers over the table. 'So, shall we have some more wine?'

She shook her head. 'I have to go. I probably shouldn't have come in the first place.'

'Stay with me for a little longer, Emilie.'

'I have to get back home. I really do.'

Their lunch had already lasted hours, and the one member of staff still there was standing by door wishing they would leave.

Joachim tentatively took her hand which rested on the table and looked into her eyes.

'I think I've fallen in love with you, Emilie. And no, don't speak, I know you don't feel the same, but maybe, there's some little part of you that could love me. Not now, not with things being the way they are, but later, when the world is well again.'

Emilie felt her eyes well over and she didn't know why. In or out of uniform, he was a German and she should hate him, but she didn't. Instead she moved her chair over and felt his face under her hand, his hair between her fingers.

A cough from the doorway brought them back to reality.

'Shall we go?' Gerber asked.

She nodded and rose from her chair.

Gerber paid the bill whilst the waiter mumbled something about disappearing morals.

Outside, the streets were quiet, but still they both looked around to see if there was anybody around to challenge either one of them.

'Come with me.' Joachim said and took her hand.

They walked for a few minutes and ended up outside a boarded up little house.

'It's not the Ritz I know.'

Emilie looked up at the broken shutters and knew how wrong it would be, but God she needed it. A little love away from it all and nobody had to find out. His love for her was almost too tempting to resist, there hadn't been much of it recently.

'I can't Joachim. You will find someone one day....' Her words drowned as he suddenly kissed her. Her body tensed for a moment before she closed her eyes and found that she actually enjoyed it. She pulled away slightly looking up at the old building. 'How do we get in?'

***

There had to be something hidden here somewhere. He knew she was up to something, her and that sister of hers. That cow Anaise would know about it, would be laughing at him behind his back. They both must be laughing. He knew she didn't have any family except for that sister so how could Kluger have information of a cosy 'cousin' living with them in Marseille? He hadn't wanted to ask for a description, hadn't wanted the German to think he didn't know about it. It was however the conversation that followed that had initiated the search. Kluger had tapped a thin file on his desk and declared that there was some flimsy report showing Emilie to be taking part in some anti-German activities. Emilie, really? Gerard had almost laughed out loud at this point. His wife was not the sharpest tool in the box, and even though he knew she didn't like the Germans, let's face it, who really did, she didn't have the brainpower or the conviction for the resistance. They wouldn't want her anyhow. He had mentioned this to Kluger who said he was glad and that he'd leave the file for now. Her singing in Berlin would put the whole thing to sleep anyway. Gerard had not mentioned the fact that Emilie had decided she wasn't going. He'd find something on her, and if he didn't, he'd make something up that he could use to blackmail her into doing it. He relied on the mutual business relationship he had going with Kluger and very soon there would be bigger fish to fry. Kluger had hinted heavily at it.

He stood up by the door and leaned his head back on the frame when his eyes fell on something as obvious as the large flower pot by the window. The setting sun threw an uneven shadow at the bottom of the green ceramic and he walked towards it. He looked at it for a moment before lifting it off the mahogany cupboard it stood on. It had a double bottom and when he inserted a penknife the false part fell onto the bed together with photographs and letters. The pictures were of Em and that Tom Lancaster before Gerard had married her. He remembered those times and how he'd hated him then, there was no reason for him to hate him less now. It didn't prove that he was the cousin Kluger had talked about though, the pictures were old and no matter how annoying he found it that she'd kept them it didn't prove that she was still seeing him. There was this nagging feeling in his stomach though that it was just what she was doing, maybe he was in Paris too, maybe she was with him now. He felt his pulse race and forced it to calm down. She was no different to Lilou, both performing for money, at least Lilou had been honest about it. Lilou was still hiding somewhere in Paris, but he had no doubt that they would find her.

First thing first, he sat down on the bed and glanced through the letters. They stopped in '37, the year he'd married her. He picked up the photos and at the bottom he found one that must have been taken quite recently. She was wearing the hat he'd got her for Christmas only four months ago, and cosying up next to her was Tom Lancaster.

He'd been in Marseille when his wife had been there only weeks ago.

He felt strangely calm considering that he held in his hand proof of her infidélité. The sun had set whilst he'd sat on the bed staring at the photo, but when the doorbell rang, and he heard Louise open it, he quickly put the hoard back in the pot and placed it carefully on the window frame. He then went downstairs and warmly greeted his surprised wife.

~ 14 ~

Soft sunlight edged its way through the rail carriage as it reached the end of the Pyrenees Tunnel des Balitres. Their last stop had been the south eastern French town of Cerbere and now they had entered Franco's Spain. Portbou, the Spanish border town came within view against a shimmering blue Mediterranean sea and Tom prepared his nerves for the border control.

He'd done this before, he'd done this before with forged identity documents, but never had so much been at stake. If they got caught with the film he carried in a cigarette case in his trouser pocket they'd be sent right back to France and most likely treated as spies. Worse if Perrault got hold of them.

Time was also of the essence, he needed to get the film to London and find out what was on it before Perrault decided to give the information they had on Emilie to Gerard and the Germans. He only hoped that Father Michel had got his message to her through to Paris, and that both the sisters had left the capital. He didn't even want to consider that it might already be too late.

The train slowed down before roughly stopping on the eastern platform where they would all have to alight and change trains. Out of the dirty window he could see the border control check point. The papers they had got from Marcel were good, but the travel documents were still forgeries and he tried not to think about it. They travelled as a newly married couple on their way to Lisbon. From Lisbon they had decided that America was their final destination as they were not in the war and would cause less scrutiny than London. Once they got to the Lisbon border they would have to come up with something else as they sometimes insisted on seeing onward travel visas for people entering. He'd worry about that later.

The previous evening they had gone through Sophia's new identity and the reason for their travels until she'd lost her temper and gone to bed. This morning she'd been very quiet, pale and nervous about the crossing.

He still didn't quite know what to make of her. At times she worried about everything and seemed younger than her nineteen years and at other times, there was a steely determination in everything she did. Mostly that happened when Tom voiced doubts about their journey and then she became over positive and rather bossy. When he talked about anything personal she'd stop listening, he'd shrug his shoulders and silence would settle over the small damp room they'd shared in Perpignan. He still knew very little about her and maybe that was for the best, their paths would separate soon enough.

The train came to a halt and Tom took their two borrowed suitcases off the overhead shelf and they stepped out into the late morning sun. They both wore clothes donated by Marcel and his wife. Tom's brown trousers were just a hint too short and his shirt a little too tight, but then again most people re-used and mended old clothes these days.

Sophia pulled her jacket closer as if she was cold in the heat and Tom wished she didn't look so jittery.

'Take it easy, it'll all be fine.' He looked at her and smiled as a husband would to his wife. 'You need to breathe, dear.'

Sophia took a deep breath and tried to smile back. 'Of course. Is that the town down there?' She looked over the far side of the end platform and pointed towards the rooftops.

'It is. It had quite a rough time in the Spanish war, but it's still here. Maybe not as it would have liked, but it's still here.'

After this attempt at conversation they both fell silent, concentrating on what lay ahead. An orderly queue had formed and they were in the middle of it. The low, tense chitter chatter of their fellow travellers were at times drowned out by the seagulls swarming to and from the sea, calling out to each other as they passed. There was slow progress and the barking of two guard dogs at regular intervals kept everybody tense. Then it was their turn.

The man checking their papers looked smart and efficient whilst the two men in basic army uniform standing beside him, blocked the way out until the smart man gave the go ahead.

'Have you been to Spain before,' he looked at their papers, 'Señor and Señora Prideux?'

'Yes, I was here in the late twenties. In Pamplona to watch the bullfighting.' This was partly true, he had been to Pamplona, but not in the twenties and not to watch bullfighting. 'It was very good.'

The man was still looking between them and the photographs on the papers.

'And you Señora, have you been to Spain before?' He looked up at her.

It took a moment for Sophia to answer. 'No, I haven't.' Her clear voice was confident.

He turned his attention back to Tom.

'And, you are travelling to Lisbon?'

'Yes, we are.'

'What are your plans once you get there?'

'We are just travelling through on our way to America.' The man nodded.

'Just make sure you don't linger here.'

With that he dismissed them. They had only moved a few steps away from the border official when he rose and called out, 'Señor Prideaux.'

Tom's heart had done a double take as he heard the man's voice and he turned around.

'Come back to Spain one day, Señor. There are many many bullfights to be seen.' He smiled before sitting back down again. Tom managed a polite smile and a nod in return.

He was too relieved that they had got through the check point to notice the narrowing eyes of one of the guards following him onto the next platform.

When the Spanish train finally arrived they managed to get a seat each in the full carriage and relaxed a little. Their conversation had run out at the station and now they were both in their own private thoughts as he train moved along the tracks towards Valencia and Madrid. At times they would fall asleep on the long journey only to be jolted awake by the train stopping or its whistle blowing. By the time they reached the outskirts of Madrid they were both awake looking out of the window at a city that still bore the scars of a destructive Civil war.

Tom had not been back since 1937 when Madrid had been under siege and almost constant shelling had left most of it in ruins. Even if he'd wanted to he couldn't have returned, he had been on the losing side in the war and Franco had promised to eradicate his every enemy. He was doing a good job of it too. The ones he hadn't had shot or imprisoned were struggling to stay alive on next to no food and no work. Their broken dreams of a free Spain had killed their souls.

It would only be a quick stop over. A bed for the night and some food before getting on another train for the Portuguese border first thing in the morning. He didn't like being back, it made him more nervous than the whole Perrault business. His life had changed there and even breathing Madrid air brought back memories that he should probably have buried deeper. If only they'd trekked over the Pyrenees they would have avoided it all together.

'Are you ready for a good night's sleep and proper food?' Tom asked.

'I am so hungry. When did we eat last?'

'Must have been those oranges in Barcelona. We'll find somewhere that does good Spanish food.'

'Yes, let's. And a proper bed to sleep in.'

The train pulled into the station and once again Tom lifted down their cases and stepped out onto the platform. There was a lot of noise and activity. At first Tom thought it was just travellers, but as his eyes focused on the station side of the platform he could see they were Civil Guardia, checking and re-checking everybody's papers.

Both of them had thought they would be clear until the Portuguese border, but something had drawn out this police presence and even though he doubted it was them, something in his stomach told him it was bad news.

'Alphonse, what's happening?' Sophia asked quietly whilst staring at the bulk of people and police ahead.

'It's just a checkpoint. No different from Portboa.'

The train had been full and there was a throng of people waiting to go through the guard barrier. Moving around the edges of this mix of people were more Civil Guardia police looking intimidating in their three pointed hats and well used blue uniforms.

There was no other way out of the station. Whoever it was they were after, they were doing everything possible to catch them.

Tom and Sophia were in the middle of the throng of travellers, hoping that some distraction would come up to allow them to slip away.

'Sophia, we need to split up. If anything happens to me, you have to go to the British Embassy and tell them. Do you understand?' He handed her one of the suitcases.

'What if they arrest both of us? What then?'

'You will be fine. Just stick to the story but say, if they ask, that you're meeting me here in Madrid for the journey to Lisbon.'

'I don't like it.'

Before Tom had a chance to respond there was shouting from the front as two men were roughly led away towards the exit whilst shouting their innocence.

'Let's hope those two were the reason for all of this. You'll be better off without me here. I'll see you outside.' Tom slunk away towards the back of the queue which was now moving a lot quicker. Sophia was at the front and he saw her move through the barrier and out the other side without any problems. He felt a little calmer as he stepped forward with his papers.

The man inspecting his papers and travel documents was overweight, and even at arm's length, he smelled as if he hadn't washed for days.

'This is not you.' He stated matter-of-factly.

'What do you mean? Of course it's me, who else would it be.' This was all going wrong. His documents were good ones and he might have understood if they had stopped him at the French border or even at the Spanish one in Pourtbou, but they hadn't. Why now?

'The man in this photo is not you. The papers are very crude forgeries.' He nodded to his colleagues and they took hold of Tom's arms and yanked them up behind his back. The pain took him by surprise.

'What are you doing? Let go.' He tried to get out of their grip.

The fat man stood up in front of him and before Tom realised what was happening his fist landed with force in his stomach. Tom lost his breath and doubled over. He screamed out in pain and anger as the fat man grabbed hold of his chin and pulled him back up.

'You were recognised at the border.' The guard's face was still full of war, of hate, and of spite as he hit him once again before the two guards dragged him away from the barriers and towards the station exit. It was a sign of what Spain had become after the war, that nobody even stopped to look.

***

It was remarkably calm outside Madrid Atocha station, at least compared with the noise inside it. Sophia's nerves were in tatters, but there was no other choice than to continue.

After their escape from the beach she'd started smoking to calm herself, and she needed one now. She'd ask Alphonse for one as soon as he came out.

He must have been right, they were after the two men that were taken away, as they'd let her through with only a cursory glance at her papers. He'd be there any minute now.

She looked back into the station and saw some poor man doubled over and held up by two policemen. The queue was almost gone and there was no sign of Alphonse. She took a couple of steps back into the station and looked around. A low scream from the man they had caught made her look again, and only as they dragged him along towards the exit where she was standing, did she notice it was Alphonse they held between them.

He'd noticed her too. She stood frozen to the ground, where just a few meter away, Alphonse managed to release one arm and head-butt one of the policemen. The commotion attracted the attention of other policemen and they came running towards them. Tom was on the floor and after a few kicks from all of them he was back between the two officers. Within seconds they were out of Sophia's view.

She couldn't believe what had just happened before her eyes. Her eyes were glued to the point where she'd lost sight of him. A Spanish woman came up to her and spoke in

Spanish. Sophia assumed she was asking if she was alright so she nodded and turned to go outside before she was sick right there in the station.

The Spanish woman came running after her holding out a cheap cigarette case, indicating that she thought Sophia had dropped it on the floor. It was Alphonse's case, she'd seen him with it on several occasions. She politely took it from the woman and started walking away.

That must have been the reason for Alphonse trying to get his arms free, he didn't want to get to the police station with it on his person. After dropping it into her purse she started walking towards the town centre and the British Embassy. The soles of her shoes were so thin that she felt every stone on the cobbled streets. All around were people dressed a lot worse than her going about their business. She asked around for directions to the Embassy but she didn't speak Spanish and she didn't get very far. Finally she found a man in a large black hat that explained to her in French how to get to the Embassy and she set off in that direction.

It was getting late and she would have liked nothing better than to lay down in a bed and go to sleep, but when she thought about what Alphonse must be going through in that police van, and in the police station she hurried her steps.

What she didn't understand was what a French person would need the British Embassy for. She could only assume that because France was under occupation, he was part of the British resistance. Whatever the reason, she'd make sure they got him out quickly.

It was a long walk, but finally the substantial building that was the British Embassy in Madrid appeared in front of her.

Even though it was late, there were still one or two lights on in the upstairs windows. With determined steps she walked past the two Spanish guards standing by the open gate and went up the steps leading to the front door. It remained closed even though she rang the bell repeatedly, but she couldn't give up. There were people there and she needed to help Alphonse quickly.

'Hello, is anybody there.' She yelled towards the top window in a mixture of French and English.

'Deja de gritar. Ellos están cerradas.'

One of the guards from the front called out before walking towards her.

Sophia threw her hands in the air. 'I don't understand.' She knew he was telling her to go away and come back when they were open, but she had to continue. 'Hello, can someone come down and talk to me.'

'Bien, usted-tiene que irse ahora' He started ushering her towards the gate.

A middle aged man in a blue security uniform emerged from the side of the building. 'Excuse me, what's going on here?' he asked angrily.

'I need help. My friend who works for you has been arrested.'

'You will have to come back tomorrow. There's nothing we can do now.'

'No, you don't understand. We've just managed to get out of France. He works for you. He's very important.' Alphonse was, if nothing else, important to her.

The man looked at her and sighed. 'Right. Wait here.' He repeated this last sentence to the Spanish guards and went back indoors.

Minutes past by and in the end Sophia couldn't help it. She turned to the Spanish guard and smiled. 'Do you have a cigarette please?' She moved her fingers in a smoking action.'Cigaretta?'

The guard hesitated before pulling out a packet from his pocket.

They were nothing like Alphonse's cigarettes, this one almost tore the lining from her throat, but somehow it seemed to fit in with her experience of Spain so far. Harsh and unfriendly.

The guard came back and looked with displeasure at Sophia smoking before asking her to follow him.

'This does not normally happen,' he said as she followed him down a path to a side entrance. 'But Mr White thought it was best we listen to what you have to say.' He held up the door for her and continued up some stairs.

'It's very kind of you,' she said even though she'd only understood a few words.

'Yes, that gate should have been shut. In fact, I'm sure I locked it earlier.' He turned to look at her as if she'd opened the locked gate guarded by two people. 'Well, maybe I didn't.'

He ushered her into a room where a pale, thin haired man sat and read a large document. 'Here we are, Sir.'

'Thank you very much. Maybe you can wait outside for a few moments.'

'Yes, of course.' He shut the door.

'Please sit down Miss...?'

'Apfel, Sophia Apfel.'

'My name is Mr White and I look after various things here at the Embassy. I understand you have a friend that works for us and that he's been arrested.'

'My English is not very good. Do you speak French?' she asked.

He nodded and repeated what he'd said.

'Yes, we've just come from France and at the railway station here in Madrid, the Police beat him up in front of everybody and then took him away.'

'I see. How unpleasant for you, well for both of you. Does this friend of yours have a name?'

'Yes, of course he does. His name is Alphonse Prideux and he was with the resistance in Marseille.'

'Did he give you a contact name? Anyone back in London that would be able to give us more information?'

She shook her head. 'No. When we split up at the station all he said was that I was to come here and tell you if something went wrong.'

He thought for a moment. 'We'll contact London and see what we can do.' He put his pen down. 'You must understand however that if he's been arrested there is very little we can do. We will let the Spanish authorities know that we are aware that they hold him, that way, at least, they can't just get rid of him.' He saw the shock on her face. 'It is highly unlikely that they would do that anyway with a foreigner, but it's always better to be prepared. If it's only a case of entering the country illegally they will hold him for a month or two and then he can be on his way to... where was it?'

'We're on our way to Lisbon and then to London. Alphonse organised it all.'

'Well, that makes sense. Best not to hang around here if you can avoid it. Apart from contacting London I can't do anything else for you right now. If you come back in a few days I'll let you know how we got on.'

He stood up to indicate that her time was up.

'A few days? I saw what they did to him at the station, he might not live in a day or two.'

He came around the desk and stood beside her. 'I know how you must feel but you must realise that this is not Britain. Our scope of influence here is very limited indeed.' He helped her up from her chair. 'Now, go and have a good night's sleep and try not to worry.'

The shock of realising that the British Government would not be able to help gave way to anger. How dared he patronise her. He's been sitting in his office whilst the rest of Europe was either fighting the enemy, on the run or dead. 'Don't tell me not to worry. My family is probably in a concentration camp in Germany, I'm in a foreign country with nowhere to go and my only friend was beaten up in front of me before being dragged into a police van. No, I won't worry.' She opened the door and turned back to look at him. 'Enjoy your tea.'

She followed the guard back outside and took a deep breath. There was only one way out of this. Something she didn't want to do, but there was no other option. She started walking towards the town centre, her spirits getting lower with every step.

~ 15 ~

Every stone and pot hole in the road hurt. He ran his tongue over the rough edge where he used to have a tooth and spat out some more blood. They had repaid the head butt in kind, several times over, in the back of the van before they set off from the train station. Now he could hardly keep himself upright on the floor of the filthy van where more men than him had taken a beating. Images of his friend Eduardo, dead on the floor next to him in a hut outside Madrid and his Maria resting in his arms both floated in front of him. Even Bea appeared briefly in images he'd suppressed for years. He still missed them all.

Madrid, it was always bloody Madrid. Would he have to add Emilie and Anaise to these pictures in his head? Friends, whose life had been taken because of war, grit and sodding madness.

The film, he'd dropped it by Sophia's feet and he hoped she had picked it up. If she hadn't there'd be trouble even if he did get out of this. Maybe it had been a stupid thing to do. He could have kept it with him, hidden it, at least he would have known where it was. There was no point worrying about it now.

What he did worry about was that Sophia didn't know his real name and he hadn't given her a contact name in the UK. He only just realised that she didn't even know he was British.

The van stopped and seconds later the door opened. It hadn't been a long journey, ten minutes maximum and judging by the city noise he could hear now that the van was open, they were in central Madrid.

'Come on, get out.'

Tom didn't move fast enough so one of the guards from the station, the one he hadn't attacked, leaned into the van and pulled him out by his arm. Bumping down on the ground in the courtyard outside the police station was unpleasant and undignified, but he managed to get back on his feet before they dragged him into the station.

Inside the station, the smell of unwashed bodies and cigarette smoke seemed ingrained in the once white walls. The dim lights and scuffed brown floor tiles enhanced the misery that lived there.

In a corner was one of the other men arrested at the train station. His face didn't show a mark, he'd obviously gone with them willingly.

The police men had a few words with a man behind a desk, Tom couldn't hear what they were saying, before pushing him along a long corridor. Only a few lights were attached to the bottle green tiled walls, just enough light to see where you were going. The cell doors that lined those walls every two meters were metal and there was silence behind all of them.

They pushed Tom into one of those cells at the end of the corridor and slammed the door shut. It was cold, dark and smelled vividly of previous occupants, but he'd rather be there than in an interrogation room. The door back to the front of the station slammed shut loudly as the policemen left, letting a heavy wall of silence settle. He thought it wouldn't be long before they would collect him from his cell and take him somewhere more unpleasant. Just long enough for him to worry about what they knew and what Sophia was up to.

He must have nodded off because when he next opened his eyes he could hear doors opening and shutting. Someone turned the key in his door and a thin man in a Civil Guardia uniform stepped inside and slammed down a bowl of something runny and a very small piece of bread.

Tom cleared his throat. 'Why are you keeping me here?' he asked in Spanish.

The thin man shrugged his shoulders before shutting the door behind him. Once again there was silence and Tom put his feet onto the floor before standing up slowly. Every bone in his body ached and he slowly walked over to the door where his breakfast was on the floor.

The dirty metal bowl was half filled with an almost see through liquid and Tom left it where it was. The bread even though hard and dry was edible, but it hurt to chew where one of his front teeth had snapped off the night before. Pulling the bread with his hands and placing it in the left hand side of his mouth worked but it was so dry it was hard to swallow.

He couldn't stay in this place any longer, either they'd have to tell him why he was there or let him go. Even if they threw him back into France it would be better than staying another day here. If he hadn't listened to Marcel and taken the mountain route instead, he would not be in this situation now. Fair enough, they might find themselves in a different situation, but at least they would have had some control over their crossing. Keeping to low population areas and places he knew, places where people would help them.

There was no point in thinking of what could have been. He went up to the door and started banging until his hands hurt on the hard metal. He continued doing this every time he heard other doors opening or shutting in the corridor, every time he could hear voices of other prisoners being taken out or thrown in to their cells, but still nobody came.

Hours that seemed like lifetimes later, the breakfast man opened the door with a guard in tow.

'Come on, you're going to see the Captain.' The thin man said with a grin.

'Well, it's about time.' Tom tried to smile sarcastically at the man but found his face hurt too much pull it off.

'I don't think you will like him much.' He stood to one side to let Tom pass through the door.

The guard pushed him along in front of him back through the green tiled corridor and into another part of the station. Through one of the windows he saw Civil Guarda officers milling around in the courtyard outside. The sun was low in the sky. Tom didn't know if it was morning or afternoon.

'Hey, stop here.' The guard said and knocked on a door before opening it.

It was a room with only a desk and two chairs. The man behind the desk spent some time looking through a fairly thick brown file without acknowledging Tom's arrival. He assumed the file was on him and if it was, he was in trouble.

He stayed sitting on the chair quietly until the man behind the desk looked up.

'Alphonse Prideux it says here in your papers.'

'Yes. That's my name.'

'What were your reasons for coming back to Madrid?'

'I haven't been to Madrid before. I was only travelling through on my way to Lisbon. It's all there in my travel permits.'

The desk-man looked back down at the papers in front of him.

'They're not very good are they? However, your identity papers are in order and we are still inundated with republican scum here.' He indicated to the guard that he was done. 'But trust me Señor Prideux, if you ever set foot in Spain again I will make sure you regret it.'

'I'm free to go?' Tom couldn't believe it. With those comments they knew about his past and still they were letting him go.

The man in charge didn't acknowledge his comment.

Tom had been sure this would be a nightmare situation, interrogation and several further nights either here in the station or in a prison, but they were letting him go. He stood up and left the room. They took a different route back to the front of the station where the guard escorted him to the front gates and went back indoors.

Never had he been so glad to be out of somewhere. He had no idea why they let him go and he didn't care, at least not right there and then.

'Alphonse. Over here.'

Tom turned around to see Sophia standing behind a street corner, hiding from the police station. If anything would catch their attention surely that would, but he was pleased to see her.

'What have they done to you?' She impulsively touched the cut on his cheek.

'It's fine, really. Have you got the cigarette case?' He looked hopefully towards her hand bag.

'Yes, it's in the suitcase.'

He looked around the pavement but saw no suitcase there. 'Where's the suitcase then?'

'Come on. I'll take you to it.' She turned around. 'I had to find somewhere to stay last night and this woman I met agreed to let me have a room for a whole week.'

'How did you pay for it? You had no money.'

'It doesn't matter. All that matters is that you are free and I have arranged a lift all the way to Lisbon.'

He stopped. 'You've done what? How and with whom?'

'It's a long story. Their chauffeur is picking us up in an hour. Plenty of time for you to have a wash.'

She looked at Tom who was still not moving.

'Well, come on then.' She tried to hurry him along.

'Who are we getting a lift from?'

'I'll tell you back at house.'

He sighed and followed her. An uneasy feeling was spreading in his stomach and he was sure it wasn't just hunger.

The room was small but better than spending the night on the streets. She had managed to get hold of some fruit and bread and whilst they ate she told him what she'd been up to for the previous 24 hours. The British Embassy had been as good as useless so in desperation she'd gone to a Jewish refugee association and they'd helped her.

'They wouldn't have given you the room and lift for free though would they?'

'Why wouldn't they?'

His eyes fell to her hand.

'I can see you're missing your rings. And I guess one of them paid for my release from the police station too.'

'What are some rings worth now? Nothing is what it was and it never will be again, therefore only staying alive matters.'

'But you said they were your mother's.'

She shrugged her shoulders and he put his hand on hers.

'I appreciate it. Thank you.'

They sat there for a moment both of them deep in thought before Tom got up on his feet. 'Right, I'd better wash my face before the driver arrives.'

He splashed some water on his face and shaved before lighting his first cigarette since they arrived in Madrid. He was still enjoying it when the car arrived and it was time to go. Who were these people that would help them across the border, risking their own freedom for a ring?

By the time they got to the Portuguese border Tom still had no idea who their travel companions were. Señor was a Portuguese diplomat who had, together with his wife, been in Madrid on official business. They were middle aged, both dressed in dark clothes and they would both be in terrible trouble if they got stopped.

Apart from a greeting and some basic instructions for the border crossing they had travelled mostly in silence which suited Tom. He'd fallen asleep before the car even left Madrid. Sophia had spent most of the journey looking out of the window into the darkness whilst the car sped un-challenged through the night towards freedom.

Even though it was early morning, a queue of cars had built up in front of the border barrier. Their driver sighed and left the car for a few minutes before returning with a smile. He backed the car up and around the vehicles in front and manoeuvred it into a space created for him at the front. They had decided that Sophia would be a friend of their daughter's and Tom her husband if anybody asked. It seemed the most sensible way to do it.

The border guard did not even bother looking into the car. He shared a joke with the driver and lifted the gate for them to pass. If Tom's body wasn't quite so achy from his arrest and the many hours spent in the car he would have thrown his hands in the air with relief. As it was, all four of them just looked at each other and smiled a little.

The hours remaining until they reached Lisbon went by very slowly. Now that the main concern about the journey had been dealt with Tom felt his aches and wanted to stretch his legs out fully.

Finally they entered Lisbon and after a brief thank you Tom and Sophia stood on the broad, palm tree lined main street, not knowing which way to go.

~ 16 ~

Paris

Two days had passed since her lunch with Joachim and a message from him had just arrived. She had no intention to repeat what had happened after that lunch. She couldn't deny the excitement that had swept her away that afternoon but she'd felt so very guilty afterwards. This was a good opportunity to tell Joachim Gerber that they couldn't see each other again.

Gerard had acted strangely since she'd returned home that evening and she hoped he didn't suspect anything. Why would he, they were living more and more separate lives and very soon she'd be gone. For some reason it didn't make her feel relieved, she wanted to stay in Paris.

Gerber wore his uniform this time and the meeting place was more upmarket in the middle of town.

'Very formal Oberleutnant Gerber. I hope all is as it should be.' She smiled awkwardly as he pulled her chair out.

'Of course it is Madam. I wish we could meet like last time but there was no opportunity.' He sat down opposite her. There was not a wrinkle to be seen on the crisp white table cloth and a waiter took their order. Silence fell heavily between them before Emilie asked him why he had asked to see her so urgently.

'When we met last you mentioned that you weren't going to Berlin, is that still correct or have you changed your mind?'

'No. I couldn't possibly go.'

Gerber lit a cigarette and looked at her through the smoke. 'You are still on the list to go.'

He gave her a moment to let it sink in.

'There's been some mistake that's all. My husband will talk to them again.'

'Emilie, he won't.' He whispered across the table. 'Your husband is involved with something, I don't know what, but my uncle is talking as if the war with Britain could be won or lost because of it. And soon.'

'He doesn't decide what I do. I'll tell Kluger myself. It's not yet a crime to decline an invitation, is it?'

They waited as coffee was poured and a variety of cakes delicately put on the table.

'No, but it would be seen as a slight on the friendship between your husband and Kluger. My uncle can just take from him what he wants, but Monsieur Valoise needs his connection and he will make you go.'

'What do you mean by Kluger can take something from him? What does he have that your uncle wants?'

'I don't know. There was some mention when we first arrived in Paris last year that Monsieur Valoise was involved in blackmailing. Something about a brothel where pictures had been taken for years of budding politicians, both from France and elsewhere.'

'And you think my husband is involved? Running the brothel maybe like some lowlife pavement crawler.'

'I don't know,' Gerber said taken aback by her reaction. He'd been sure she didn't even like her husband, not after the afternoon they'd spent together. Yet, he'd had to tell her. 'I think that is exactly what he is doing.'

She took a deep breath and rose from the table. 'Well, Oberleutnant Gerber, thank you very much for the coffee but I have to leave. I'm sure you understand.'

'Please sit down Emilie. People are looking.'

She nodded a goodbye and left him staring after her. The worst thing was that she had no doubt that it was all true.

Outside The Ritz, Jacques rose from the bench he'd been sitting at ever since she went into the restaurant. He noted her pale and upset eyes before continuing his mission of following her.

***

The front door echoed shut behind her. The house was dark and she called out for Louise but got no answer. She'd been there when Emilie had gone out and wasn't due to leave until late, but there was no sign of her. It was probably for the best, she could do with a little time to herself. In an hour or so she'd have to get ready for the nights show, and Anaise was coming along this time. She would have to tell her what Joachim had said even though it cut through her pride to have to do so. They had all been right about him, she'd always known he was a bastard but not this low. She went over to the cocktail cabinet in the lounge corner and poured herself a large brandy even though she didn't much like the drink. It would be part of her punishment for being so gullible and selfish. She'd had every chance to leave him and spend all her time with Tom, but was he so much better? He'd left her so many times and was so unreliable, but she knew deep down that they were meant to be together. She loved him enough for the two of them. It was only pride that had been in the way, the pride that he'd shattered when he left her for Spain. She knocked the brandy back and it burned the back of her throat as it went down. Her glass went crashing to the floor, shattering in a million pieces as she noticed Gerard sitting in the corner, quietly observing her.

A life time seemed to pass before either of them spoke.

'You look like you've seen a ghost dear. It's only old me sitting here in the corner waiting for my wife to come home from some rendezvous or other.' His head leaned back in the chair, his blank face only slightly lit by the fading light outside.

Emilie became aware of the shattered glass on the floor. 'Damn. Louise seem to have gone out.' She wanted to bring a bit of normality to the room. She recognised the look on his face and quickly weighed up her options. She could stay and take her chances, his moods did change back to normal sometimes, or she could make a dash for the street, but why should she. After the conversation with Gerber she had to stand up to him, he was a lowlife creep that had been around her too long. Any pain he could inflict on her was nothing to the pain she felt on the inside. All caused by her blindness and obstinate will to seem happy and normal when she wasn't, when nothing was.

'I gave them the day off.'

'Again, dear? Our staff has more days off than you.'

The provocation lit a fire in his eyes and he slowly stood up as Emilie tensed, readying herself for a fight. The only weapon she could see was a large piece of glass on the floor.

'We are in a playful mode today aren't we?' He was standing right in front of her now. 'I will however let that comment and your activities today go unmentioned. Pour us a drink and sit down will you.'

She poured two large measures of the brandy and went to sit next to him on the sofa.

'What do you want Gerard? Let's not pretend anymore that everything is as it should be between us.'

'Whatever you think Emilie, I did love you in the beginning you know, and I still do in a strange way. Look how well we've done, us two alley cats from the other side of the river.' He tried a forced smile. 'The trouble is that everything has changed now, the game has changed. It's no longer just about getting a nice house and invitations to places that would have pushed us away before. Now it's also about power and influence, all the things I couldn't have dreamed of having before the occupation. It's all possible now though, it's all possible.' He looked at her. 'The only trouble is that you insist on sitting on the fence. A perfectly good opportunity to further your career and my influence with the Germans and you refuse to do it. You do see how silly it is, don't you.'

'I'm not going to bloody Berlin Gerard. And this whole scene, who do you think you're kidding? You've always taken exactly what you want anyway. Do you really think they see you as an asset? They probably just look on you as a lackey giving them the odd blackmailing photos and I bet you don't even ask for money, just to be their special friend.'

Gerard had winced at the mention of photos. 'So I see there is no talking to you. I need you to go to Berlin, will you go?'

'No.'

'Can I do anything to change your mind?'

'No.'

'Right. That's what I thought you'd say.' He sat down next to her. 'Here's something that might change your mind. They have a file on you, I saw it Em.'

She looked at him and wanted to ask what he meant but her lips wouldn't move. Her head was spinning and she closed her eyes.

'A file full of what you've been up to since last June.' He lightly slapped her face. 'Keep awake.'

She opened her eyes but had lost the will to talk.

'They will put the file away darling if you show your support for them by going to Berlin. Now doesn't that make it worthwhile?'

Her eyes shut slowly and her head fell backwards against the back of the sofa, her glass falling on the floor.

'I have a feeling you're still not fully understanding the situation my dear.' He sighed. 'But you will.'

He picked the glass up from the floor and called for Jacques.

~ 17 ~

The British Embassy, Lisbon, Portugal

'Mr Lancaster.' A short, fair haired man in glasses called out from the doorway and Tom stood up. He noticed the short man taking in his face that still bore the signs of his troubles in Madrid. Most of it had healed up, but there were still some soft bruises, and the cut on his cheek that kept on re-opening. It would leave a nice old scar. This was the fifth daily visit to the British embassy in Lisbon since they had arrived and still there was no sign of a ticket out. He knew flights were few and priority given to officials but he had no intention of hanging around the city for months or even years like some poor, desperate refugees were. The trouble was that he couldn't tell them why he needed to get back to London. Pierre, or rather Erik had made him promise to tell nobody apart from Charles Johnson at CJ Films.

He followed the man up some stairs and into a small, messy and stuffy office where they both sat down. Tom sighed, he had no choice but to ask them to contact Sir Arthur.

'Are you suggesting I send a message to Sir Arthur at the war office in London just like that? I don't know that you are who you say you are. You could be an enemy spy for all I know.'

The man tapped his pen to V for Victory and Tom could happily have rammed it down his throat.

'This is important you stuffy little man, and if you don't, I will go above your head.'

'Not really the way to get help is it?' He paused. 'I don't think we can help you Mr Lancaster, please leave.'

'I'm not going anywhere until my message is sent. Go on, try to move me.' He'd had enough of queuing to get in there every morning only to be told to come back in a few days time. Enough.

'I don't have to.' He picked up the phone. 'Mr Trebble, could you come to my office please, there's a troublemaker here.' He put the receiver back and turned his attention to the scruffy looking hooligan in front of him. 'There's a prison sentence for threatening government employees.'

'As long as the prison's in England.' Tom replied.

The door opened and a tall slim fellow wearily looked Tom up and down. 'What's the trouble now?'

'This man threatened me, Sir.'

'I did no such thing. All I said was that I'm not leaving until I see someone more senior.'

'Well, you said it in a threatening way.'

'Why don't you leave this to me?' Mr Trebble stepped out of the doorway indicating that the clerk should leave.

'We have to take action. If one gets away with it Sir, they all will and we will have chaos on our hands.'

'I quite agree, but let's see if we can avoid all that paper-work eh?'

The clerk stepped outside and the door shut behind him. Mr Trebble sat down in his vacated chair and looked Tom over. 'So, how can we help?'

Tom explained that he had urgent information he needed to get back to London, but he couldn't tell him what it was. To arrange a speedy exit from Lisbon he needed to contact Sir Arthur at the War Office who would get him and his friend a flight out.

'I've waited here for days now and I can't wait any longer.'

'So have a lot of people Mr-'

'Lancaster.'

'There is a war on you know.'

'I'm well aware of that, I've been right in the firing line of it since last summer. My network in Marseille and friends in Paris might already have paid the price for my bloody delay here.'

'So why not use ordinary channels.'

Tom just shook his head in exasperation. He'd explained this at almost every visit and he was getting annoyed. 'I can't tell you. For God's sake, what do you have to do to get a message sent?'

'Right, what's the message?'

Tom wrote it down and handed it over to Mr Trebble who read it and nodded.

'I hope for both our sakes that you really have something of importance or we'll both be in trouble for wasting radio time.' He handed the note back to Tom. 'Write down where you're staying.'

Tom grabbed the pen and dotted down the name of the shabby little hotel where he and Sophia had managed to get a small room in this city that was overflowing with refugees. He handed the note back.

'Thank you very much Mr Lancaster. As soon as we get a reply I will send for you.'

They both got up and Tom thanked the man before heading down to the nearest bar.

The bright red cocktail tasted awful and he shouldn't have bought it, but it was the cheapest alcoholic drink on the menu. He'd contacted his bank in London and asked them to wire over some funds, but it still hadn't arrived. Now he was running low on both money and patience. There were a few coins still in his pocket and he used them to order a proper drink, a large whiskey, no ice. When it arrived he lit a cigarette from his last pack and tried in vain to relax. If he had the money he would have asked the barman to leave the bottle. He never thought he'd have anything to do with Sir Arthur again, not after the last time in Morocco, but what choice did he have?

He'd been tense, on edge ever since he'd first met Perrault in the club. It seemed such a long time ago now, an eternity since he'd watched Emilie walk down the street towards the station. He should be with her. For all he knew they could have been sent to a camp somewhere. He quickly pushed those thoughts from his mind. As soon as he'd found out what was on the film he'd get himself to Paris and get her and Anaise out. Maybe they'd left already and he clung on to that thought. At least in London he should be able to get some information on what was happening.

He heard the bar door open but didn't turn around as Mr Trebble entered and joined him at the bar.

'Mesmo outra vez por favor.'

The barman filled Tom's glass and found another one for his new customer.

'So, we sent the message.'

'Thanks.'

'You must have some friends there. Within fifteen minutes we had Sir Arthur's personal assistant on the phone telling us to put you and your friend on the priority list out.'

Relief flooded through Tom and he couldn't help a smile. 'Thank God for that. When do we leave?'

'Hold on. The priority list is still quite long and planes get cancelled regularly. Should be within the next few days though.'

Tom smiled and lit another cigarette. It would all be ok.

'It was all quite impressive. I gather they have moved you to The Palácio Hotel in Estoril to make the waiting easier for you.'

'Who has done what?'

'That's why I'm here. I'm to drive you and your friend to the hotel and stay with you until you leave.'

'Sounds like I'm under house arrest or something.'

'Nothing of the sort. See it as extra protection.' He looked at Tom's now threadbare and shabby suit. 'I assume you had to leave all clothes behind in France.'

Tom nodded.

'And your friend too?'

He nodded again.

'Right, we'd better stop off and get some new clothes for both of you.'

'There's no need. It's only for a few nights.'

'You've never heard of the The Palácio Hotel? Trust me, you will need a whole new set of clothes even for a few days or you'll look like the cleaner. Actually, the cleaners will look and smell a lot better. Come on let's go, lots to be done before dinner and blackjack.' Mr Trebble smiled broadly.

Tom followed him out the door and into his car convinced that Mr Trebble had volunteered for this particular job.

The tailor's shop was on the Avenida da Liberadade, the wide palm tree lined main street in Lisbon. Mr Trebble, or Nick, as he insisted they called him now that they were to spend such a lot of time together, had driven Tom and

Sophia to it before setting off to his own apartment to collect a few things.

'It's a little tight.' Tom moved shoulders around. The tailor stopped his inspection of the suit he was wearing and pinned his busy eyes on his customer.

'You give me one afternoon to get both day and evening wear and complain that it does not feel as if I had made it for you from scratch? You should be happy I did not turn you away. I do have a lot of other customers you know.'

He went back to adjusting the length of the trousers before asking Tom change back into his old clothes and sit down.

'Give me half an hour to get this suit ready and the rest I will send on this evening.' He looked at Tom and shook his head. 'I think you will want to change before you leave for the hotel.'

'I guess I will.' Tom said and changed back into his old clothes.

A little while later, as he sat waiting for his new clothes, a girl brought him coffee and a custard cake. She couldn't be more than ten years old but she carried the tray confidently.

'Señor, this is for you. My father says you are not well and need cake.'

He smiled at her serious little face. Her father had commented on his extensive bruising and been content with the explanation that they had arrived in Lisbon via Madrid. That must be what her father must have meant.

'Thank you very much.'

'My sister makes them. I can also make them, but I'm better at bringing them to customers.'

'Yes, I can see that. Have you got many brothers and sisters?'

'Five sisters.' She held up all the fingers on one hand before running off to the back room.

The coffee was strong and hot. It had been a long time since he had real coffee. Lisbon was a haven if you had money. Everything that wasn't available in the rest of Europe was freely sold here. Unfortunately for Tom and Sophia, they didn't have much to spend before his money arrived.

When Tom and Nick had arrived at their modest hotel and told Sophia the news, she'd been happy. She'd liked the idea of staying in another hotel and even happier that they were finally on the flight list out. The issue of new clothes had not gone down so well though. He'd known a lot of women and not a single one of them would have been upset at having a few new shoes and dresses. Whatever was wrong with her, he was sure she'd come around a little later on.

The tailor came back with his new suit and shirt hanging over one arm and a bag of sundry items in a bag. He handed it all to Tom.

'Go in the back and change. You should leave the clothes you're wearing in this bag.' He held up an old sack. 'I will burn them for you.'

Tom did as he was asked and thanked the tailor for his help before leaving.

Outside he found Nick waiting in the car and he quickly went into the larger shop next door where Sophia was getting her clothes. He asked a lady at the front desk if Sophia was ready yet and she went up some stairs to see.

She quickly came back downstairs. 'She will be ready in just a few minutes. Please, take a seat.'

He sat down and must have been waiting ten minutes before he heard her come down the stairs. She wore a plain green dress and a well cut cream coloured coat without any embellishments. The assistant walking down behind her held an armful of bags explaining to him that ladies need more clothes than men. Maybe she could get some help with her hair at the hotel.

'Now remember to use the nail file. You will tear,' she looked over to Tom and whispered, 'your stockings if you don't.'

Nick had already sorted out the bills before he'd gone to his house and now all they had to do was join him in the car for the drive out to the hotel.

'Here are some pointers for your stay,' Nick said whilst looking into the rear view mirror frequently. 'One. Don't hand your passports over to anybody. You can show them, but don't let them keep hold of them, you might never see them again. Two. Your rooms will be searched frequently so if you have anything you don't want the Portuguese secret police or the Germans to find, you'd better keep it with you. They don't normally steal things, but most of the PVDE, that's the secret police, are on the Germans side. Three. Try to stay near me. We have had the odd kidnapping here. A few people that the Germans wanted back have disappeared after being arrested on the streets of Lisbon. At least if I'm there it might put them off.' He looked briefly at Tom and laughed. 'I know I don't exactly look like a fighter, but I've got a good gun.'

'I'm relieved.' Tom replied with just a hint of sarcasm.

The hotel was magnificent in crisp white. The lawn covered park area in front lined with palm trees that gently moved in the breeze seemed like a different world.

That evening they dined in the hotel restaurant on food that neither Sophia nor Tom had eaten for years. Afterwards they played Blackjack at the casino next door on money Nick insisted they borrow from him. It was impossible not to stare at the guests. They wore diamond jewelry and evening dress, their hair styled and champagne glasses in their hands. It truly was a different world. Sophia had been acting odd ever since they left the hotel in Lisbon. She smiled when she thought she should, but it never reached her eyes, and in conversation, she contributed only the bare minimum. She did look quite lovely in the dark blue silk dress she was wearing, but he could tell that she didn't feel comfortable.

Nick on the other hand thrived.

'Some more champagne please.' Nick called over to the barman and took out a cigarette. 'It's all quite interesting, isn't it?' He looked out over the crowd. 'Germans, British, Jewish, everyone with money that comes to Lisbon stays here. Even Royalty.'

'Quite the hotpot then.'

'It is indeed. As long as Spain doesn't join Germany or invade Portugal it will just continue until the end of the war.'

'Why would Spain invade this country? They've only just had a civil war.' He glanced over to Sophia who looked pale and tired before turning back to Nick.

'I don't know. These dictators get power mad. There's been rumours ever since the beginning of the war that Spain is about to invade. A few weeks ago there were people who swore they'd seen Spanish forces marching this way. It was all untrue.'

'So, are the Portuguese really neutral or do they have a preference? If it came right down to it and they had to choose, where would their loyalties lie?'

'I don't think they know themselves. Salazar just wants to keep his country out of war altogether and in the meantime we try to get on his, and his police force's, good side and so are the Germans. For goodwill, I think Germany might have the upper hand at the moment. We even gave Salazar an honorary Oxford degree last year, that's how far we'll go. I had to work for my degree there you know.'

Sophia put her glass down on the bar and looked at Tom. 'I'm tired. It's been a long day.'

'Of course. I'll walk you back to the room,' Tom said. 'It's always best to retire on a win I find.' He smiled at Nick who'd lost more than he'd won. 'I assume you're staying here for a while, to try and get your losses back.'

'No,' Nick replied. 'I have to go with you. Wouldn't want anything to happen to you because they'll send me back to London. I mean that in the nicest way.'

Back in the room Sophia thanked him and went straight to bed. As Tom turned the lights out in their little lounge area he could hear her sobbing through the thin door.

He knocked lightly and when there was no response he carefully opened the door. She was in the bathroom, he could hear water splashing and he called out to see if she was alright.

'Yes, I'm fine. Go to bed please.'

He walked up to the door. 'I don't think you are. I'll wait out here for you.'

He sat down on the bed until she came out. She'd splashed water on her face to try and eradicate the signs of crying but her eyes were still red.

'Come, sit down and tell me what's wrong. We're friends now aren't we?'

'There are so many things wrong Tom. So, so many things.'

'I know. But there's something especially wrong today, isn't it?'

She nodded and crossed her arms before the emotional pressure that was building up inside her came out in great big sobs. Tom handed her a handkerchief and put his arm around her shoulders. He could tell she was trying to get it under control but couldn't. After a little while she calmed down and took a few deep breaths.

'Look at me. I'm wearing a night dress that I could never have afforded before the war, and the same with the dresses and lovely undergarments. I've been eating wonderful food and drinking champagne. All this whilst my mother and father are somewhere that even my darkest nightmares can't imagine.' She lit a cigarette. 'In my old clothes I was just trying to survive, just like them. Now I feel like I've betrayed them.'

Tom sat next to her in silence.

'I want to feel their pain Tom. I want to scratch the skin of my arms and scream.'

'I don't know what to say Sophia. I can tell you that this is necessary, that we have to be close to the airport just in case there is a flight for us out of here. You're still fighting for survival, you know, wearing posh clothes doesn't change that. Besides, once we're back in London you'll be with your brother and the two of you can help each other.'

For a moment she looked confused, but she recovered very quickly.

'I'm sure that's true.'

'Sophia, you do have a brother in London, don't you?' He'd noticed the look on her face.

'Yes. I told you that I did, and I do.'

'Ok. Are you feeling better?'

She nodded.

'Well, goodnight then.' He went over to the door. 'And Sophia, keep those nightmares at bay.' He smiled and closed the door. He turned the lights of in the lounge and wandered into his own room. The girl has no bloody brother in London. What was he supposed to do with her when they got there?

***

Cold water dripped onto the marble swimming pool surround as Tom returned to his chair to dry off in the Portuguese spring sunshine. He'd only done a couple of laps before his bruised ribs had protested and he'd had to have a break. Even out of the water his body still hurt at certain angles, but it was better now than it had been. In this luxury haven, the bruises still on his body drew attention from some people, but most of them were too caught up in their own problems to notice.

It was difficult to relax, both of them were just waiting for Nick to give them the good news that there were two seats on a plane out. They ate well, they slept well and Tom had won and lost in equal amounts in the casino, but there was no denying that they felt a little edgy. Every time he saw Nick approach he hoped he had some news, but so far there had been nothing. With nothing to do all day he had plenty of time to wonder about his arrest and quick release in Madrid. It seemed silly to keep on wondering why they'd let him go when obviously they knew about his past, but it kept niggling at him.

Nick, who was enjoying himself at the hotel, out of the office and on expenses, had suggested they relax by the pool for a while. Sophia had refused to get into the water and sat herself down at the table with a book and a drink. Tom noticed that she didn't turn the pages very often.

'Tom, over here.'

Nick was standing on the hotel balcony and waved for him to join him up there. The few people sitting outside looked towards the noise and then at Tom with disapproving looks.

'I'll be back shortly.'

'Alright.' Sophia looked up from her book.

Tom put on a bathrobe and entered the hotel through a side door before joining Nick at a window table in the bar.

'So, we have take off.' Nick declared with a smile.

'Thank God for that. All this relaxation is giving me high blood pressure.'

'Well, going back to the office will give me great pleasure.' Nick looked around the hotel. 'I shall miss this.'

'When do we leave?'

'Tonight. If we leave here at seven we can have an early dinner before we drive to the airport. You should eat as much as possible, the food back home is not what it was.'

'It's the same everywhere, eh? Apart from here obviously.' He looked out of the window. 'I should go and tell

Sophia... the good news.' He looked back at Nick. 'Do you know who the man speaking to her is?'

Nick shook his head. 'No, but judging from his tan and stance I'd say he's German. I wouldn't worry about it, you've been talking to several of them during your stay here.'

'All the same. I'll go back down.' He headed back towards their poolside table but there was no sign of the German.

Sophia was sitting where he'd left her, but the book was on the table and she was looking into space.

'Are you alright?'

'Of course I am. Why wouldn't I be?'

'Who was that man?'

'I don't know. He just asked me for a light, in English.' She sat up. 'Should I be worried?'

'No, not at all. I have good news. We fly to England tonight, after dinner.'

It took a moment for it to sink in. They were finally leaving.

'Tonight? That's wonderful. 'Her eyes narrowed.' You don't look happy.'

'I am. Come on. Let's have a drink to celebrate.'

'A drink? It's only 11 O'clock in the morning.'

'Sophia, it's never too early for a celebratory drink. You won't get a Manhattan like these in London you know.'

'Well, just the one then. I don't want us to miss the plane because you're drunk.'

'When have I been drunk on our little journey?'

'Many times. Maybe not drunk, but certainly tipsy.'

'I guess I just like it.'

'I guess you just do.'

'So you'll have a Manhattan with me?'

'Of course. You'll never get one as good as they make them here in London you know,' she said with a hint of sarcasm.

'That's what I thought. I should probably change first.'

'Yes. You should. I'll meet you in the bar when you're done.'

He turned and walked back to the hotel. As soon as he'd disappeared from view the German walked casually up to Sophia.

'No balls up, Jew girl,' he whispered before diving into the pool.

~ 18 ~

Paris

Anaise knocked loudly on her sister's front door one more time. She had tried to get hold of her throughout the day but there was still no answer and the house remained dark and silent. It had been a few days since she last saw her and she'd acted strangely then. Anaise cursed herself for not making her leave Paris right there and then, because for all she knew, her sister could be lying dead in there on the cold floor. Where was Louise and the cook? And Gerard for that matter.

She'd attracted the attention of some neighbours passing by and she took the opportunity to ask if they'd seen Madam Valois recently. They hadn't and Anaise walked on towards the south side of the river and Madam Carter.

She looked up at the battered old building which housed the flat where the American lady lived. She'd given her address at the Salon party and insisted that Anaise came to visit. This was probably not the visit she'd envisaged. It was only a twenty minute walk from Ballou's flat but whereas her friend's flat seemed chic, this road was crumbling. She'd thought Madam Carter was well off and she looked around for some hidden building around the corner, but this was it, this was the address she'd been given. Oh, well there wasn't much choice so she pushed the once imposing front door open and went in. Only a small stream of sunshine reached into the stairwell through the small window above the door which shut with a bang behind her. The light was enough for her to walk up the stairs, and once she reached the first floor everything changed. It was still dark, but the apartment doors were well polished and the black and white floor tiles clean. A flickering electric light showed the numbers above the door and on the top floor she found apartment eight and knocked on it.

A male voice asked who it was and she answered, hoping it was the right flat. A moment later the door opened and a tall, thin, elderly man in a black suit invited her in. Noting her reluctance to enter he explained that Madam Carter was in the sitting room and expected her.

So, even living here, Madam Carter had kept her butler. Anaise wondered if there was more to it than that but very quickly pushed those thoughts from her mind, she was here for more important issues.

The hallway was dimly lit and led into a large sitting room dominated by a green velvet sofa and paintings of all descriptions crowding the walls. The brown shutters were closed and only a little daylight peaked in through the cracks in the old dried wood.

Madam Carter almost blended into the sofa where she sat dressed in a green ankle length dress with deep 1920s pearl necklace reaching her waist and a glass of something pink in her hand.

'Oh, do come in. I'm so glad you came.' She got to her feet. 'And just in time for a lunchtime drink too.' She signaled to the man who'd opened the door to bring drinks and for Anaise to join her on the sofa. 'I do apologise for the state we have to live in now, dear.' She lit a cigarette and offered one to Anaise who accepted. Maybe it would help settle her nerves.

'Madam Carter, I'm going to come straight to the point.' She paused briefly, not wanting to worry the older lady. 'I'm looking for Emilie. Has she been in touch with you?'

Madam Carter looked at her for a moment before answering. 'Has that husband of hers done something?'

'I don't know that anything has happened, but she's not been home, or in touch with me for days. She acted a little odd when I saw her last, but she didn't mention going away.' Anaise felt so guilty for not calling around earlier.

'We need to talk to her husband. Oh, what is his name? I normally just call him the pig.'

'His name is Gerard, and I agree, he's a pig but he's nowhere to be found either.'

'I'd like to help dear, but I really have no idea where she can be.'

Anaise finished the drink that the butler had brought her and bid a worried Madam Carter goodbye.

'They're closing in on all of us.' Anaise sat at the top of the table with Albert and Christophe in their Latin Quarter flat. The atmosphere was tangible, and even though they knew nobody could hear them, they spoke with hushed voices.

'They arrested Max this morning and two others at lunch.' Albert looked to Christophe on his right. 'Any news on Marseille?'

'Only what we found out yesterday. Nothing has come through since.' Christophe looked to Anaise. 'They got Remy a couple of days ago. And his son and wife too.' Anaise's face fell and Christophe shook his head. 'Father Michel's body was found a few weeks ago. He'd been shot a couple of minutes' walk from the church. Everything seems to have fallen apart down there, and I guess it won't be long before it's our turn.'

She knew they just wanted the bad taste of Marseille out of their house, but she couldn't leave yet.

'What about Tom?' she asked, worried what the answer might be.

'He's gone. We had a message mentioning that he's left for London. Running away most likely,' Albert said.

Christophe poured them all another drink.

'He might be the informer.' Albert looked at the two of them. 'He had all the information, all the trust and now he's gone. Speaks for itself really.' He held out his hands to show the simplicity of his theory.

'That's rubbish, and you know it.'

'No, Anaise, I don't know it. You and your sister brought him in, and now all hell's broken lose and he's disappeared. - Come to think about it, your sister's disappeared too. My guess would be that she's gone to London to be with him. Deserted. Left you here with us, dangling bait before the Nazis.' He stopped only when Anaise whacked her hand across his face and burned her eyes into him.

'Don't you ever imply that about her again.'

She sat back down and Christophe put his arm around her shoulders.

'We're just tetchy. Nobody thinks Em's switched sides or run away. Have you any news on her whereabouts?'

Anaise shook her head whilst still glaring at Albert who was glaring right back.

'Well, I'll go then.' She got up from the wooden chair she'd been sitting on.

Christophe nodded and Anaise left knowing that no help would come from them. To hell with them, her world was crashing and she didn't need any half brained men to help her. She'd find Em on her own.

She went straight back to her sister's house and knocked on the door. This time it opened. Louise, dressed in normal clothes asked her in and Anaise explained her worries.

The maid shook her head. 'I don't know where she is. I'm not supposed to be here, I got fired yesterday afternoon. There were a couple of my things still here so I used my key to get in. You know we can't be here when Monsieur or Jacques return.'

'Who fired you? Emilie?'

'No. Monsieur Valois just said they were going away and that I wasn't needed anymore. There was something odd though, apart from the fact that I know Madam wouldn't have let him fire me without saying goodbye, there was broken glass on the sitting room floor.'

Anaise rushed up the stairs to check if Emilie was lying there somewhere and Louise followed. When she threw the door open, the first thing she saw was the photos of her sister and Tom lying on the bed next to a broken flower pot. There was no doubt now, Gerard had done something, and Anaise hoped it wasn't final.

Louise opened the wardrobe. There were no clothes missing.

'I have to get hold of Monsieur Valois, Louise. Have you any idea where he might be?'

She shook her head. 'I'm sorry.'

Anaise tried to think what to do next. Normally she would have contacted the police, but she didn't want to draw attention to them, and anyway, they were only doing the Germans work these days.

Before returning downstairs she went into Gerard's room, but couldn't find any clues as to what had happened. Both of them were just about to leave when the front door opened and Gerard stepped inside. He stopped in his tracks when he saw them standing at the bottom of the stairs. Seconds passed slowly before Gerard ordered Louise to leave or he'd call the police and she reluctantly left Anaise on her own. Gerard quietly shut the door behind Louise, and when he turned around, his face cracked into a grin.

'So, it's just us. Just you and me here.' He took a step into the hall and involuntary Anaise backed a couple of steps up the stairs before steeling herself. Who did he think he was?

'Don't think you scare me. You're just a bully who would run a mile if someone of your own size challenged you.' She stopped as Gerard held up a hand.

'I don't really care what you think. You're here to see my wife I expect?'

'Where is she?'

'She's gone away. She should be crossing the border into Germany for the opportunity of a lifetime by now. I'm sure she would have told you, but I think she was getting quite tired of having you around.'

'Rubbish.'

'Oh really? So why didn't she tell you then?'

'I know you found the letters and photos.' She waited a moment to see how he reacted.

He just shook his head and laughed. 'Why would I care about what she did in the past? You forget, I was her manager when they went out, I know everything about the Englishman. Everything.' His smile had gone, and in one quick move he'd caught hold of Anaise's hair and pulled her down the stairs. She tried to get free, but he'd grabbed her by surprise, and before she knew it, he'd dragged her outside and pushed her down the front steps.

'My wife has moved on. She doesn't need useless family members hanging on to her.'

For a moment she thought he would come down the front stairs and she quickly stumbled onto her feet. With one last look of contempt Gerard closed the door.

From nowhere Louise appeared and touched her shoulder. 'Come, let's get away from here.' She tried to take her arm but Anaise shook it off.

'We have to find her before it's too late.' She'd hurt her hand in the fall and it was throbbing but she didn't think it was broken. She turned to Louise. 'Will you help me?'

Louise looked at her. 'Of course I will. Do you really think he would have done something bad? I know he's got a temper but I think he loved her in some strange way. It's only recently he's gone a bit mad.'

'I know he has. The only way we can find out is by following him when he leaves.'

Louise nodded and looked down the street. 'It's a long road with nowhere to hide.'

'Well, that just means he has to come out either on that side,' she pointed to the right, 'or on that side and there's two of us.'

Was it right of her to involve Louise? She'd need to find herself a new job, not spend her time following her old employer. 'You don't have to, I know life's difficult.'

'No. I'll help. I always felt a little sorry for her, so beautiful and talented, but she always seemed a little sad, always trying to please everybody. As if she was missing a little piece of herself.'

Anaise's stomach twinged when Louise said her sister always seemed a little sad. 'Ok, I don't suppose he's going to stay in very long so if you go that way and I'll go this. If you haven't seen him by sunset come and tell me and we'll come up with another plan.'

They went their separate ways and Anaise eased her bruised behind into a cafe chair and ordered some wine. She shouldn't drink this early, but it had been that kind of day. The wind picked up and flapped the ends of the red awning and she pulled her coat tighter.

The cafe was full and judging by their clothes most of them were well to do members of society. She'd chosen her table well, it had a good view of the exit from her sister's road. Twice now Valois had felt the need to prove that he was stronger than her and she was seething inside.

The two women sitting behind her talked loudly about the food shortages and how anything worth having from the shops disappeared before they had a chance to even ask about it. Daily, mundane and utterly boring. If they had something to really worry about they wouldn't be talking about it in front of the whole world.

Where was Em? She would never leave without telling her. If only she had kept her mouth shut, if only she'd never met Fleur. Maybe things would have gone wrong anyway, that was the nature of their game, but at least it wouldn't have been her fault.

Anaise was engrossed in her thoughts and only just noticed Gerard disappearing down the street. She threw some money on the table and rushed off after him. She could just about see him as he strode purposefully down the street but she was gaining on him. Just as she was about to slow down to make sure he didn't notice her, a man stepped out from a building, a German man whom she ran straight into. He was very tall, and once she'd recovered her balance, she saw who it was, and couldn't even open her mouth to apologise.

'Watch where you go.' The waiter from Marseille said brusquely. His eyes narrowed slightly. 'I know you from somewhere.'

Anaise shook her head and looked downwards. 'Please Monsieur, I am late for work.'

'Well, go then.' He stepped out of her way and she moved past him and made sure she was well down the street before she turned around. He was supposed to be dead by now, what was he doing in Paris? Further up the street, The Waiter was still standing in the same spot, but now there was another man there with him. A chill travelled down her spine as she recognised him. The man from Marseille, the one whose cold face she'd never wanted to see again.

Martin Perrault lifted his gaze and looked down the street towards her. She knew she should leave, but her legs wouldn't move. Only when the two men started walking towards her at speed did she turn around and start to run.

There were Germans all over the place, she wouldn't stand a chance of trying to outrun them on the main streets, so instead she ducked into a side alley. She had no idea where it would lead to, and still she could hear them behind her. There were more of them following her now and she couldn't run much further. The cobbled side streets were narrow and dirty and smelled of old rubbish and damp. She turned a corner, and at the end of the street stood a woman. When Anaise reached her, she ushered her in through a door which, judging by the smell, was the back entrance of a restaurant. She slammed the door shut and ran ahead of Anaise up the stairs. Halfway up she stopped and looked down at Anaise who was still catching her breath at the bottom. 'What are you waiting for? Come on.'

Anaise followed her up the stairs and through a windowless corridor which seemed to lead into a different house entirely. When the woman stopped running they were in a small room where the afternoon light beamed in through the high window. Anaise couldn't stop staring at her, the woman who had undoubtedly saved her. She was the most beautiful woman she'd ever seen. Her skin flawlessly pale and blonde hair piled on top of her head with a handful of it escaping down her shoulders. Anaise looked nervously around the room. This woman might just have lured her into a trap, but what choice did she have?

It would only have been moments before the men chasing her had caught up, and God alone knows what would have happened then.

She leaned her head back against the closed door and looked at her rescuer. 'So, who are you?'

****

It had been two days since she'd been rescued by Lilou, and Anaise had laid low since then. Apart from sending a message to London, hoping it would reach Tom, she'd spent her time pacing Ballou's flat and wondering how she could hurry the new identity papers and travel documents on. She was sure there would be a warrant out for her arrest and frustration was building up inside her. What was happening to Em? Lilou had sworn that she wasn't involved and that she didn't know where her sister was, but she would try to find out.

The bar was busy but not full, and even though there were no Germans in sight, she choose a table in a corner by the back exit and waited. Half of the people in the bar would be pro-German or just looking out for themselves and they would hand her over if they knew she was wanted by them. The other half were just trying to get on with their lives as best they could. Anaise tried to tell herself that it was no crime to look out for your family and just get on with things but bloody hell, that was how they'd ended up like this. That was how the Germans had just been allowed to walk in and take over their city and their lives. Look at Britain, they'd been fighting on even though their cities were bombed daily by an army so much bigger than theirs, but they didn't just give up. Right now, helping them was helping France.

She ordered a drink and waited. Finally Lilou arrived and sat down next to her so that she too would have a view over the bar.

'Here.' She handed a small parcel to Anaise under the table. 'Don't look at it now. Put it in your bag.'

Anaise did as she was asked.

'What about my sister.'

'I will tell you in a minute, but first you have to promise me to get these photos out of Paris and to someone who can deal with them.'

'What are they?'

Lilou started telling her in a low voice of the work she'd done for and with Gerard for the last eight years and how he'd tried to get her killed.

Even Anaise, who had such a low opinion of him to start with, was surprised.

'And Em, what about her. You have to tell me.'

'I've been keeping watch over the house since he tried to get rid of me. An old client of mine lives opposite and he's let me stay in the attic. About five nights ago I saw her come home, and less than an hour later, Gerard and Jacques carried her out into a waiting car. I kept on watching the house, and that's how I saw you being thrown out into the street. When those men started chasing you I took a chance on your route and luckily enough got to you in time.'

'The bastard. I knew he'd done something to her. Are you sure she's alive?'

'I don't know, but she was at the time, and I don't think he'd kill her. She's too valuable to him alive and he's very possessive of her.'

'You don't know where they took her?'

'No, I'm afraid not, but they were back within half an hour so I don't expect it was very far away.'

Anaise finished her drink. 'What are you going to do now? Will you be safe?'

'Who's safe these days? I can look after myself though and I have friends who will help. I have a plan for a whole new life. I'm going into fashion.' She put her hand on Anaise's. 'After you find your sister, promise me you'll hand the photos over to someone who can undo some of the things we've done. Don't get me wrong, I'm no angel, and I like money like everyone else, but I'm not a killer.'

Anaise nodded and wondered how someone as beautiful as Lilou could have fallen as low as this. She probably stood a much better chance to survive the war than most though. She knew where to hide and seemed to have a lot of friends. She'd be alright. Anaise had to find out what Gerard had done with Em, and she could only think of one way of doing that.

Lilou stayed on and had another drink in the bar. She wasn't quite sure of Anaise. Most people were easy to read, easy to manipulate if one wanted to, but not this woman. She had built up some kind of wall around herself to confuse the rest of the world as to her true self. Oh well, it was done. She felt relieved now that the pictures were handed over and she could concentrate on surviving. She drained the last few drops from her glass and paid the bill. The sky had clouded over and she hoped it wouldn't start raining before she got back to her attic room. Actually, maybe she would go to some shops first, see what her future competitors were doing. It was all quite exciting.

The first thing she knew about the man that had been following her for most of the day was when he appeared behind her and pulled a scarf tight around her neck. He pulled it harder and tighter until her head felt like it would explode. Her hands tore desperately at the scarf, and the man behind her but it was no use. The last words she heard were 'Bye, bye Lou' as Jacques used all his strength to finish the job.

She lost her life and her dreams right there, by the side of the Seine, under a Sycamore tree.

$$\sim 19 \sim$$

The Savoy, London

Tom could feel her presence in the foyer even before she softly spoke his name. Her voice brought back a thousand exiled memories of a life he'd once known. Ever since his run in with the police in Madrid and the painful van journey to the unknown, he'd hoped to see her again. A chance for both of them to save whatever was left of their friendship.

'Tom, darling. It's been so long.' She approached him in the shimmer of the chandeliers above with a tentative smile. 'I'm so glad you're here.'

'So am I, believe me. You look well, Bea.'

Her hands automatically went to make sure that no strands of her fair hair had escaped from the up-do that framed her face. She wore a dove blue chiffon dress that reached just below her knees and matching shoes.

'Well, apparently one still has to dress for dinner. The world may be collapsing outside these walls but heaven forbid you'd wear day clothes for dinner at the Savoy.'

She looked over towards the entry into the American Bar. 'We can't stand here and talk. Daddy isn't here yet, but he promised to join us shortly. That's just because you're here you know, I'm lucky to see him at all these days. Come, let's have a drink whilst we wait.'

She led the way up a short set of stairs to the bar. There they were met by a tune played on the piano, groups chattering over White Ladies and a waiter that seated them by a window.

'This feels very surreal.' He lit a cigarette after offering one to Bea which she accepted.

He leaned back in the chair and looked out of the shatter proofed window where the shimmer of the Thames could be seen between the branches of the Plane trees lining the walkway.

The journey from Lisbon had been a long one, and as soon as they'd arrived in London, he'd set off to find Charles Johnson and hand over the film. The stern lady receptionist at the CJ Film Company had however told him that Mr Johnson, wasn't available for some time. He'd tried to argue with her but it had gotten him nowhere.

Downheartedly he'd wandered back to the hotel, through streets with bombed out buildings and hurrying people. He would ask Sir Arthur's help in getting in touch with this Mr Johnson and if he couldn't help, he'd just have to hand the film over to him.

He brought his eyes back to Bea. She hadn't changed at all and he could see the odd hotel guest stealing an extra-long admiring glance at her when they thought nobody was looking.

Maybe this awkwardness between him and her would disappear with a few drinks.

For so long he had forced himself not to think of her, or what she'd done, but she had been like his sister and his best friend for so many years that he couldn't help but miss her.

The bar bustled with couples in evening wear drinking cocktails and enjoying themselves. It set a very strong contrast to the bombed out houses and their former inhabitants further down the road. It must be a good place to spend the war if you had the money.

'So tell me, what have you been up to since... well, since... Spain.' Tom asked. The bare mention of Spain tore little holes in both their souls, but it was the only way forward if they were to spend some time together. The only way to move forwards.

After a few moments she smiled. 'Avoiding marriage mostly. Helping out with the war effort where I can.' She took a sip of her Pink Gin before continuing. 'And worrying about you.' She touched the scar on his cheek. 'You do always get yourself into trouble Tom Lancaster. Promise me to keep in touch from now on.'

'It's a bit difficult with the job I do, but I shall certainly try.' It was nice to have someone worry about him. 'I have missed you.' The words came out before he had a chance to stop them.

'Oh Tom.' Her eyes welled up. 'I was so afraid that you still hated me.'

'I don't hate you. Can we just leave it at that? Can we just agree to be friends again without mentioning the past?'

She nodded. 'I would like that. I would like that very much.'

They sat in silence for a few moments. 'I brought a girl back from France. Did the driver mention to you if he got her a room?'

'Oh yes, I almost forgot about her. Don't worry. She's resting in one of our rooms upstairs until dinner.' She laughed. 'Who is she?'

Tom got the attention of a waiter and ordered another drink. 'I'm sorry, it's been a very long day.' He relaxed back in the chair. 'She's a girl that needed to get out of France, so I took her with me. I didn't want to at the time, but a friend of mine, Father Michel blackmailed my conscience into it. She's a nice girl.'

'I'm sure.' Bea said raising her eyebrows.

'No, it's nothing like that. She's a Jewish refugee. Her whole family was rounded up and taken away to some god-awful camp somewhere. She managed to escape to Marseille.'

'And that's where you met her?'

He nodded. 'This Priest, Father Michel, takes in quite a lot of refugees and we end up having to find a way out for them. The world should have more Father Michels.'

'I agree. It's all been quite dreadful here too.'

'How come you're staying here and not at the house?'

'Well, it's just impossible to run without staff, and they're all, quite rightly I might add, doing war work of one kind or another. I still keep in touch with some of them, but until for now, we're stuck here.'

'That must be awful for you.' Tom shook his head and grinned.

They caught up on each other's lives until Sir Arthur arrived. His once well filled face showed the stresses of his job at a difficult time. His hair and beard were now fully grey and the pounds lost from his weight showed gauntly in his face. When he turned his eyes on Tom, he could see that the changes were only skin deep, his eyes were as intense and strong as ever.

'What does a man have to do to get a drink in here, eh?' he jostled Tom's side as a waiter came over and took his order. 'Now, to what do we owe this honour young Tom?'

Tom smiled at the comment, he was almost thirty years old. He felt sure Sir Arthur would still call him that when he was sixty. He hesitated to tell him why he was in London whilst Bea was still there. It was not that he didn't trust her, but if anything was to go wrong, he didn't want to think that she had anything to do with it. If he'd learnt something from his past it was to never trust anybody completely.

Silence settled over the table for a few moments before Bea excused herself. 'I must go and fetch Sophia. We'll all die of hunger if we don't eat soon.'

Her father looked at her. 'Who's Sophia?'

'She's Tom's friend.'

'Ah, yes. You'll have to tell me all about her sooner rather than later. I had to pull quite some strings to get her into the country you know. She could even be a spy.' Sir Arthur's drink arrived and he lit a cigar. The smoke curled up towards the high ceilings.

Tom laughed. 'She's no spy. Just one of millions of refugees in need of a bit of help.'

'All the same. I'll organise for someone to come and see her here at the hotel tomorrow. It won't do for her to wander around the streets without proper papers. The same probably goes for you.'

'I'm only here for a few days and then I'm going back to France.'

Arthur nodded and smiled at someone he knew before turning his attention back to Tom. 'So you've come all the way back to London just for a couple of days? It must be important.'

Tom checked there was nobody in listening distance. 'I have a film from an agent in France. It's very important that it reaches a Mr Charles Johnson at CJ Films and nobody else. A matter of national importance I believe. The trouble is that I can't find him. The receptionist at CJ Films in Wardour Street told me he was away for some time. Naturally, I didn't tell her why I wanted to see him.'

Sir Arthur gazed out into the room. 'I do happen to know Mr Johnson and what he used to do. He might well still be doing it I guess. That's the business I used to be in as you know.' He paused. 'Mr Johnson worked, or works, for another part of the security services, one that operates lower and under more layers than our official departments. I hate to admit it, but when they started operating after the '14-'18 war I was highly against them. Now, I'm actually pleased to have them on our side.'

'Will you help me find him?'

'Oh, I know exactly where he is. I'm just not sure that a request from me will be warmly granted.'

'It is very important. Tell him I have something for him from Erik Tag. He'll know who that is. At least, I hope he does.'

'I'll see what I can do. A matter of national importance eh? Well, we'd better get that film to him as quickly as possible.'

A waiter informed them that the ladies were waiting for them in the restaurant.

'Well, come on then old chap. Let's see what's on the menu today.'

***

Tom opened his eyes and blinked against the bright sunlight streaming in through the window. There was someone knocking on a door but his head hurt too much to care. He pulled the cover back up over his face to shut out the light.

The previous night, as he stumbled into bed, he'd forgotten to pull down the blackout lining. The saving grace was that he'd not turned the light on before instantly falling asleep.

Whoever wanted him to open that door wasn't going away. Reluctantly he sat up and screwed his face up in pain until his brain had settled. He still wore the clothes from the previous day and he desperately needed some water.

'I'm coming,' he said towards the door. 'Bloody hell.'

The cold water from the polished bathroom taps travelled fast down his parched throat. If only he had something for his head. He splashed a couple of handfuls of water over his face before vigorously drying it with the fluffy white towel folded on the side of the sink.

When he finally opened the door he found Sophia leaning against the wall outside.

'You look terrible.' She pushed past him and looked around the room.

'Thank you. Do come in.' Tom said sarcastically and shut the door behind her.

'It is nearly midday and I thought you had to get to London in a hurry for some reason or other. I didn't realise it was to spend your days in bed with a hangover.'

'Oh, for God's sake. One overslept morning and - excuse me.' He turned around and disappeared into the bathroom.

Sophia opened a window before sitting down on the bed where she tried to ignore what was happening in the bathroom.

Finally Tom appeared, looking pale but feeling better and he sat down next to her on the bed.

'I'm so sorry about that. I only meant to have one drink before going to bed, but there was this man who told the most amazing stories. It was very difficult to leave before he'd finished.'

'Oh, I'm sure. Well, you'd better brighten up quickly. Your friend tells me you have a meeting with someone at one O'clock. She said her father had organised it and you'd know who it was with.'

'Did she say where the meeting was to take place?'

'No. I don't think she knew.'

Tom looked at his watch. 'It's twelve now. Do you know where my clothes are? I left them in the car yesterday.'

'I'll get them. They're in my room. You left me too remember.'

'Sophia, I have things I have to do. Bea will look after you for now. She'll probably help you look for your brother and find somewhere to stay too.' He decided that pretending he believed her story about her brother was the best way forward. Otherwise he'd have to sort something out for her permanently.

'Yes, she seems nice.'

'She can be. Now be a good girl and run along and get my clothes please.'

'Yes, sir.'

'Thank you.'

He remained seated on the bed as she left. Coffee was what was needed and bacon. Would that be available here? He picked up the internal telephone and ordered breakfast.

***

Charles Johnson didn't look anything like Tom had expected. He was forty-ish, tall, slim and there was a certain arrogance that Tom instantly took a dislike to. There were pictures of famous film stars on the brown walls and piles of folders and files collecting dust on the carpet underneath them.

'They are film scripts and letters from writers. Most of them are rubbish, but I must look through them when there's time. You never know where there might be a diamond script just waiting to be discovered. It may well take me until the end of the war to get around to it though.'

Tom sat down opposite him. 'So you actually make films? I thought this might just be a cover.'

'A cover for what, old chap? Of course we make films. Some are very successful too.'

This was the man he had to hand the film over to. He didn't seem quite dedicated enough. Not dirtied enough by what went on around him. Still, that's what Erik had asked him to do. 'I have something for you.'

'Yes, so I gather.' He held out his hand across the desk.

Tom hesitated for a moment before pulling the old cigarette case from his pocket and handing it over.

Johnson had a quick look before putting it back on the desk. 'Now, do you want to tell me what it is and how you came about it?' It wasn't a request.

Tom pulled out a cigarette and was about to light it when Johnson held out a hand. 'Not in here please. Can't stand the filthy smell.'

Tom put the pack back in his pocket and started to tell him about the signalling house and Erik's death.

He'd toyed with the idea of ignoring the bomb part of the story, but he'd done nothing wrong. Erik had been posing as a German and therefore a legitimate target.

'This is what he gave me. I in return promised to hand it safely to you, and you alone. He said there were moles in the London office which is why, I guess, he didn't get in touch with you to say he was on his way back here.'

Mr Johnson sat quietly for a little while whilst taking it in. His eyes faced the desk and for a moment Tom thought he detected something real about this man. Some kind of affection for a lost soldier. When he looked back up at Tom he seemed more human, a little more professional, and certainly more direct. 'So he died because you blew up the house?'

'Yes. But as I understood it from Erik, it wasn't supposed to happen like that. He was supposed to survive and escape to England. Perrault told me to press the plunger too early.'

'This man Perrault that wanted him dead, do we know why?'

'Erik had been blackmailing him for a while. That would be enough for anyone to kill.'

Johnson nodded behind his desk. 'There was always a big chance he'd get found out. It could have been worse, the Germans could have found out about him and the information he'd sent us through the years. At least now it's been sealed. The information is safe.' He stood up. 'I understand from Sir Arthur that you're staying at the Savoy.'

Tom nodded. 'Yes, for now.'

'I will need to talk to you again once I've had a look at this.' He held up the film.

'Of course. Just bear in mind that I'll be going back to France shortly. There are things on that film I need to know about too. There's the blackmail information that Erik had on Perrault, and I need it to save what's left of my network.'

'Trust me Mr Lancaster, you won't be going anywhere until I'm happy to let you go.' Suddenly he smiled. 'I am sorry, I didn't mean to come over as some company sergeant, but I'd like to politely ask you not to leave London.'

Tom hesitated, but he could see the man's point, and he wanted to know what was on that film as much anybody. 'Alright, but bear in mind that people's lives depend on me finding out what's on that film.'

'What people?'

'My network in Marseille and another connected one in Paris. It might be too late already.'

'What are their names?'

'Masalia in Marseille and The 52 in Paris. They're very closely linked, but not run directly from London. The leak we had can be fixed, but we need the information that's on that film. That's what your Erik said, and that's partly why I travelled all the way here.'

He'd tried so hard not to think of Emilie and Anaise and what was happening across the channel that it all seemed like a different world. He too stood up. 'Have you heard any news from Paris about the singer Emilie Valois? Any large crackdowns by the Germans on the networks there?'

'There's always news like that. Sometimes they just fall like dominoes. Never makes it any easier though.' He came around to Tom's side. 'I will try to find out some news from Paris for you if you write down everything you remember about your meeting with Erik. And remember, do not talk about this to anybody but me.' He kept hold of Tom's hand whilst shaking it. 'Nobody, understand.' Tom nodded and Johnson let him go. 'You can always find me here. Day or night in case you remember anything else.'

A minute later Tom found himself back outside the CJ Film office on Wardour Street in the sunshine with nothing to do but wander back to the hotel.

~ 20 ~

Tom had spent the last two days at the hotel, letting Bea and Sophia beat him in various games and getting cabin fever. He had to get out and seeing his mother was something he should do whilst he was in London. It had been too long since he last saw her, and time had put up a barrier which he would have preferred to leave where it was. It was easier to just get on with what you had to without thinking about the people that mattered most to you, but it would be wrong to leave without visiting.

From the window of the South Kensington flat his mother was staying in he watched a procession of demonstrators pass by. The rain and the wind tore at the placards whilst Tom tried to see what they were protesting for or against.

After this visit all he could do was to return to the hotel. If he hadn't heard back from Charles by the end of the day, he'd go back to Wardour Street. Things needed to speed up, he couldn't just sit around waiting any longer. Besides, he felt lost and lonely in London. He never used to. The streets had changed along with people's lives and his friends were all in the services somewhere. He'd been gone too long.

He put on a smile as his mother returned to the table.

She'd just had just had her fiftieth birthday, but apart from a few laughing lines she didn't look it. Her hair was still jet black, her eyes glinting, and a smile was never far from her lips.

'So, what is this?' She reached over and ran her finger along the scar on his cheek.

'It's nothing mama, an accident that's all.'

'I don't believe it,' she paused. 'But if you don't want to tell me that's fine.' Her Spanish accent was still audible even though she'd not been back there for over thirty years.

'Alright, it's a little momentum from our stopover in Madrid.'

'Oh Tomaz, why did you go back there? Nothing good ever came from there.'

'I had to. It was the quickest way through to Lisbon.' He smiled at her. 'Something good came from Spain.'

'Ah, you sweet boy. That was a long time ago, and I left.' She poured them tea into plain white teacups. 'The good china is in Orrington. With all these bombs falling I thought it best to remove them from the house. The cakes are good.' She nodded towards the flowery cake stand that held a variety of small cakes. 'I don't know how Mrs Wilson does it, or maybe I don't want to know.'

Tom took a bite and agreed with her. 'So how have you been? I'm sorry I haven't been in touch as much as I would have liked.'

'I haven't heard a word from you since '39. You could have died for all I knew.' she paused. 'I know it's your job, I know it's all for the war, but it doesn't make it any easier.' She picked up a cake. 'I pray for you every night. For you to come back home safe and sound.' Her eyes welled over and she picked up a tissue. 'I'm sorry.'

'Don't be upset, mama. It's not what any of us would want, but the world's gone a bit mad.'

'But not a word in two years. Even before the war you were bad at keeping in touch, but at least I knew you were safe.' She paused and tried to smile. 'I have some news of my own.' She held out her left hand. 'I'm engaged.'

Tom almost choked on the last bit of a carrot cake. 'Engaged. To whom?' He couldn't help a bit of indignation filtering through to the surface.

'He's a very nice man. His name is Henry Seymore and we met when my London house was bombed. I had nowhere to go and he was very helpful.'

'You have a large country house in Sussex, I assume that's still standing.'

'It is Tom, it is, but I felt lonely there since you, Bea and Arthur left the village. Here in London I have my friends, committees and parties.'

'What about Arthur? I always thought there was something between you two.' He'd never approached this subject before and he had no idea how she'd react.

'I am not going discuss that with you. Suffice to say that I'm on my own now. In fact, he'll tell you he doesn't approve of Henry, but then again, he was your father's best friend. I have to think a little about myself now. You understand?'

'So when can I meet him?'

'He's up north right now doing something or other for the war. It is a shame as I know he wants to meet you darling. Are you here long?'

'I don't know. I'm hoping to go back to France within a few days.' He lit a cigarette. 'I have a favour to ask you.'

His mother leaned back in her chair. 'Go on, what is it?'

'There is this girl I know who needs...'

His mother sat straight up. 'Oh no, you haven't got some girl into trouble?'

He was a little taken back. 'No. She came with me from France. She needs somewhere to stay whilst she looks for her brother. I wondered if she could stay with you perhaps. Just until she finds him.' He didn't mention his misgivings about the existence of a brother. It would solve one of his problems if she was to say yes. He quickly explained a little of how their paths had crossed.

'How can I say no? We've all got to help as best we can now, don't we?'

'I'll pay for her keep until she leaves.'

'No, no there's no need for that. It'll be nice to have someone here. Especially a girl now that I don't see Bea very often.'

When Tom left, with the promise of returning before he went back to France, he felt his shoulders relax a little.

The demonstration had come to a stop outside his mother's house and he edged his way past them.

'Deep shelters for all, not just the rich. Open the underground for shelter.' The chants went on in a very individual way even though the police were doing all they could to disperse the protesters. Tom managed to push his way past them and onto the main road. It was still crowded with people and not much of a chance to get a taxi, but a stroll back to the hotel might do him good. He'd walked a few steps past a Lyon's corner house when he remembered his promise to Erik. His stomach might have been full of cake from his mother's house, but these days there seemed to be no stopping him with regards to food. He stopped and turned around when a suited man bumped into him rather harshly before apologising and moving on. For a moment he wondered where he'd seen the man before but forgot all about it as he entered the Corner House. He'd only taken a few steps inside the door before realising that he was bleeding. Almost instantly it began to hurt and he bent over sideways, trying to stem the flow of blood. His thoughts raced all over the place trying to figure out what had happened.

Two soldiers from a nearby table rushed over and grabbed hold of him before sitting him down on a chair.

'Quickly, call for an ambulance.' One of them called out to a Nippy. The entire clientele of the House had by this time turned to see what was going on.

'What happened to you then?' the other soldier asked Tom calmly.

Tom lifted his head slowly. 'I think someone just stabbed me.'

'Right, let's see what's what.' He lifted Tom's jacket and asked his friend to get some serviettes to stem the blood flow. 'I'm Lieutenant Balding by the way.'

Tom didn't really care, he just concentrated on breathing. The serviettes arrived and Lieutenant Balding pressed them hard against the wound. Tom gasped briefly but as they were held steady, the pain eased a little. 'I can't thank you enough,' he said to the two of them.

One of the Nippys brought over a cup of tea. 'It's sweet tea, good for shock I'm told.'

'Any sign of the ambulance?'

She shook her head. 'Not yet. Is he going to be ok? What happened to him?'

'He'll be fine. Only a flesh wound in his side. We do need it to stop bleeding though.' The soldier turned his attention back to Tom. 'Do you know why someone would do this?'

Tom shook his head. 'Could I have some of that tea please?'

The sweet liquid helped keep the nausea that had threatened to make him faint at bay.

What an appropriate way to keep his promise to Erik.

***

The pain of the wound overtook his annoyance at the un-sympathetic doctor at the hospital. The ambulance had taken its sweet time to arrive whilst Lt Balding's chit chat had gone in through one ear and out of the other. He'd found himself incapable of concentrating on anything other than keeping calm and breathing. He'd been so scared it was a fatal wound and that he'd never see Em again that he'd nearly panicked. Now that he was all patched up he thought back to that moment and the fact that it was her he'd been worried about, and how much she actually meant to him.

He sat on the edge of a hard bed waiting for the doctor to say it was alright for him to leave. It was only a flesh wound, more blood than damage and they'd put some stitches in to hold him together. It had been at least an hour since the doctor had to rush off and told him to wait where he was. He'd had enough of it now and decided to leave without the official sign off. He passed the nurses station and the young girl there came rushing after him.

'Mr Lancaster, where do you think you're going?' Her dark hair was pinned up tightly and covered with a white cap. He stopped for a moment.

'The doctor that was supposed to sign me out seems to have gone missing and I can't wait any longer.'

'I'm sorry, but you can't just leave.'

Tom started walking again. The nurse, torn between following her escaping patient and leaving the nurses station unattended, decided to find a more senior nurse or doctor in the next ward.

He felt a little sorry for her, but not sorry enough to stay. If he walked carefully, his wound didn't even hurt. Still, he hoped to find a taxi to take him back to the hotel. Evening had fallen outside and the lack of lights made the streets of London hazardous to walk along. He kept on walking towards the Strand without finding any mode of transport to help him along. The question of who and why kept on racing through his mind with every step he took.

Mistaken identity, a mad person, or someone who intentionally wanted to kill him. If he hadn't done a total turn around to go into the Corner House the knife would have gone through the upper left hand side of his back. Then it would have been a totally different game, well not for him, he'd be dead. How sad would it have been to die on the streets of London after everything he'd been through. Now he felt a little paranoid walking slowly back to the hotel on his own in the dark. Finally though he turned the corner to the main entrance of the Savoy and walked through their black out painted revolving doors.

He didn't fancy company so he ordered a bottle of whiskey to be sent up to his room on his way through the foyer. The concierge didn't bat an eyelid at Tom's bloody clothes when he asked him to get it sent up as quickly as possible.

He struggled with his room key door until he realised it was unlocked. It creaked as he slowly opened it and saw the outline of Sir Arthur against the moonlit window. He sat in the dark waiting for Tom's return.

'So, is this your revenge for Morocco?' he asked in a neutral voice before Tom had a chance to say anything.

Silence settled completely until Tom replied.

'I don't understand what you mean. What have I done?'

'Oh don't play innocent with me.' He stood up to pull the blackout blind down and Tom lit the main light to see a bottle of port almost gone next to Sir Arthur.

'Where did you get them from?'

Tom still stood in the short hallway that led into his room. He went in and sat slowly down on the blue silk covered chair opposite the man who'd been like a father to him.

'Get what, Arthur? What am I supposed to have done? You need to tell me because I haven't got a clue.'

Arthur stood still and stared at him. 'I know you think I let you down back then, but to do this, to hate me so much that you want to ruin my life. And Bea's too.'

A fire crept into Tom's eyes as he pulled a cigarette out of the case.

'You're mad. Do you think I've spent the last four years plotting something against you? I'll tell you what I've done,

I've spent every day trying to keep you and Bea out of my head. Seeing you here was not my plan at all but when I saw you in the bar when I first arrived I thought that we might have another chance to make up for everything in the past. And yes, I hated both you and Bea for a long while, but I missed you too. I can't forget what happened but I have no wish to bring it up again. You, it would seem, have different ideas.'

Sir Arthur studied his face and after what seemed like minutes his face softened slightly. 'You really don't know what was on that film?'

Tom shook his head and Arthur finally noticed the blood on his shirt.

'What happened to you?'

'Nothing,' Tom said brusquely. 'If you know what's on that film you have to tell me.'

'Nothing? Very well.' He looked quizzically at Tom for a while before speaking. 'What I am about to tell you goes no further.'

'Of course not.'

'If this got out I'd be ruined.' He lit a cigar after offering one to Tom who declined. 'The Prime Minister came to see me this afternoon. He told me that Johnson had been to see him with the content of the film which he believed that I knew about.' He paused. 'I've always had a very good relationship with the prime minister and I could tell that something was wrong and that he found it difficult to tell me. He talked around the subject for some time. In the end I got the picture, quite literally, he handed me an envelope with photographs. My stomach turned when I saw what was on them Tom. They were of me, taken years ago, in Paris... with a prostitute.'

He let this sink in. 'The shame of it. In my day it was quite normal to go to a brothel whilst in Paris, I mean, more important people than me visited the Paris houses. But to have been photographed. God knows how many copies of these are around.' He drained his glass and refilled it. 'As if that wasn't enough, there was substantial evidence to show that I've been blackmailed and in the pocket of the Germans for years. It's ridiculous, but there are notes from my so called 'handler' and meeting dates that corresponds to my travels in my diary. How they got that information I don't know. It's only due to my seniority, and the state of our country, that they allowed me to come back here rather than go to a police station. If this was to get out it would be awful for the moral of the British people at a time when we're supposed to be in it together. One of their ministers working for the enemy.'

He sank back into the chair. All strength and ambition gone from his eyes.

'I had no idea what was on that film.' Tom knew Sir Arthur's integrity was solid and this was all too difficult to take on board. If he had been someone else it wouldn't have mattered, but he was a minister in a country at war, and this would break him.

'What are you going to do?'

'I don't know. Wait and hope that they find some evidence somewhere that it's not true. No, I'm going to find out who got the details from my diary and start clearing my name from there. How did you come by this film, Tom?'

He'd promised not to discuss it with anyone, but Sir Arthur was as close to a father to him as his own. He knew that he would never have allowed himself to be blackmailed. So he told him about Erik. Sir Arthur seemed none the wiser after he'd finished but he nodded calmly to himself.

'You're a good man, Tom. I'm sorry for doubting your intentions.'

'The way we left things in Morocco I'd probably have thought the same thing. - Why would the Germans have this information and not use it until now?'

Sir Arthur sighed. 'We have been bombed since July last year. Everybody knows someone who's been injured, killed or bombed out of their home. The bombs are dropped to kill whatever is near and you never know when it's going to be you or your family. After a very short time it starts grating on your nerves. Morale needs to be kept high, it's the only thing that will get us through this and the Germans know it. It might look like a desperate ploy on their part but only one lit match is required to set off mayhem on the streets. - What I'd like to know is how those pictures ended up with....'

A loud knock on the door echoed through the room and made them both jump. Tom rose slowly and painfully from his chair, but didn't move towards the door.

'Have you got a gun?' he asked Sir Arthur.

'No. Do we need one? This is the Savoy.'

'Let's leave it. They'll go away.'

Tom looked around for anything that could be used as a weapon until Bea's voice came through.

'Are you alright? I know you're in there. I'll get someone to...'

Tom walked over and opened the door where he found Bea with an urgent look on her face. Then she noticed Tom's shirt.

'Oh, no. What's happened to you?'

He really had to change his clothes.

'It's nothing, I'll tell you later.' he said rather more brusquely than he'd intended.

'Alright. Can I come in?'

'Yes, of course.' He stepped out of the way. 'What's the matter?'

'There are crowds of people outside with placards...' she stopped as she noticed her father. 'I didn't know you were here. Thank God you're alright.'

'I'm just talking to Tom. What's happened, you look upset.'

'There are a lot of angry protesters outside the hotel. The police are there too, but it's what they're saying that's...' Her voice trailed off.

Her father stood up and walked over to the window.

'What do they want? Is it the communists again, about the hotel?'

'No it's not about the hotel.'

He turned from the window. 'Come on girl, spit it out.'

'Their placards say you're a fifth columnist, a spy for the Germans.' She paused. 'They know you're in here.'

Sir Arthur closed his eyes. When he opened them he looked at Tom. 'Take her back upstairs to our rooms and stay with her.'

'What will you do?'

'I'm not sure. I need to see the PM.'

'Wait here whilst I take Bea upstairs. Then I'll go with you.'

'There's no need. I'll take the driver with me. There are more exits out of the Savoy than you'd think.' He put his matches back in his pocket and pulled out a neatly folded piece of paper. 'I nearly forgot. This arrived from Paris for you.' He handed the note to Tom just as the air raid siren went off. 'Go on, get in the shelter with you.'

'What about you. You can't go out in a raid.' Bea tried to stop him leaving and he took hold of her hands.

'Get in that shelter Beatrice. I will see you later.' He turned to Tom. 'Go on, get her down there.' And with that he walked out the door.

Tom quickly grabbed a fresh shirt. 'I'll be one minute.' He disappeared into the bathroom. He removed his bloody shirt and put a new one on as the ack ack of the anti-aircraft guns started up.

He stepped out of the bathroom, grabbed the piece of paper from the table and looked at Bea.

'Where's Sophia?'

Bea shook her head. 'I don't know. I haven't seen her since breakfast.'

Loud explosions that pulled at their nerves and rattled the windows came from all around them.

'Come on then, let's go downstairs.' He took her hand. If he could have he would have run but he didn't want to start the bleeding again so they walked quickly towards the stairs. When a bomb made the floor move, they ran.

The other guests had done this before and gathered in their usual places in the large underground Savoy shelter. The occasional glance over towards Bea showed that they were aware of the demonstrators outside. They must have scattered with the raid and he hoped they wouldn't be back. He ordered a large whiskey from a waiter before pulling the note from his pocket. From Paris. He twisted it between his fingers and pulled at its sides before laying it on the table in front of him. Bea watched him in silence for a while and when their drinks arrived she put her hand on his.

'You should read it.'

'I know. I'm just scared of the contents. What if something has happened to them?' He tore his eyes away from the note and looked up at Bea. 'I can't do it again.'

'It might be good news.'

'Good news from Paris? Is there such a thing?' The golden brown liquid made his throat burn as he emptied the glass and put it back down.

Finally he unfolded the note and read the contents. When he looked back up at Bea he noticed her eyes falling instantly to his side. When he looked down, a small patch of blood had appeared on his fresh shirt.

'Let's get you to the nurse's station. They'll look after you there.'

'I have to go out. I need to see Johnson straight away.' He stumbled as he tried to get up from the chair. Bea took his arm and led him down a corridor into a brightly lit room where two nurses were having a cup of tea. It smelled of disinfectant and efficiency and Tom let them look at his wound without arguing.

'How did this come about?' one of the nurses asked whilst putting a few stitches through to keep the bleeding down.

'I fell onto a metal gate.' He answered shortly.

'It does help to know how the wound happened. This was caused by something sharp. Don't worry, we won't get the police involved. Unless you've done something illegal of course.'

'I was stabbed in Kensington. I don't know by who or why.' That was the only explanation he offered.

When they'd patched him up and put him in a bed to rest, Bea came and sat next to him even though there were no women allowed in the men's sleeping quarters.

'It'll be fine until the snore guard comes along. It's still quite early so not a lot of the men are in bed yet.'

Tom's eyes were heavy with tiredness and the last thing he heard was Bea asking him what had really happened.

~ 21 ~

There was no daylight anywhere, only the small lantern at the end of the thin corridor and that would stay the same whether it was day or night. It took Tom a few moments to remember where he was. The hard wooden back of the sleeping cupboard dug into his back when he sat up. He pulled the cover up to warm himself. It was eerily quiet down there now that all the guests had all left. The smell of cleaning liquid reminded him of boarding school. How long had he been there? He could so easily go back to sleep in this place where time seemed to stand still, but before he had a chance to lie back down he heard a door open and footsteps coming towards him. In the low light he swung his legs over the side and stood up.

'Well, there's never a dull moment with you around is there?' Sophia appeared from around the corner. 'Bea said you were down here and not very well although she didn't mention what was wrong with you.' She put down a tray with tea and sandwiches without spilling any on her green Lisbon coat and pulled up a chair.

'What time is it?'

'About half past eleven.' She started pouring the tea.

'In the morning?' He sat back down.

She nodded. 'So, what's wrong with you?'

'Someone tried to stab me yesterday. Luckily he only got my side, but it keeps opening.'

It felt normal talking to Sophia about it. After their journey and previous lives it didn't seem like such a big deal.

'We thought that might be the case.'

'What do you mean?'

'We discussed it over breakfast and decided it would be best for you to stay down here and get some rest.'

The note. Where was it? His suit jacket was gone and so were his socks and shoes.

'Where are my clothes?'

'They're being cleaned. Best not to have temptation around, don't you think? Now, drink your tea and then you can read this book. It's supposed to be awfully funny.' She handed a well-thumbed copy of some tat to him. 'Here, drink your tea and eat something. Then you can go back to bed.' Bea said she'd come down and have dinner with you this evening.' Hot tea splashed on her arm as Tom grabbed hold of it. 'Go back upstairs and pick up some clothes from my room.'

'I can't do that.' She removed his hands from hers.

'Oh, for God's sake I'll go out like this if I have to. Just do it.' He was losing his patience.

'Don't snap at me Alphonse Prideaux, or Tom Lancaster, whichever name is the one you answer to now. I can't do it because your room is off limits for the time being. They need some engineers to check the hotel before guests in your area are allowed back in. The bombing last night was the heaviest one so far and a mine landed on the embankment. You should be glad you're able to sit up never mind anything else.' She stood up to leave. 'You'll just have to go out in what you're wearing.'

Tom's heart sank a little, but he wouldn't be stuck here.

'I didn't mean to snap. Do you know where Bea is?' She'd understand.

'No. I saw her briefly at breakfast. She said she'd be back as soon as she could.'

He nodded. 'Thank you very much.'

She'd turned to leave when Tom remembered to ask, 'Where were you last night? Did you find your brother?'

She shook her head. 'No, but I'll keep on trying. Goodbye Tom, I'll see you later on.'

'Goodbye Sophia.' he replied quietly.

She had left the room before he realised that she hadn't answered his question.

Luckily enough hotel staff are there to make your life easier and a chamber maid, for a handsome tip, ventured upstairs to his room and returned with a set of clothes. He didn't need the note itself, he knew what it said. The waiter was alive and in Paris with Perrault. At least he knew Anaise was alright for the time being, but she hadn't mentioned Em. Right now he just had to get on with what he could. He struggled into his clothes and left the shelter behind.

It was lunchtime and the sun shone down on the previous night's devastation. There were still fires burning and the smell of building dust and smoldering timber hung heavily in the air. The maid had informed him that the mine that had made the whole Savoy building stagger the previous night had indeed made a number of rooms inhabitable for now. He'd think about what to do about that later.

He walked up the Strand towards Wardour Street and the CJ Film office, avoiding broken glass and debris as he made his way through the London streets. Roads were closed off and he had to make his way up to Shaftesbury Avenue and back down towards Piccadilly. Conscious of the number of people on the streets and what had happened to him the day before, he kept a keen eye out for the chap that had tried to finish him off.

Three giggling young women came out of a Lyon's Tea shop and Tom wondered how long it would be before he could see a Nippy again without remembering the stabbing and thinking that he might die there.

He stopped for a moment to light a cigarette and give himself a chance to have a look for any shadows behind him. The only one he saw was Bea who was running along the street behind him, waving. She took a few moments to catch her breath before she spoke.

'Why aren't you in bed?'

'I have something I have to do. I am a grown man Bea, I don't need you and Sophia nursing me.'

'Well, I was only trying to be helpful.'

'I know, but go back to the hotel, or to lunch, or whatever it is you normally do.'

'I'm going to let that go Tom Lancaster,' she said sternly. 'I'll walk with you.' She put her arm in his and resignedly Tom let her.

'So, was it a knife?'

Tom nodded. 'Yes.'

'Who did it?'

'I don't know. I was lucky really, I'm sure he meant to kill me.'

'Why would he do that?'

'I don't know. There's been too many things happening and I haven't had a chance to think about it.'

'You come back here with that film, cause a lot of problems - I'm not blaming you for it - and then someone tries to kill you. It must be connected.'

'It must be,' he said tiredly and turned into Wardour Street. 'Have you heard from your father?'

'He's gone to Orrington to 'collect his thoughts' apparently.'

Orrington Manor was the house where Bea grew up with her father and her constant friend Tom. Tom and his mother had a large house closer to the village but he'd spent most of his time at the Manor with Bea. His mother had taken over as a surrogate wife to Sir Arthur and mother to Bea whilst they grew up.

'You should have gone with him.'

'I didn't want to leave whilst you're here. Besides, what help would I be in all of this?'

They walked in silence until they reached the CJ Film office.

'If he's there, I think it would be best if you waited outside the office.'

'Here in the street?'

'No, in his secretary's room. I'm sure she won't mind. Maybe you can make her more human.'

'Super darling,' she said as Tom pushed the door open for her and they stepped inside.

'I really didn't expect to see you here.' Charles poured them a drink and sat down behind his desk. 'I did hear about your... accident shall we say.'

'Are you just showing me how well informed you are?'

He just smiled tiredly at Tom. 'What I don't know is what brings you here.'

'I had a message from France that I think will interest you. It certainly surprised me.'

Charles leaned back. 'So, what is it?'

'You tell me what was on that film first. There must have been something else, something other than the load of rubbish about Sir Arthur. I need to know what it was.'

'There was nothing else on there. Just plenty of dirt on Sir Arthur which I believe you know already.'

'I'd like to see it.'

'That's not going to happen. It's all classified information and we're trying to sort out the mess that the former Minister of War has caused. Erik was right to get this back here at whatever cost.'

'You don't really believe that Sir Arthur has been sending information to the Germans? He's one of the most upstanding people in the country.'

'That's what makes him more susceptible to blackmail. I don't think for one minute he's on the Germans side, but I do think he would do anything to keep his family name clean.'

'Well, let me throw something else into the pot. Erik Tag is still alive.'

Charles' eyes narrowed. 'What do you mean? You said he was dead when you left him.'

'He was. At least I thought so, but my friend saw him in Paris. He was together with the man who blackmailed me into blowing the signalling house up. There's something really quite wrong with this whole thing.'

'Tell me again what happened in France. Minute by minute, word for word.'

Tom told the story once again.

'And he asked me to have some tea at Lyon's for him, which funnily enough saved my life yesterday.'

'You didn't mention tea when you recounted your meeting with him last time.'

'I didn't think it was important. Is it?'

'What else is there that you haven't told me?' Charles stood up and paced the room.

'Nothing. There was nothing else.'

'So tell me exactly what he said about Lyon's.'

Tom shrugged his shoulders. 'That he would miss London and especially Lyon's tea. And cakes I believe. No, scones with cream.'

'His exact words Tom.'

Tom thought for a while. 'That's what he said, and then he asked if I would have tea and scones there for him. I only remembered it yesterday afternoon when I walked past a corner house on my way back to the hotel. Why? Is there something wrong?'

Charles stared at the wall in front of him until Tom thought he'd forgotten about him. Then suddenly he stood up. 'I think there might well be.'

~ 22 ~

Paris

'Oh God, what some people get up to amazes me.' Ballou screwed her face up as Anaise flicked through the photos Lilou had given her. They didn't make for pleasant viewing and Anaise tried to concentrate on their faces, but apart from Lilou she didn't recognise anyone of them. The note from Lilou explained how Gerard had blackmailed the men and then handed some of the photos to the Gestapo for a second wave of personal gain. Lilou was hardly recognisable in the pictures and Anaise felt as if she'd intruded into her personal life, embarrassed that she'd seen her like this.

She'd partly explained to Ballou what had happened, leaving out the Tom and The Waiter part. She didn't want to get her friend into the trouble she found herself in so she limited her story to Emilie's disappearance and Lilou's pictures.

'I'll come with you. It'll be better with two of us following him.'

'You might get into trouble Ballou, and I need you here and clean from suspicion just in case I need to hide. You do understand, don't you?' She couldn't tell her that her Zazou look would only attract attention to them.

But Ballou didn't understand and kept on arguing until Anaise gave in and agreed that she could come along. There was nothing they could do at this time of night anyway.

As soon as the first rays of sunshine poked through the shutters Anaise crept out of the bed they shared, pulled on her clothes and scribbled a note to her friend. She felt a little bad about it, but she couldn't worry about her as well right now.

Paris was as quiet as it ever got at this hour and Anaise cycled along the river before crossing the Pont Neuf and Les Halles and on towards Emilie's house.

She had hardly slept a wink after she got back and had tried to hide the bags under her eyes before leaving Ballou's flat, but it hadn't worked very well.

She wore glasses together with a brown hat and dress hoping it would show her as a woman on her way to work in an office somewhere. Someone that blended in with everybody else. She got off the bike and stood next to it a few houses further down from her sister's hoping nobody would find it odd. Gerard would probably still be asleep and so she got back on the bike and cycled past the house. She looked up towards the attic rooms on the opposite side where Lilou said she stayed. They were all dark. She once again settled down in the cafe she'd been in a few days earlier and tried to think where she could go after her second coffee. They would find it odd if she had more than two and she didn't want attention drawn to herself.

After an hour or so she cycled back down the street, trying to not stare at the house but noticed that the shutters were now opened.

When she got to the other side she stopped. There was no cafe or anywhere else to hide so she stood on the side of the road trying to look as if she was waiting for someone. She'd only been there a few minutes when a tap on the shoulder made her jump.

'Good God Louise, you scared the life out of me.'

'I'm sorry, I didn't mean to make you jump. I didn't know where you were staying but I thought you'd be back here at some point.'

'Well, here I am.' She looked over to the house to make sure she didn't miss any movements.

'I know where he's keeping her.'

Anaise quickly turned all her attention to Louise. 'Where?'

'It's only a possibility. I've been waiting here on and off for a few days to see if you had any news, and yesterday I saw them come out.'

'Gerard and that Jacques?'

Louise nodded. 'They both got in the car and drove off,' she paused. 'Luckily, my little brother Alexandre was here and he gave me a lift on his bike all the way to the near end of the 18th Arrondissement. Monsieur Valois' car couldn't move very fast with the gas converter at the back so it wasn't too difficult to keep up with them. Anyway, they stopped and he went into a house without knocking. Nobody seemed to live there so I tried to get in once he'd left, but it was locked. My brother has been watching it since then.'

'Can you tell me where it is?'

Louise nodded and got on the back of the bike.

'I'll show you.'

After what seemed like a long journey on the bike they finally arrived in a poor part of Paris. The short street was empty and the houses lining it were grey and in places windows were broken. It reminded her of a ghost town and she briefly wondered where the former occupants had gone. They'd probably left Paris in the rush to get out before the Germans arrived last summer and they might still be stranded down south without the correct documents to return. Louise pointed to a ramshackled house at the end of Rue Lapier.

'That's where he went in.' She pointed towards a black painted door with a black metal bar over the broken glass window. 'Alexandre should be here somewhere.' She looked around.

'Let's have a look around the back.' Anaise said, leaving the bike against the rusty railings on the house opposite.

The two women walked around the side where they found Alexandre sitting behind a tree in the overgrown small garden belonging to the house. He looked a lot younger than his fifteen years. His clothes had lost most of their colours and his trousers had mended tears in places. When he stood up they only reached the top of his ankles. It was hard to imagine that this skinny boy would be eligible to be called up within a year or two.

'How did you get over the railings?' Louise asked as he came towards them.

'Here, there's a gap, but I don't know if you'll get through. You shouldn't eat all those cakes.' He grinned.

'As you can tell, this is my little brother Alexandre.'

Anaise said a quick hello before squeezing through the gap, closely followed by Louise.

'Is there anybody in there?' Anaise asked.

Alexandre shook his head. 'Not that I've seen.' He turned to his sister. 'Shall we go in?'

'No, you go home and wait there.'

'Yeah, that's likely.'

Anaise who'd been busy trying to find a way in turned to the two of them. 'There's a window to the right of the back door which has no glass in, but it's too small for me to fit in.' She looked at Louise and Alexandre.

'I'll do it,' he said and ran towards it. Putting one foot on an old metal chair and another on a horse holding ring he pulled himself through the window and landed with a crash that made the two women wince and look around.

Shortly afterwards the back door opened and the search for clues as to what had happened to Emilie begun.

It smelled of damp and they moved quietly along the hallway. There were several doors along it but none of them held any clues as to the whereabouts of Em. Where the windows were broken leaves had fluttered in and the flowery wall paper had come lose.

Anaise was just about to go up the stairs when Alexandre came running from nowhere.

'Come with me,' he whispered.

Anaise and Louise followed him to the front of the house and down some stairs to the basement. It was a large place and the light coming in from the small windows at the top of the high walls was enough for them to look around.

Alexandre ran up to a door at the far end and beckoned them over.

'It's locked,' he said.

Anaise pulled the handle and tried to push the door but it wouldn't move. It was a sturdy door and it was fitted with a brand new lock.

'Em, are you in there?' Anaise shouted towards the bottom of the door where there was a gap.

It took a few moments before Em answered and relief flooded through Anaise's body.

Outside a shiny black car stopped. Its owner wasn't worried that anybody would steal it even in this part of town. Kluger stepped out from the driver's seat onto the pavement and was shortly afterwards followed by Gerard.

'So, this is where you keep your wife these days Valois?' He looked with distaste on the ramshackled old house.

'As I said before, I think she is indeed part of some resistance network and I didn't want her to escape. Now, I'm not doing this lightly, but I want you to know where my loyalties lie.'

'Why didn't you just let me know earlier?'

'I hoped I was wrong. She is my wife and I guess I just wanted it to be some horrid mistake.'

Kluger nodded. 'Well, let's see what's what.'

Gerard opened the front door and held it up for Kluger. 'I'm sorry to have to take you all the way out here, I really am. I didn't want our neighbours to see...' he paused. 'Well, you know. They're snooty at the best of times.'

Gerard led the way down the stairs and through the large basement room and to the thick door at the end of it. There was a different smell than normal but he put it to the back of his mind and turned the key.

The darkness of the basement room eased as he pushed the light switch outside the door and instantly wished he'd gone there on his own first. For a second all he could do was stare at her.

'What have you done to yourself?'

Em stood in the corner covering her eyes from the light. Her clothes and face were dirty from the sooty dust that covered the room but what really shocked her visitors was that she'd chewed, cut and pulled out chunks of her hair.

'Not so keen to get me to Berlin now then?' She still hadn't seen Kluger standing by the door, but now he stepped forward and looked at Emilie with disbelief.

'Madam Valois.'

Em was taken aback by the German's presence, now there would be no way back for her, and Gerard would know this. He must be trying to get rid of her properly.

From the under stairs cupboard, Anaise carefully peeked out and got quite a shock when she saw who was there. Behind her, Louise and Alexandre were squeezing together in the small space, keeping very quiet.

Anaise indicated to them to stay where they were. She pulled a small gun out of her bag and quietly walked up to the door.

The two men stood with their backs to her. She would get Em out, lock the two men in and then loose the key. The element of surprise would be hers. The moment Em's eyes flickered towards her sister standing in the doorway, pointing a gun towards them, the two men turned around. The look of surprise on Kluger's face quickly gave way to amusement. Gerard's turned to thunder.

'Ah, I wondered when you'd show up,' he sneered.

Anaise's mouth was suddenly dry. 'Em, come over here,' she said, her voice shaking.

Her sister moved towards the door when Kluger, who had no intention of letting them get away, grabbed hold of her and held her in front of him.

'Go on then, shoot.' His voice was mocking, as if he was so damn sure that she wouldn't.

Anaise wasn't sure how to handle the situation and so pointed the gun fully at Gerard instead.

'Let go of her. Don't think that I won't do it. 'She let off a shot and the bullet ricocheted off the wall and then went through Gerard's leg. The noise had taken them all by surprise and Emilie struggled to get out of Kluger's grip but couldn't. He lifted her off her feet and started walking, with her as a shield in front of him, towards Anaise.

Gerard was in well-deserved agony but tried to pick himself up from the floor to follow his German friend out of there.

Anaise backed out of the room as Kluger came closer. When he was only inches away he pushed Em towards her sister. Anaise, taken by surprise, moved the gun to the right and caught hold of her sister. Kluger had grabbed hold of his own gun and was now pointing it at the two women. Anaise had no choice but to put her own gun on the floor and kick it over towards the stairs.

'Now what?' she asked.

They were all standing in the larger basement room and Anaise had moved herself and Em towards the smaller room so that both the German's and Gerard's attention would be away from the stairs where Louise and Alexandre were still hiding.

'Now, we finally have a chance for a chat.' Sturmbann-führer Kluger said. 'Third time lucky some would say. First in Marseille, then here in Paris and if I may say so, it was a very clever escape. Where on earth did you get to?'

'None of your business.' She needed to keep him talking for a minute or so, just whilst she tried to find a way out of this. There had to be one. 'What is it that you want Perrault? We have nothing of interest to you.'

'That's not true. Don't put yourself down. If it hadn't been for you we would never have found out about Lancaster, his past and his connections. Now that we have that and the plan is going, well to plan, we don't need you two girls anymore. In fact, we don't need your friend Lancaster either, but he's been taken care of in London already.' He smiled when he saw the effect of his words on the two women. 'Oh, and one more thing Anaise. Did you tell your sister about Fleur and how you betrayed them all for some depraved obsession?' He laughed. 'No, didn't think you would have. Chin up, as our late friend Father Michel would have said, there'll be plenty of time in heaven to confess to sins.'

So, her secret was out. Well, at least it was overshadowed by their current predicament. If they got out of this alive there would probably be some explaining to do.

Kluger waved his gun towards Gerard who, even though his thigh hurt, was enjoying every moment of this. 'Sorry Valois but your time is up too.' We have no need for your blackmail anymore. The fact that the victims know there are photos is just as powerful.' He pushed all three of them back into the room. 'Besides, it was only your connection to the lovely Madam Valois we needed. If we wanted dirty pictures of politicians we'd get them ourselves.'

Gerard was too stunned to argue and moved towards the far wall together with his wife and her sister.

Kluger held the gun up to fire when Alexandre leaped onto his back and pressed his arms around his neck. Kluger's attention was momentarily diverted as he pushed the boy's arms away from his neck and threw him off. The second Alexandre fell to the floor with a thump, Louise pulled the trigger on Anaise's gun and the German looked around with surprise before toppling forward.

There was stillness for a few moments before Anaise rushed over to check that he was actually dead.

'I didn't mean to shoot him, really I didn't.' Louise still stood by the stairs where she'd picked up Anaise's gun. 'We are in so much trouble now.'

'If you hadn't, we would all be dead now, so thank you. It'll all be fine, nobody will know.'

Anaise and Alexandre started dragging the body into the smaller room where Gerard was edging his way towards the door in the confusion.

'You stay right there,' Em said to him as he tried to leave. 'We'll see how you like being locked in here shall we?'

He leaned against the wall, holding his jacket tight across his wound to stem the blood loss.

'You're going to leave me here with him?' He pointed towards Kluger's lifeless body that Anaise had left in the far corner. 'If you do that, I'll tell them exactly what happened here because they will find us. Let me go and I swear I won't breathe a word. I promise.'

Em leaned close to his face and spat 'I hope you rot in hell, I really do.'

She turned away to walk out the door when he landed a punch in her side. She managed to keep upright through the pain of the blow and didn't turn around. He'd get what he had coming to him.

The sudden movement had caused Gerard more pain than Emilie and he fell to the floor clutching his leg. It was not until they'd locked the basement door, leaving him and Perrault's body in there that she noticed the blood stain spreading through her blouse.

~ 23 ~

There could be nothing prettier than the English countryside in spring. Buttercups, Bluebells and Primroses lined the space between the road and the spaced hedgerows, under old gnarly trees where robins and sparrows flittered between the branches and sang in the sunshine.

Bea was at the wheel of her blue Lanchester with Tom next to her. Charles was in the backseat with his head in one file or another, making the most of the time spent travelling. Tom almost wished he had some files to go through too. Bea was in a bad mood and had hardly spoken a word the whole journey and it was all due to Charles' reaction of finding her waiting outside his office. He'd alienated her by doubting her trustworthiness rather loudly. In the end Tom had calmed her down and she'd agreed, just to help her father you understand, to drive them down to Orrington. Tom couldn't be bothered to care and leaned his head back and tried to relax for the remainder of the journey. All he was supposed to do was deliver the damned film and return to France. It had been over four weeks now since he'd blown up the signalling house and left The Waiter for dead. Even in the event of someone finding him, it was un-likely that he would still have been alive. Still, he wasn't dead. If there hadn't been some sort of meaning with the Lyon's corner House comment he'd be inclined to think that Anaise had been mistaken. He knew however that un-less she was sure, she would never have sent that message.

The car finally came to a stop on the gravelled drive in front of the substantial red bricked building where he had spent most of his childhood. A little further down the coun-try road, towards the village High Street, was his mother's house. He could understand that she preferred to be up in London from a social point of view but why she stayed up there with bombs dropping regularly was beyond him. If he had a chance he'd pop in before returning to London, it had been too many years since he last visited the place. Maybe he'd have a pint at the White Hart. He had a feeling that Charles would want to return to London as soon as their business with Sir Arthur was completed though. Maybe that was for the best, it was always better to look towards things to come rather than back at what had been.

Sir Arthur emerged from the house to greet them and if he was surprised to see Charles he didn't show it.

'I assume you have business to discuss?'

'Of course. We need to have Mr Lancaster with us as well.'

Arthur enquired about Tom's state on the way indoors and stopped when Tom explained what had happened.

'Did they catch the man?'

'I didn't report it. Let's get this over and done with first.'

'Well, that simply won't do my boy. People don't get stabbed for no reason. Bombed yes, but not stabbed. We'll deal with that before you go back to London.'

The study was the smallest room in the house and smelled of ingrained cigar smoke and charcoaled logs. A painting of Bea that he'd never seen before hung above the fire place and a variety of books were piled on top of the grey stone surround.

Tom and Arthur settled into the old leather arm chairs whilst Charles remained standing. His exterior was calm but his darting eyes betrayed a tension that had been there since Tom told him about the message. As soon as he was sure he had their full attention he began to tell them about Erik Tag, the best and deepest spy he'd ever run.

'I'll start with the obvious, he's German. He had a job offer in London and left his two sisters and parents in Friedrichshafen, Germany behind. It was all down to me. I had organised it all for him because one of my other agents highly recommended him for our kind of work as his brother in law was the Gauleiter for that area. It would be many years before Britain decided to officially do something about the Nazi party, be it the Munich peace treaty or declaring war. Our little group however had special permission, going back to the end of the Great War, to infiltrate and take note of any threat to Britain. The old secret services were mostly made up from the old boys network. They did the work for King and country, but there were not a lot of controls in place to ensure that their work stayed secret, and all too often they were, and still are, too gullible.' He held his hand up to stop Sir Arthur who wanted to defend the services he'd spent most of his life working for. 'Once Erik was here in Britain we trained him rigorously and then we sent him off back to Germany. He had asked his brother in law for a job helping the Nazi party and he got one. He did very well and went far above his brother in law, reporting everything of any interest back to me for several years before he went quiet for a little while. That was back in '39 and we thought that he probably just had trouble getting information through to us here, and we were right. A few months later he was back briefly, and then he left the airways for another few months. His information became increasingly more important to us and more difficult for him to send. Ever since the occupation of France we've had a lot of good regular information from him which is why I did not doubt the information we received on that film Sir Arthur.' He quickly explained to him how Tom had come across Erik and the film. Tom was pleased to note that Sir Arthur didn't let on that he already knew. 'The reason I'm telling the two of you this is that between the three of us I hope we can understand why he used the emergency code in that forest, how he came by those pictures and how he can still be alive in Paris. There is obviously something odd about the relationship to this man Perrault too.'

'The code was something to do with Lyon's Tea Rooms was it?' Tom had noticed Charles reaction at the office.

'Yes, but it was slightly different. Had he forgotten after such a long time? I don't know, but I doubt it. The correct code was 'Mrs Line's tea' in a sentence. He wasn't English and the Scottish pronunciation of her name might have made him say Lyon. It's not impossible and certainly we have to take this as a distress signal.'

'Can I have a look in the file?' Tom indicated to the file on the chair next to Charles.

'By all means.' He handed the file over.

Whilst Tom opened it up Charles and Sir Arthur were exchanging ideas.

There were personal notes that he glanced through. No transmission details, no information on anything of national importance, only the notes from his training time in the UK and the odd note throughout the years from Charles. It was at the back of the file that Tom stared at the photo of Erik. It was an amazing likeness, but this person was not the Erik he'd helped up the hillside and watched as he faded away. He looked up at Charles and Arthur and their conversation stopped.

'This isn't the Erik Tag I met.'

Charles' eyes went to the file.

'That was back in '35 he would have changed in six years.'

'Even so. They are almost the same person, but there are differences. The main one is just a gut feeling because they are remarkably alike but the man in the photo has a thick scar on his left hand, this is also mentioned in the medical notes, the man in France had a scar on his right hand.'

'You're sure about this?'

'Yes, definitely.'

Charles closed his eyes. 'If someone is impersonating him he must have been lost quite some time ago. He must have worked the code in there somewhere, hoping that it would somehow get through to us.'

Sir Arthur stood up. 'I won't pretend I'm not relieved. This will just be a trick by the Germans to ...' he looked at Tom. 'They tried to get rid of you - the only person who could tell us that the man in France wasn't the real Erik.'

'It's starting to make sense. The Germans wanted to secure the information they'd already sent us as real, they needed someone who would be trusted by us, i.e. Tom with his connections, to tell us that the real Erik died there on that hillside. End of true messages, end of the true messenger.'

'So you're telling me that it was all a set up?'

'It could be. It'll need a little more investigating, but that would make sense. Especially as the man Tom here thought was Erik is alive and well in Paris. How trustworthy is your source that spotted him?'

'Very. She saw both Erik and Perrault in Marseille.'

'What if this is all true? All the information we've received since God knows when could be false.'

Sir Arthur walked over to the stone fire place. 'There's something I thought about the other day after the Prime Minister had delivered the photos. I was going over any-body who had access to my diary and apart from my staff there's someone else who could quite easily have accessed it. He was with me in Paris at that time and he went to that house too. In fact, he's the one that brought me there.'

'Who are we talking about?'

Sir Arthur hesitated.

'Lord Allcotte. We shared an office for a short time last year. There would have been plenty of opportunities for him to root around my diary if he wished. It's not kept un-der lock and key.'

'There are surely a number of people and staff that would have access to it. We can't just go around accusing people.'

'All I'm saying is that he was at that Paris house too and he had access to my diary. I'm not telling you that he's been leaking secrets.'

Silence settled. 'So, there is a possibility of another member of the cabinet being a security risk.'

Sir Arthur nodded. 'Maybe some discreet questions could be asked. We don't want another scandal like the one that's been my life for the last few days. Anyway, without proof there is very little we can do.'

'Quite right. I'll deal with it as soon as I get back to Lon-don.' Charles too stood up. 'I do think it's for the best if you stay down here in the country side for a little while Sir Arthur. Let us sort this one out first.'

Tom lit a cigarette and ignored a look of disapproval from Charles. 'There seems to be nothing left for me to do here.'

'You're itching to get back to France aren't you?' Charles asked and Tom nodded.

'You should be in a British network though.'

'Can you organise my return? I'll travel back through Portugal and Spain if I have to.'

'I have a couple of little errands I need running in Paris. If you're up for it I'll have you parachuted in as quickly as possible. Obviously you'll need a full medical to make sure you're well enough.' He indicated towards his side.

'Thank you.'

'Both of you realise that, if it is indeed the case that some of Erik's information has been sent by the Germans, it is imperative that they don't find out that we know. If they find out we'll have nothing to fight back with. As it is we'll have a huge task on our hands to find out when he died and if they fed him false information beforehand.'

'Of course, we're not stupid Mr Johnson. We have been in this game before,' Arthur said.

Charles looked a little taken aback by the comment. 'Yes well, it doesn't hurt to re-iterate it. That includes friends, family and club members alike.'

Sir Arthur rose from his chair. 'I wondered how long it would take you to bring that up. Still got a bee in your bonnet about how the secret services are run.'

'I haven't got a bee in my bonnet, as you so kindly put it, about anything.' His voice kept steely low. 'There is room for a lot of improvement though as you well know and one of them is the Old Boys Network. Ministers, members of parliament and security services chatting over a drink at the club, sharing gossip and secrets like peanuts. It's a security risk, and you know it. The three of us, in here, are the only ones that know about this and all I'm saying is that we should keep it that way.'

'Don't get on your high moral horse here Johnson. I will not be lectured on National Security issues from you. - Now, let's calm down.'

The only noise notable was the little Robin singing loudly in the holly tree just outside the window. Charles' mask of professionalism had returned and he held out his hand to Sir Arthur. 'Please accept my apologies for that outburst. I stand for every word I said, but it's neither the time nor the place for discussing it.'

Sir Arthur nodded in response and sat back down.

'Also, I realise that this will be hard on you for a while. Staying down here when you probably want to get back to London to clear your name. I just ask that you give me a little time to gather some more information together before returning to London.'

'A lifetime of work for this country and this is how it ends. It's not easy.'

'This doesn't have to be the end. Just let it all rest for a while and then... well, who knows, you could have your old post back.'

'No, I think I'm done. How could I demand even an ounce of respect from parliament, never mind the public. There would always be someone remembering the demonstration and my retreat down here like someone with something to hide. Maybe it's for the best,' he looked over to Tom. 'Do you think she'll come back to the village for a while? I think I've been rather neglectful of your mother in recent months.'

Tom smiled. 'You might have a job on your hands, but I'm sure she will in the end. I'll tell her you're back down here when I see her tomorrow.'

A knock on the door made them all look over towards it. When Sir Arthur's booming voice confirmed it was alright to enter, Bea stuck her head in and asked if they were ready for dinner.

'Well gentlemen, it's too late for you to return to London tonight.'

Charles looked most upset at this and Sir Arthur continued. 'Come now, we have good food and wine here. It'll do you good to have a night off, especially as you haven't got a choice. I won't have Bea drive you back in the dark.'

'Very well,' Charles said with good grace.

They all walked towards the dining room when Charles stopped.

'One moment Sir Arthur, why were you in Paris with Lord Allcotte?'

Sir Arthur shrugged his shoulders. 'Because he asked me.'

~ 24 ~

The Savoy was running as if nothing had happened. Tom's room was still in the no go zone but his belongings had been moved to Sir Arthur and Bea's rooms. Sir Arthur had stayed in Sussex whilst Bea had driven himself and Charles back to London. She was under orders from her father to make sure Tom rested for a couple of days before returning to France and took her instructions seriously.

She sat him down in an armchair and made him promise to call reception if he needed anything at all.

'I would stay with you darling, but if I don't go to this meeting there will be chaos. Lady Brown will rule high and mighty and everything will fall to pieces. No more embroidered handkerchiefs sent to our brave officers on the front line.'

'I beg your pardon?' Tom raised his eyebrows. What was she on about?

'It's a joke darling. Are you sure you don't mind being alone?'

'I'll be fine. An early night and then tomorrow I'll see my mother as I promised her. And she can meet Sophia as well.' He just remembered that he hadn't actually told Sophia yet of his plans for her.

'She'll be here soon I'm sure. TTFN as Mrs Mopp says.'

'Who?' His face still remained blank.

'From ITMA, the radio program. It's That Man Again.'

'Just go to your meeting Bea, maybe they'll know what you're talking about,' he said with a hint of a smile.

After she'd finally left, he leaned his head back in the chair and closed his eyes. He would have dozed off if his head hadn't been swimming with the implications of Perrault and Pierre's actions and his imminent return to France.

He must have been deep in thought as he didn't hear Sophia come in and jumped when she spoke.

'So you left your sickbed in your pajamas then?' She looked pale and drawn standing in the low lights of the lounge.

'Not quite. That would have warranted an arrest I guess.'

'No thoughts for me wondering where on earth you had gone to?'

'I'm sorry Sophia, but I came to London for a reason and that had to take precedence over all else. Which brings me onto another matter.' He looked around for his cigarettes. 'My mother is coming here tomorrow and she has agreed for you to stay with her until you find your brother. I think the two of you will get on well.'

'Sadly I don't think I'll be able to meet her.' she paused. 'You really need to come outside with me. Now Tom.'

'Why, what's happened.'

He could see thoughts whirring around her head before she finally spoke. 'Because in my pocket I have a gun, which I know how to use. This isn't my idea, I think the world of you, but they want to talk to you.'

'Who are they?'

'The people that are holding my parents' lives in their hands. The Germans.'

He sank back into the chair trying to take it all in. Really he wanted to laugh, but that might break his stitches. The very idea of Sophia with a gun was ridiculous. Still, she looked serious enough. 'Have they been directing you all the way from Marseille?'

She nodded. 'I didn't escape from the round up in Vienna. I was picked out, given instructions and sent on my way with the lives of my parents hanging on how well I did. You would have done the same. Now come on, they're waiting.'

'They organised my release in Spain.' It was a statement not a question. Well, that answered that. The look in Sophia's eyes convinced him that she would shoot him, she might miss but he was a little curious to see where she would take him. She was right in a strange way. He'd travelled through war torn Europe to deliver a film to London mainly because he wanted to save his friends from arrest. What a joke that had been. They must really have wanted to secure the information sent from the fake Erik to stage such a show. He got up with a wince. 'Well, we don't want to keep your friends waiting.'

'They are not my friends. I don't want to do this, but I have to. You understand, don't you? You would do the same for your mother.'

He didn't answer, instead he walked out of the room slightly in front of her and headed towards the lift.

'We'll take the stairs at the end of the corridor.'

That was the hotel staff's stairs. They wandered downwards catching the odd glance from a chamber maid or waiter. They reached the bottom and she indicated that they should exit through a side door leading out to the Embankment where a car was waiting. Just outside the door he hesitated. He wanted to see where she was leading him but getting into the car would be bad mistake. He turned around and swung Sophia in front of him. She wouldn't be able to turn the gun around in her pocket very easily and the chap in the car wouldn't shoot because he might hit her.

'Now, now Mr Lancaster. We've gotten so far in a friendly manner. Let's not spoil it here.' The voice came from the side door they'd just exited and he felt the hard edge of a gun in his back.

He let go of Sophia who stepped aside whilst they bundled Tom into the car.

'Come on, you're coming too.' The man with the gun said to Sophia. 'We have business to discuss still.'

She nodded and sat down in the back seat next to Tom who was squeezed into the middle. The man with the gun gave the order to drive and then sat back. The gun was under a folded coat, but it still pointed at Tom.

'They'll kill you too you know,' he whispered to Sophia who ignored him. 'Why wouldn't they? What more can you do for them?'

'Shut up,' the man next to Tom said.

The setting sun threw a pink glow over the London skyline as they drove eastwards towards the river. When the car stopped it was outside a large bombed out building. It's arches were still standing intact but the main building had the front missing and the rubble from it spilt on to the street. They climbed over some of it and entered the remaining building through a hole in the wall. They must have made some procession, and if the area was inhabited they would have been noticed, but it wasn't. The driver led the way, followed by Sophia, Tom and finally the man holding the gun.

Inside it was gloomy and Tom nearly fell over as a rat scurried across the floorboards in front of him. Old brick dust crunched under their feet as they walked through the huge old building to the back.

They trundled along in silence down some stairs that led to a basement. Before he had a chance to look around, the driver threw his fist into Tom's side. Luckily it wasn't on the side where he'd been stabbed, but it hurt none the less. Whilst Tom bent over, the driver kicked his legs so that he fell onto the floor. Very quickly Tom's hands and feet were tied up and they turned their attention to Sophia who was still standing at the bottom of the stairs.

'Give me that gun you've got.' He waved his gun at her. 'Come on. Quick now. I have dinner reservations at the Ritz and we don't want the lady kept waiting now do we.'

'Will you still let my parents go? I've done what you asked me to do.'

'You stupid girl. They were never going to get released. They are most likely dead already. Now, I don't approve of how the Jewish issue is dealt with but there is a war to win and we all have to sacrifice something.'

'Just let her go.' Tom had his head turned towards them. 'She doesn't know anything about the film.' He couldn't tell them that their plans had failed whatever happened however desperate he got.

'I'm only following orders Mr Lancaster. Now,' he turned back to Sophia, 'hands please.'

She held them out in front of her and he tied them tightly and then her legs.

'This building used to be a soap factory until it got bombed a few weeks ago. It's a no entry zone as it's structurally unsafe. Now what we're going to do is set fire to it so that the few remaining beams holding this large building up will collapse. However, we also need to make sure your bodies aren't identifiable so therefore we're going to start the fire down here and lay a trail of camphene to lead it upstairs. That should give you enough time to frazzle. These wooden stairs will be the first to go so don't even try to escape.'

The driver lit a match and waited by the stairs.

'Come on, let's go.' The man with the gun said before lifting his hat in goodbye to the two tied up bundles. 'Sorry, it's just one of those things.'

The man with the gun reached the top of the stairs before the driver threw the match onto the camphene and a bluish flame appeared immediately.

The two men disappeared and the only sound was that of the fire speeding along the path of the lighting liquid and down the fragile stairs. It quickly took hold and spat out glowing bits of wood and smoke along its trail.

Tom rolled onto his back and sat up. His hands were tightly bound and he needed something sharp to cut them. The large cellar was full of rubble and he scanned the room for anything useful.

The smoke was starting to fill the room and he knew they didn't have long if they wanted to survive.

Sophia was trying to open her handbag, her tied hands pulling at the catch.

'There's a nail file in here. Will that help?' she asked breathlessly. 'It's very sharp.'

Tom moved over to her and emptied the purse onto the floor. The ivory nail file fell out together with her compact and new identity papers.

'Hold out your hands.'

She did as he asked and he started filing.

'I'm sorry for this,' she said.

'Apologise when we're out of here. Right now it's probably best to conserve whatever air we have.'

Several times he scratched her arm with the file, but it didn't take long for the rope to come apart.

She rubbed her wrists quickly before freeing Tom. They untied their legs and got on their feet.

'Try to keep as low down as much as possible.' Tom coughed as the smoke from the wooden floors above them increased.

They wouldn't be able to get out of there. The stairs were gone and the heat was so intense they had to move. It was a big cellar, there must be another exit. They followed the walls to the other side of the room, tripping over debris and coughing as they went.

'There's a door. Just here.' He pulled the handle and tried to open it, but it was locked. He tried to kick it, but it was too sturdy to give way, and in the end he gave up. There was a large crash as the ceiling where they had just been crumbled and the dust mixed with the smoke and fire.

The door they were trying to get through had survived the bombings with flying colours, but the walls around it were less intact.

He started whacking at some cracked bricks with a stone from the piles of rubble and Sophia did the same. Breathing was difficult now, almost every breath ended up in a coughing fit and their eyes stung. If this didn't work they'd had it. Bloody hell, to die down here when there was still so much to be done. For his mother and Emilie never to know what happened to him.

'Come on you bastard.' He cracked the stone as hard as he could, and finally the brick crumbled. The others followed fairly quickly and when he put his hand through he found the door key and turned it. It was still a struggle to open it as the frame had warped but it did open with a kick and they went through. Tom went back out and picked up a burning piece of wood before shutting the door from the inside.

It was a coal storage room. It was empty, but there must be a trap door where the coal would be delivered. He looked around and found that it was right above where they were standing and there was a ladder attached to it.

'Hold this.' He handed the lit piece of wood to Sophia and stepped onto an old metal chair. The latch undone, the ladder folded down and the door moved upwards letting a stream of cold night air in. There was something holding it back from opening fully but the ladder, propped between the door and the floor held it open enough for the two of them to climb out. For a minute they just sat there, breathing in the fresh air and glad to be alive.

The flames stood out against the dusky sky, sending plumes of smoke up into the air. Sirens could be heard approaching and Tom grabbed Sophia's hand before running down the street.

'We don't want them to find us here. Just think of all the questions.'

They ran until their smoked lungs couldn't take any-more, and then they ran some more, towards the city cen-tre.

The Ritz foyer was shimmering in the light of two chandeliers as Tom and Sophia walked in. Halfway back to the hotel they'd found a taxi to take them the rest of the way. A quick change of clothes at the hotel before he dragged a reluctant Sophia along to the Ritz where they knew that their kidnapper had a date.

He hadn't wanted to leave her on her own in the state she was in. She'd hardly said a word since their escape from the factory and he didn't have the time to sit her down and tell her that he understood why she'd done it. He would do that later, but what he couldn't do was tell her that all everything would be fine because they both knew that for her it wouldn't be. Her family had been taken away and all her dirty work had been for nothing.

'A table for three. Discreetly placed.'

The maître di led the way towards a table in the corner behind the stairs.

Bea, who had been at a committee meeting at the hotel, joined them.

'You still smell of smoke.' Bea said as they sat down. Tom had explained a little of what had happened, he'd left out Sophia's part as he needed them to get along.

'Well, at least I'm alive. Look discreetly over there.' He nodded towards a table in the centre of the room.

She turned her head as if to look at the back of her dress whilst scouring the area Tom had indicated. There was another man and two women together with the kidnapper. Dressed in evening wear they laughed at something one of the ladies said.

Bea returned her attention to Tom.

'I don't know who the ladies are. Tarts no doubt, but the man with the beard is Lord Allcotte.'

Sophia was still quiet and staring at the table in front of her.

'I'll go and make the phone call to Charles.' Tom left Bea and Sophia at the table and discreetly made his way back out into the reception area.

When he got through to Charles' office his telephone was answered by an unknown man.

'Who's calling?' His voice rasped on the other end of the line.

He knew this voice, but couldn't place it. He quickly hung up without saying a word.

There was something not right. He glanced around the reception area before asking the operator to connect him to another number.

He then quickly scribbled a note to Bea explaining that she should stay with Sophia and that he'd be back later.

The concierge supplied him with a car and driver for the short distance to Wardour Street. To avoid drawing attention to himself, Tom asked the driver to let him out a few doors away from the CJ Film office and he waited there whilst the car disappeared up the street towards Oxford Street. There was no moonlight and no streetlights as Tom quietly opened the door to the CJ Films building. He could see light coming out from under the door to the office and muted noise escaping with it. By the sound of drawers opening he'd say CJ Films were being burgled, but why would a common burglar answer the phone.

Back at the hotel Tom had collected his gun and now he pulled it out of his pocket. He took a deep breath and kicked his foot into the door. The drawers of filing cabinets were open and its contents lay strewn over the floor and on top of the reception desk. Behind the desk sat the man who had driven them to the bomb site earlier. He looked up at Tom with surprise.

'Well, aren't you the bad penny.'

Tom stepped into the room and held his gun steadily pointed at the driver.

'Get up and keep your hands in front of you.'

The driver stood up slowly and a smile formed on his lips.

'How did you get out? We watched the flames take hold properly before we left.'

Unnerved by his smirk Tom quickly glanced around the reception room to find the other person he knew was in the office somewhere. He'd heard two voices and the driver was not the one who'd answered the phone.

'Get in there.' Tom waved the gun towards Charles' office. The door was shut to and it was the only place that other man could be.

The driver sat back down.

'I'm not finished here yet.' His hands disappeared underneath the desk.

'Get your hands back up. I will shoot.'

His attention was focused on the driver and it was only in the corner of his eye that he noticed that the door to Charles' office had opened.

Within the blink of an eye the driver had his gun up and the man in the doorway pointed another one at him.

'You again?' The man in the doorway said.

Tom had seen him before, in Portugal. He was the German that had talked to Sophia by the pool, the same raspy voice that had said sorry when he'd driven a sharp blade into his side.

Tom had no choice but to throw his gun on the floor.

'Come on, get in here.' The tall man in the doorway moved out of the way to let Tom pass. 'Maybe we can get some use out of you.'

On the floor by his desk sat Charles. Hands tied behind his back and blood from his nose dripping onto his once white shirt.

The driver had joined them and stood guarding the doorway whilst the other one sat on the edge of the desk.

'I believe you two know each other,' the tall man said. 'This is getting very tiring. Maybe third time lucky, eh?' he addressed the last comment to Tom.

'What is it you're after? You know your scheming has failed.'

'Well, it hasn't failed as such has it? You see, that for one side to win, it has to have another side to fight. Divide and conquer.' He stood back up. 'You see if you hadn't turned around so unexpectedly nobody would have been any the wiser. They would have taken the information we sent over as true and correct. I don't think Mr Johnson here has had the time to tell anybody about your little discovery yet, but he won't confirm it. It's really quite unfortunate as I've heard an awful lot about him from Erik before he died.' He paused as if to reflect on the sadness of these events. 'It would be such a shame if this operation went bad, a lot of work has gone into it on both sides of the channel. Not the end of the world though. Even if the information we sent over after the sad decline of Erik is now being questioned, we still have a break in moral, a disgraced Cabinet Minister and ...'

His voice drowned in an air raid siren.

'It seems we'll have to find out if you've told anybody from other sources.' He nodded to the driver who brought his gun up, pointing it at Charles and pulled the trigger. The bullet went wide of its intended target as the house shook by what must have been a direct hit further down the street. Tom took the opportunity and launched himself on the tall man who had stumbled towards the wall. He slammed his fist into his stomach and forced his knee upwards into his head as it bent forwards from the punch. He grabbed the gun and turned around as the driver was about to fire another shot, this time at him. Expecting a bullet to come his way he dived behind the desk just as a shot went off. With his gun ready he quickly got back up, ready to pull the trigger when he saw the driver flat out on the floor in front of Sophia.

She just stood there for a moment before entering the room, gun still held in front of her.

'Bloody hell, what are you doing here?'

She just shook her head as she noticed the tall man on the floor where Tom's kick had landed him. His nose sitting at an awkward angle he got back to his feet. Silence filled the room as Sophia, with steady hands, held the gun in front of her and without hesitation pulled the trigger.

This time the shot echoed throughout the room and probably down the street through the broken windows. When he fell back onto the floor she put another bullet in his head.

Tom walked slowly towards her. 'Sophia, can you point the gun to the floor.'

At first she didn't move, and then she did as he asked. Her eyes didn't leave the man on the floor.

He went to stand beside her. 'He's the man from Portugal.'

She nodded. 'And Vienna. The promise to save my family if I did this came from him. What choice did I have?' She handed the gun to Tom and sighed. 'I would happily turn that gun on myself. Right here and now, but what purpose would that serve?'

She walked up to the doorway. 'You should get him an ambulance.' She nodded towards Charles who still sat, leaning against the wall with his eyes shut.

'Where are you going?

'I'm going to fight, Tom. I'm going to rescue somebody else's family.'

How could he argue with that? 'I won't see you again will I?'

'Never say never.'

'No, I guess not. Take care of yourself.'

She nodded and smiled. 'Thank you. For everything.'

With this she disappeared out the door and out of his life.

~ 26 ~

Anaise peered out through a crack in the brown wooden shutter. It was still raining and she had run out of ideas of how to get herself and Em out of Paris. Her sister was still weak, but the temperature that had resulted from the infected stab wound had started to give. If it hadn't been for the infection, a quick patch up would have sufficed, but as it was, it had made her very ill. Every day they stayed in Mrs Carter's flat they put her and themselves in danger, but the papers they needed to leave Paris didn't materialise. She'd gone to see Christophe twice, glad that Albert hadn't been around either time, but the papers he could get weren't of very good quality. Even so, it would be at least a couple of weeks before he could get them. He promised to let her know if he could get something quicker for her. She wasn't quite sure how that would work as she hadn't told him where they were staying.

It all felt like the end. A darkness had settled over her and everything that had once been was no more. Tom was no more, it was probably safe to say that a lot of their friends in Marseille were no more, and their old happy, dysfunctional lives were no more. They had to leave before she went mad. The trouble was that she was almost scared of even leaving the flat.

Sighing she went to sit next to her sister's bed and stroked what was left of her hair. What must she have gone through in that basement to do this to herself. Anaise had cut some of the longer strands to even it all out but even so, at the top of her head were bald patches where she'd torn at it.

Em opened her eyes.

'Has it stopped raining yet?'

Anaise shook her head. 'No, it's still coming down.'

'You know you have to leave Anaise. Don't wait around for me.'

'I'm not going anywhere without you. If you mention it again I shall ignore you. Anyway, you're getting better, the doctor says so.'

Em closed her eyes. 'Try Oberleutnant Joachim Gerber.'

'Pardon?' Anaise had heard what she said but thought she must still be feverish. Ask a Nazi for help? 'The German from that party?'

Em opened her eyes and smiled weakly at Anaise's expression. 'I know what you're thinking, but he's a nice man and he might be able to help.'

'There's no such thing Em. Do you think he'd still be nice now? He must know what happened. We killed a German Officer.' Her sister stayed silent so she continued. 'Even if he is a nice man as you say, where would he get what we need?'

Anaise had no intention of going anywhere near a German of any kind. Not only was The Waiter still out there somewhere, but Perrault would at least be noted as missing if not dead. If they'd found him, they wouldn't rest until they got whoever had done it. Em would be noted as missing and how could they explain their whereabouts for the last eight days, never mind her sister's injury. They should have shot Gerald too. If he was found alive, he'd talk.

Alexandre had moved the car before heading home together with Louise. They had all sworn never to discuss what had happened. If Anaise ever got a chance, she would thank her properly, and her brother too. Emilie had just had enough strength to walk a couple of blocks where they'd got into a horse drawn carriage that took them almost to Mrs Carter's house. As soon as they'd got there she'd collapsed on the floor, leaving Mrs Carter with no choice but to put them up. She said she was glad to have the opportunity to help and to be fair, the woman hadn't had an alcoholic drink since they got there. Instead she'd spent most of her time looking after Emilie, sending her butler out to find a suitable doctor and supplies. Bringing a doctor into their little secret made Anaise nervous. If he didn't inform the authorities he could be shot for treason. However, if he hadn't come, her sister would not be laying here talking rubbish.

God, they had to get out quickly before her nerves shattered.

She hesitated for a moment and then picked up her jacket.

'I'm just popping out for a bit Em. I'll be back in a couple of hours.'

She was out of the door before Em or Mrs Carter had a chance to ask where she was going.

Her wooden soled shoes clinked along the cobbles and even that noise made her worry that someone would notice her. She didn't have anything else to wear though. During their stay at Mrs Carter's she'd washed her clothes bit by bit, declining the offer of their host to borrow something of hers. She had a whole bag full of clothes at Ballou's and she'd bring it back to the flat after her visit. Hopefully her friend wouldn't have taken her absence as another one of Anaise's goodbyes. She hoped there would be no shouting because she had sneaked out, leaving her friend sleeping soundly that morning she'd gone to find Em, when she knew she wanted to come along.

The Vichy Government had renamed the traditional May Day, Fête du Travail et de la Concorde sociale, a day to celebrate work and social harmony. Normally the workers and their unions would be demonstrating on the streets all over France. She wondered where they all were today. It was quiet and the narrow streets alongside Rue Moufftard were almost deserted. It all seemed so sad when the streets should be full of people having a well-earned day off.

She was pretty sure there was nobody following her as she went into Ballou's doorway. She knocked on the door but there was no reply so she dug down in her handbag and found the key Ballou had given her.

'Hello, it's only me.' She walked into the dark hallway. There was no answer, but it smelled of newly made coffee and paraffin so she couldn't have been gone long.

Should she wait? She really needed to talk to someone other than Em and Mrs Carter but she didn't know how long her friend would be. Maybe she'd just grab her bag and leave her a note. She'd pop back another day if she got the chance.

She walked into the bedroom to get her bag and almost laughed out loud. Ballou was asleep with her bleached mop of blonde hair just about visible above the duvet. It must have been another late night, or early morning, down at the club.

She sat down on the edge of the bed and shook her gently. 'Ballou, wake up. It's me. Come on, wake up.'

Her friend didn't stir, and an uneasy feeling started to slowly spread through her stomach. Something was very wrong. She looked around the room but all seemed normal. When she pulled the duvet back from her friend she saw the thick deep purple line around her neck.

'Ballou.' She shook her again, harder this time before checking her pulse and realising she was gone. For a moment she sat there just looking at her, unable to take it in.

What had happened? Then abruptly she stood up. Whoever had done this could still be here, in the flat.

Her body was cold, the coffee newly made. She looked around the room for some kind of weapon whilst keeping remarkably calm.

She picked up a heavy brass candle stick and moved towards the door.

'Join us for a coffee.' The voice made her jump. 'We're in the kitchen.'

She knew they should have gotten rid of him properly when they had the chance. She walked out of the bedroom and into the kitchen. At the wooden table, where she'd sat with Ballou only a week earlier, sat Gerard and another man now.

'Let me put some water on.' Gerard rose from his chair and lit the paraffin light that Ballou used to cook on. 'Let it not be said that we don't look after our guests, eh Jacques?'

The other man just sat still, staring at her.

'You'll have to excuse me, I can't move very well at the moment. An accident with my leg you see. Makes me limp a bit.'

Still Anaise just stood in the doorway looking at him.

'I don't know what to say Jac; she's never been lost for words before. Maybe she's upset that we got to her friend before she did.'

'What do you want?' she asked finally.

Gerard limped over to her. 'I want my wife back. Yes, yes, I know, it's odd after what she did to me, but I'm willing to let it go. I kept her name out of it so there's no reason for her not to come home.'

Anaise laughed. 'You really are mad.' And with that she brought up the candle stick, sharp edge forwards, with all the force she could muster. It made a strange thudding noise as it hit his forehead. He fell to the floor instantly and she was for a moment upset that he didn't suffer more. After all that he'd done it would only be fair.

His friend who had been sitting on the far side of the table got up from his chair and moved towards her. She gripped the candle stick harder and held it above her head before running towards him.

This time she didn't have the element of surprise and Jacques easily moved away from her attack. She stumbled forwards on the tiled floor and lost her balance. Whilst she tried to get back on her feet Jacques was behind her and snared her throat with a scarf. He pulled her upwards until she was on her knees and then he tightened it. The two fingers she'd managed to get between the scarf and her neck didn't help and she gasped for air. A variety of colours appeared in front of her eyes and her head felt as if it was about to explode. In desperation she got her feet flat on the floor and launched herself upwards pushing Jacques into the work surface. For a moment the grip on her throat went tighter, but then she was free. She fell onto the floor gasping for breath. Behind her the work surface was on fire and Jacques was tearing at his burning shirt. The screams didn't start until he realised his hair was on fire from the knocked over paraffin light that had stood just behind him on the counter. She felt nothing whilst watching him burn, maybe one day she would, but not now. Before he reached the sink to douse the flames, his body went into shock and he fell to the floor, fitting as he did so.

She had to get out quick, the fire and the screaming would attract every neighbour and passerby there were. Even though her throat hurt and her breathing was laborious she grabbed the contents of Gerard's pockets, took her bag and ran out of the building through the hidden back door.

She could still hear Jacques's screams, but she wasn't sure if they were real ,or if they had lodged themselves in her head.

***

A great big gold framed picture of Adolf Hitler hung on the wall behind his desk. Anaise found that she could easily blur it out by concentrating on the German officer in front of her.

'You have to excuse all the activity here Frauline. You must have heard of the death of Sturmbannführer Kluger, my uncle?'

'No, I haven't but I am sorry for your loss.' Her heart had jumped up into her well covered throat at the mention of Kluger.

He nodded. 'It's very sad for all of us. Very soon though we'll have caught the culprits and they will be dealt with.'

'I'm sure you will.' She looked up at the picture behind him to avoid guilt showing in her eyes.

'I do remember you from... some party. You're Madam Valois' sister'

'Yes I am. I think it was at Madam Sager's salon party.'

'That's right.' He paused. 'How is your sister?'

Anaise didn't answer immediately. She didn't know quite how to put it without causing a commotion that would attract the attention of the other people in the room. 'She's not very well Oberleutnant Gerber. She asked me to come and see you. To see if you could help her.'

'Do you mind if we go somewhere else and talk?' He asked with a serious expression and rose from his chair.

She was only too glad to be out of this lion's den. Every moment since she had arrived she'd expected to hear someone asking for her papers or recognising her.

A couple of blocks away from his headquarters on Rue de Rivoli they stopped on a street corner. She'd rather talk to him there than in a cafe where people could overhear. The lives of four people were on the line just by her seeing him. He was German, they were all bastards, but she didn't have any choice, because it wouldn't be long before someone informed the authorities where they were. Also, she was the one who had got them into this whole bloody mess, she had to get them out. She prayed that she was doing the right thing.

'Oberleutnant, my sister tells me you're a nice man.'

His eyes fell to the ground, and if she didn't know any better she'd swear he was blushing.

'I've tried to contact her, discreetly of course but to no avail. Is she alright?'

So, this had gone further than a smile and some flirtatious conversation at a party. Well, she could understand that her sister had kept quiet about it.

'She's alright but she needs a favour from you. Well, we both do.'

His face went serious again. 'What would that be?'

Anaise looked around to make sure nobody paid them any special attention.

'We haven't got much time. We need travel permits down to the un-occupied zone Oberleutnant. We have to leave Paris quickly.' She saw his face turn stern and quickly continued. 'It's her husband. She has to get away from him. She can't go through normal channels because he'd find out. He's a horrid man Monsieur, he beats her.' There, she'd said it. As much as she hated Gerard and was glad that he was dead, she was relieved that he'd kept Em's name out of it. Her own was probably on a list somewhere, but she had a feeling that The Waiter and whatever game he was playing was being acted out in secret. No wanted notes issued until someone had won.

Gerber's face softened again as he realised his Paris dream girl wasn't involved in anything illegal. She was quite rightly trying to get away from her brute of a husband.

'Where is she now? Can I see her?'

'Oberleutnant, if you were to visit her she'd be in trouble for being a collaborator.'

He sighed, 'I can get the travel documents by tomorrow but I have to see her before she leaves. I can swap my uniform for something more French. I've done it before.'

This request annoyed Anaise, but maybe it was a small price to pay to get the documents.

'Alright, I'll meet you here tomorrow, same time. Please bring the documents then if you can.'

He nodded goodbye and she walked down the street towards Mrs Carter's flat to fill her sister in on the details. She didn't know whether to be happy for the chance to get out of Paris, or worried that the following day a dirty old cell in number 84 Avenue Foch might be waiting for her.

It was dark and he'd been standing still for a long time. Steps in the hotel corridor outside had come and gone all evening, but finally he heard a key turn in the door. The light from the spherical wall lamps outside found their way into the room before its occupant and Tom prepared himself. The door slammed shut behind him and he walked up to the window to pull down the blackout blinds which the maid must have forgotten to do. He then turned to light the table lamp and Tom tightened his grip on the Welrod he held in his right hand. He stepped out from behind the door and lifted its long barrel towards its target. The light had to come on first, he wanted him to see who it was who fired the gun. The light came on, and when The Waiter lifted his head, Tom registered the surprise in his eyes.

'No last words for you I'm afraid.'

He pressed the trigger before The Waiter had a chance to move. He was close enough for the shot to hardly make any noise, and the body of the man who'd fooled him so, fell forwards with his mouth open as if he had more to say. Tom doubted it would have been worth hearing. He quickly went through his pockets before turning the light off and shutting the door behind him as he left.

FRENCH PYRENEES

Another sunset gone. How long would it take for her to get used to this life on the run without him. They had lived in a shack attached to an old barn for almost eight months now and all they got was a very small food parcel occasionally. Anaise disappeared for hours on end with no real explanation as to where she'd been and it had driven a wedge between them at a time when they should have become closer. She had a feeling that her sister had found out about her affair with Joachim and that's why she didn't tell her what she was up to, that she couldn't be trusted. It wasn't a fair thing to do as this whole thing had been started by Anaise spilling their secrets to a Nazi agent. She'd received forgiveness, why couldn't she return the favour?

Her hair had started to grow back and her sister kept on cutting the length of it to make it into something resembling a fashionable style. Why she needed that out here she didn't know, but it seemed to make Anaise happy, and it was a small price to pay for that. There was no need to cry any more, it wouldn't bring Tom back and the odd wild boar that wandered past in the evening didn't care. She looked up at the sky where dark autumn clouds were gathering on the horizon above the high grey mountains.

She'd better get back to the hut she called home nowadays. There hadn't been a food parcel for over a week and they had discussed leaving this place behind, but they had nowhere else to go. Their papers might be alright but Anaise insisted they had to stay there. Em didn't know why. Their travel documents had expired, but surely they could get past that without too many problems. There were people who could help with these sort of things.

The back of her dress was wet when she rose from the patch of grass where she'd sat every sunset since they'd arrived and she brushed it down. The clouds were getting closer and she hurried along to the shack where she hoped Anaise would be waiting.

The door creaked open and she ducked into what they had come to call the kitchen. Instead of Anaise at the table there was a man. She instinctively took a step back outside but didn't shut the door. When the man stood up and turned around, she froze briefly in shock before flying across the floor and landing in his arms. He smelled of wood fires and tobacco, of hope and of life. She had made a deal with God, and if He chose to make good on that promise there and then, she would happily have died where she was. It was only as they finally pulled apart that she noticed Lady Ella playing in the background.

'Did you bring her all the way here for me?' she asked resting her forehead on his chest.

Tom kissed her head. 'I wanted to give you something I know you love,' he paused, 'as much as I love you.'

Anaise smiled as she glanced in through the dirty small window. There would be no room in the shack for her tonight. She turned and walked back towards the mountain pass where she'd come from, humming along to Baby Won't You Please Come Home.

Fin

9 781838 134334